THE LOST

ALSO BY JEFFREY B. BURTON

The Keepers
The Finders
The Eulogist
The Lynchpin
The Chessman

THE LOST

A MACE REID K-9 MYSTERY

‡

JEFFREY B. BURTON

MINOTAUR BOOKS
NEW YORK

First published in the United States by Minotaur Books, an imprint of St. Martin's Publishing Group

THE LOST. Copyright © 2022 by Jeffrey B. Burton. All rights reserved. Printed in the United States of America. For information, address St. Martin's Publishing Group, 120 Broadway, New York, NY 10271.

www.minotaurbooks.com

Library of Congress Cataloging-in-Publication Data

Names: Burton, Jeffrey B., author.
Title: The lost / Jeffrey B. Burton.
Description: First Edition. | New York : Minotaur Books,
    2022. | Series: Mace Reid K-9 mystery ; 3
Identifiers: LCCN 2022003996 | ISBN 9781250808622 (hardcover) |
    ISBN 9781250808639 (ebook)
Subjects: LCGFT: Novels.
Classification: LCC PS3602.U76977 L67 2022 | DDC 813/.6—dc23
LC record available at https://lccn.loc.gov/2022003996

Our books may be purchased in bulk for promotional, educational, or business use. Please contact your local bookseller or the Macmillan Corporate and Premium Sales Department at 1-800-221-7945, extension 5442, or by email at MacmillanSpecialMarkets@macmillan.com.

First Edition: 2022

10 9 8 7 6 5 4 3 2 1

To Lucy the Pomeranian—
The manners in which you've outfoxed me are too embarrassing to disclose. You may have won more battles, but the war is far from over.

Dogs and philosophers do the greatest good and get the fewest rewards.

—Diogenes

THE LOST

PROLOGUE

The guest stirred the stew of fish, crab, salted pork, okra, and herbs with a silver spoon, pushing the polenta off to the side, saving it for last. "The kallaloo is mouthwatering."

"Pairs perfectly with the Petrus Pomerol." The estate's proprietor, a Belgian expatriate and host for the weekend's gathering, held his nearly empty crystal stemware under his nose. "Blackberry . . . a hint of green olive."

The acoustics of the dining hall were such that voices need never be raised as the host sat at the head of a handmade oak wood table while his guest perched at the opposite end. Each of the four walls in the dining hall contained an unaccompanied work of art—a singular painting. The east wall held a Monet, the south a Van Gogh, a Vermeer on the west side, and, finally, a masterpiece by Francisco Goya centered on the north wall.

"Thanks again for the invitation." The guest had two additional days of negotiations awaiting him in Chicago, commencing at seven o'clock sharp Monday morning. "You spared me a long weekend of sitting about the Waldorf Astoria."

"My apologies for it being so last minute, but when I heard you were in the city, I had to invite you to our weekend soirée."

"Your call was a delightful surprise."

"Were you able to catch some shut-eye?" The host had accompanied his arrival from the single helicopter pad that passed for the estate's airport to the guest suite where the visitor would be staying, and, as arranged, picked him up two hours later to escort him to the dining hall.

"A brief nap." The guest had flown to Chicago earlier in the week—all business, no pleasure—and then leapfrogged here on the host's Sikorsky S-76C. It was the first time he'd been to the host's Geneva Lake estate, a handful of curved miles from the city of Lake Geneva in southeastern Wisconsin where, once upon a time, the city had been a favored retreat for Chicago's rich and famous.

"Outstanding," the host said, and caught the eye of the estate's caretaker, a thick-set, raven-haired man who served as his maître d', personal steward, and concierge among other roles. The caretaker, who'd been standing by the servants' entrance, read his mind, walked quietly to the center of the table, retrieved the swan decanter, and refilled the visiting entrepreneur's wineglass, then did the same for his employer, bowed slightly, and returned to his post along the wall.

The guest began digging at his polenta. "When do our associates arrive?"

"First thing in the morning. I shall wake you."

"I'll be up." The guest sipped at his wine and took in the paintings on the four walls. "You've surrounded yourself in excellence, my friend—a Queen Anne cottage, an idyllic lake, fine cuisine and wine," the guest said, then added, "as well as magnificent artwork."

"The Queen Anne has been in the family for over a hundred years—my mother's side, the O'Fallons—and I haven't the heart to get rid of it. I spent summers here as a boy, many memories of loved ones long gone," the host said. "And don't get me started on beauty and the eye of the beholder, or I'll prattle all night. But, yes, by surrounding myself with the finer things in life—my *exquisites*, if you will—I am born anew. Not necessarily Ponce de León's Fountain of Youth," he said, waving a hand at the masterpieces on the walls of the dining hall, "but I do feel years younger."

The guest took in his host as though for the first time. Although the man was well into his sixties, a bit on the pale side, he looked a decade younger. Thin, with dark rectangular glasses set on an oval face, and every strand of his salt-and-pepper hair perfectly in place. Perhaps he should imitate his host and surround himself with expensive baubles and knickknacks. The items his Geneva Lake host had termed *exquisites.*

He stared at the Van Gogh on the south wall. "These paintings are originals, of course?"

The host smiled. "What do you think?"

"Please excuse me," he said. "I meant no offense."

The host brushed away his visitor's apology. "Speaking of artwork, I heard the most provocative of rumors about stolen paintings and the like."

"Do share."

The host set down his wineglass. "Have you ever been to the Kunsthal museum in Rotterdam?"

The guest shook his head.

"A stunning gallery, designed by a Dutch genius named Remment Koolhaas. The place houses no permanent collection; instead they present exhibits on loan from the world's greatest galleries."

"I shall put the museum on my bucket list."

"You must, but my tale isn't about the museum itself, rather what was stolen from there on October sixteenth of 2012."

The guest finished the last of his polenta and pushed his plate aside. "I may have heard of this heist."

"Considering what was purloined—I do love the word *purloined*—it made the papers around the world."

The duo stayed quiet as the caretaker collected their plates and then spoke in a timbre above a whisper, "Dessert will be served momentarily."

"Take your time, my friend," the host responded and turned his attention back to his visitor after the caretaker disappeared into the kitchen. "At 3:00 a.m. on that fateful morning, the museum's alarm—a state-of-the-art alarm, at that—went off. However, the thieves were gone by the time the police arrived."

"What did they take?"

"Seven famous paintings by seven famous artistes in one of the biggest art heists in history," the host replied. "Two Monets, a Picasso, a Matisse, a de Haan, and a Lucian Freud."

"That's only six."

"This is where the plot gets a bit twisty. The seventh piece was titled *Femme Devant une Fenêtre Ouverte*—or *Girl in Front of Open Window*—and was painted by the French Post-Impressionist Paul Gauguin."

At that, the caretaker returned with a silver tray of assorted dumplings—guava, peach, and gooseberry—served with cups of Black Ivory Coffee in china demitasses. He plated their desired pastries and placed both those plates and the cups of java in front of them.

"Do let chef know the food has been first-class."

"I shall do that, sir," the caretaker said, and returned to his spot along the wall.

"Smart choice of gooseberry. It will go well with the Black Ivory."

The guest lifted his cup and inhaled. "What was so *twisty* about the piece by Gauguin?"

"Oh yes." The host dabbed at his lips with a linen napkin and continued, "The art thieves were arrested the following summer, in Romania of all places. But everything hit a dead end at that point because the mother of one of the thieves claimed she burned the pilfered portraits to protect her wayward son. And even though the mother recanted her story in court, forensic specialists found pigments and nails pre-dating the twentieth century in her fireplace."

"The coffee lives up to its reputation, my friend. Alas," the guest said as he set down his cup, "your story leaves me with a heavy heart."

"But it's not over—the story doesn't end there."

"Pardon?"

"It doesn't end in the mother's fireplace," the host answered. "That was—how shall we say?—a continuation of the heist. Evidently, it's not an arduous task feeding *undistinguished* artwork pre-dating the twentieth century to the flames."

"So if the thieves were caught and the paintings not burned—where are they now?"

"I wish to God they were here; I'd hang them in this room. Unfortunately, they are *in the wind*, as detectives like to say—the paintings have vanished."

"And the Gauguin piece?"

"A puzzlement. What I've heard about the Gauguin is one part gossip, another part hearsay, with a dash of old wives' tale tossed in for good measure."

"What have you heard?"

"That the heist was put together by a *privileged* clique of millionaires—seven of them to be exact. And, to use espionage parlance, these men employed a *cutout*—a trusted intermediary—so the police could never link Kunsthal back to them." The host pushed aside his empty dessert plate and centered his cup of coffee in front of him. "I know—it sounds like the plot of a wretched movie, does it not? However, per the rumor, each millionaire got to keep one painting for their troubles, a single masterpiece that must remain forever hidden in their private collections."

"Let me guess—the one with the Gauguin had the others killed and kept everything for himself?"

"Not at all," the host replied. "This isn't a tale of murder, rather one of spite. The millionaire with the Gauguin was in on the heist for his wife's sake. Personally, he cared not one whit for any of the artwork, but his spouse—well, she was an enthusiast, a devotee of Post-Impressionism, especially of the work of Eugène Henri Paul Gauguin."

"So the millionaire was a romantic? He did it out of love?"

"In a manner. But love, as we both know, is fluid. It grows old—and stale—and when the inevitable divorce arrived, there was the typical amount of animosity that occurs as these things unfold; however, in regard to the Gauguin, the millionaire was of good cheer. Though it would never appear in their divorce settlement, he promised his wife the portrait."

"And they divorced happily ever after?"

"Sadly, no. When his ex-wife arrived to pick up the painting, she was brought downstairs to the underground room the two of them had devised specifically for the Gauguin a decade earlier. The front half of the room was for viewing the masterpiece, but the deeper half of the room—the half containing *Girl in Front of Open Window* on a display easel—was behind glass, the room temperature set to 70 degrees Fahrenheit and all that other fancy stuff."

"To keep the portrait in mint condition."

"More accurately, to keep it from the agents of deterioration. However, that was the last thing the millionaire had in mind on the day his ex-wife stopped by. He had her wait in the viewing room while he slipped inside the glass room carrying a Gatorfoam Board, several layers of cloth, and a canvas portfolio bag to protect the painting for when his ex-wife transported it to her newly purchased villa somewhere in the Mediterranean. But instead of witnessing her ex-husband gently shrouding the Gauguin in the transport materials, the ex-wife watched in horror as her ex reached into the portfolio bag, removed a can of lighter fluid, and drenched the priceless work of art with accelerant."

"My God," the guest said.

"She ran to the door of the glassed room, but her ex had it locked. She banged on the glass wall with her fists as he took out his cigarette lighter. He'd already disabled the fire protection system so it wouldn't interfere. She begged her ex not to do it as he brought the lighter closer, ever closer, to the painting, taunting her as she collapsed to the floor, in a bundle—weeping and wailing—as the Gauguin went up in flames."

"My God," the guest repeated.

"There was nothing she could do, as going to the authorities would implicate herself in the art heist," the host said, and pushed his empty cup to the side. "Although she'd driven to his mansion—her former home—she was in no condition to drive. The millionaire sent her back to her hotel in a taxicab."

* * *

"It's a shame you have to leave."

"My deepest apologies," the guest replied. "An ownership invest-ment requires my immediate attention. In fact, I'll need to shelve my venture in Chicago until this mess gets sorted. My phone," he held up his cell, "has been ringing off the hook. I'm sure you understand."

"Indeed, I do."

The host and his soon-to-depart guest were taking a morn-ing stroll. He was giving the entrepreneur the nickel tour of his Geneva Lake estate, showing him the sights. The caretaker was bringing the guest's luggage to the helipad, where the exit-ing guest would get to spend a little time meeting and greeting the arriving entrepreneurs—many of whom traveled in similar circles—before the host's Sikorsky S-76C would whisk him to Chicago O'Hare in order to catch his flight. What was supposed to have been a day of relaxation with some of the guest's contem-poraries had turned into a harried day of travel.

The two, sipping from bottles of Veen water, paused briefly at a giant fire pit encircled with chairs of faux wood, bonded leather, and wicker before continuing their jaunt past a grill station the size of a boxcar.

"Is there a way your venture can be resolved via Skype or Zoom?"

"Regretfully, no."

The host placed a sympathetic arm on his guest's back and guided him toward a diagonal series of weathered stone steps. "I've a final surprise."

The two men took the flight of steps to the slope's peak, atop which sat a dozen acres of flatland. Once they reached the sum-mit, the guest broke into a wide grin.

Hot air balloons, three of them.

One—striped in colors yellow and green, purple and red—lay on the far side of the field waiting to be inflated, a gondola of woven wicker next to it. Another balloon in a checkerboard patch of hues laid midfield, next to a yellow-and-brown gondola. The gondola for the nearest balloon was on its side, where the caretaker was busy at work, an open toolbox at his feet.

"Ballooning has been in the family for generations, back before my mother was born." The host smiled. "Nothing but blue skies for a ride over the lake."

"Magnificent."

"The gondolas hold sixteen passengers." The host led his guest over to inspect the nearest balloon—ripstop nylon in patches of red and white—which lay on the grass. "We'll be toasting the lake with flutes of champagne."

The guest sighed. "You are making it most difficult, my friend."

The host began pointing out the various sections. "You've got the balloon—technically called an envelope—the gondola, or basket, to carry passengers, and, of course, the heat source, a burner that gasifies liquid propane and directs the flame." He tossed a hand at his caretaker and added, "There's been some trouble with the unit on this one, a busted regulator or something, but, fear not, the other two are in fine repair."

The caretaker nodded at the guest and said, "Your bags are at the helipad, sir." He glanced at his watch. "We should head there soon."

The host turned to his guest. "Another Veen for the road?"

"Please."

"I certainly hope our dinner conversation didn't sour you on staying the weekend," the host said as he headed over to a giant cooler next to the overturned gondola. "I have the gift for gab and should not have bored you with stories of art heists and torched portraits."

"No, my friend. I found your talk most *educational*." The guest stared at the hot air balloon at his feet. "In fact, a question occurred to me: How did you hear of this *rumor*? Has one of the millionaires been—what is the saying?—telling tales out of school."

"Remember when I said it was part gossip, part hearsay, and part old wives' tale?"

The guest nodded.

"Perhaps I should have been more clear—it was part *ex-wife's tale.*"

The guest's eyes shot toward his host.

"No others are arriving today. This weekend was always about you," the host said. "Don't get me wrong, I forgive the heist completely; nevertheless, you incinerated a Gauguin, *my friend* . . . you destroyed a masterpiece." He stared into his guest's eyes a long second. "Wouldn't that demand something apropos?"

And with that the caretaker hit the blast valve, activating the rigged burner, and gasifying the liquid propane. Flames shot from the burner—a dragon spitting fire—encompassing the weekend's guest of honor, setting him ablaze.

The man's screams lasted several seconds.

The scent of burnt flesh lingered until nightfall, when the caretaker dropped the remains into Geneva Lake at the point of maximum depth.

PART ONE

THE SUPERMODEL

The dog was created specially for children. He is a god of frolic.
—Henry Ward Beecher

CHAPTER 1

"Look, I'm a big enough guy to admit when I'm jealous." I spoke to Vira, my golden retriever who rode shotgun in the passenger seat of my aging Ford pickup. We were heading toward a job that, amazingly, Special Agent in Charge Len Squires—the head of the Chicago Division of the Federal Bureau of Investigation—had sent my way. We were on the west side of Lake Michigan, winding through some Glencoe roads on our journey to the Kenneth and Calley Kurtz Druckman estate. The sun was on the rise; our windows were down. It was another beautiful late-summer morning, and Lynyrd Skynyrd rocked on the pickup's radio.

"I'm not sure if you've noticed, Vira, but whenever you snuggle up to Kippy, she'll flick my arm, point at you, and say, 'She likes me more, she likes me more' or, even worse, 'Na-na na-na boo-boo.'"

Glencoe, a village in northeastern Cook County, on Chicago's North Shore, lies twenty-plus miles north of downtown. Glencoe is one of the richest, most affluent, and most exclusive suburbs in Illinois, and maybe in the entire country. Needless to say, I don't get up here much. They probably have a picture of me posted at the city limits with a couple of red lines crossing my face.

"I guess what I'm wondering, Vira, is if you could throttle it back a little bit?" I continued, though my golden retriever appeared more interested in Ronnie Van Zant belting out "Sweet Home Alabama" than in listening to my yammering. "There could be extra snacks in your future if you, say, tilted things in my direction when we're with Kippy. I know you love them pretzels of yours—crispy, salted on the outside. Be a shame not to get any more. That's all I'm saying."

Like most guys who date out of their league, I've come up with a dozen ways in which to introduce Kippy Gimm to everyone I've ever met, have ever known, or even passed on the street. Us guys who date above ourselves should form a secret society—a brethren of the blessed—where we can sing songs, shoot hoops, drink beer, and high-five. Who knows, maybe we could even get a group discount on auto insurance.

Now don't get me wrong, I like to think I'm not as clunky as some of those other lucky bastards you've spotted parading about the streets and malls—big, dopey smiles on their faces, hands entwined with their eye-catching lady friends—my comrades-in-arms who've somehow managed to date several niches above themselves. My mom once informed me I ranked a ten, though there may be some maternal bias hidden in her assessment. In high school, my older sister told me I was *maybe* a seven, which is likely closer to the mark. I'm on the ass-end of my twenties—spitting distance from the big three-o—stand at that six-foot-nothing height, am a bit on the wiry side, and sprout a disagreeable thatch of brown hair that gets brushed on days I'm seeing Kippy and finger-combed on days I'm not.

"I don't mean to dump on Kippy or anything, Vira, but, you have to admit, she does kind of screw you over on the walks," I said, glancing at my golden retriever. She looked my way, but then stuck her head out the window. "Remember, girl—the Zen walks are all on me."

Since dogs live through their sense of smell, I'll let Vira sniff each twig, every dried leaf, fire hydrant, stop sign, tree, or random rabbit turd as though she'd just discovered the Lost City of El Dorado. Thus a walk out to the mailbox turns into an hours-long odyssey. On the other hand, Kippy doesn't think a trip around the block should take the amount of time it took Magellan to reach the East Indies. Kippy walks for cardio, always keeping

Vira at a brisk pace with a half snort here or a quick sniff over there. Kippy's philosophy is that Vira has smelled enough leaves, litter, and roadkill to last a thousand lifetimes, and, if they ever truly stumble upon the Lost City of El Dorado, she'll let Vira linger a moment or two before they zip onward to the park.

The two gals—Kippy and Vira—have a special relationship. Kippy met Vira first, having been the patrol officer answering the call about a suspected suicide via carbon monoxide poisoning in a closed garage at a townhome in Forest Glen. Some unhinged drunk had been gassing my little girl—her capital offense being only that she had been picked out of a litter of puppies as a household pet by the drunkard's former girlfriend whom he himself had just chased from their home. The drunkard had even managed to off himself as the carbon monoxide seeped into the kitchen where he'd been sitting at the island, getting intimate with a fifth of Jack Daniel's and beer.

Good riddance.

Vira somehow survived, and stumbled out of the lunatic's garage and into the open arms of Officer Kippy Gimm. Soon after that fateful night I'd picked Vira up at CACC—Chicago Animal Care and Control—and adopted her into my canine family.

My name is Mason Reid—I go by Mace—and I specialize in human remains detection. That is, I train dogs to hunt for the dead. I train HRD dogs—human remains detection dogs or, more bluntly, cadaver dogs. Vira is my prize pupil, the most gifted cadaver dog I've ever trained or met, and together we help the law enforcement authorities—CPD, various sheriff departments, and, as of this morning, the FBI—hunt for the missing and presumed dead. I call my pack of cadaver dogs *The Finders* and would promote them in billboard ads had I a few extra grand lying about the dresser table.

Just last spring, Kippy, Vira, and I found ourselves in a hell of a bind, but we'd fought back—somehow managed to stay on the right side of dirt—and brought the FBI Special Agent in Charge, Len Squires, information that led to the arrest and incarceration of a corrupt police superintendent, as well as the sitting mayor of

Chicago. It also led to the execution of the head of the Chicago Outfit—evidently, his *colleagues* got it in their collective noggins that, sooner or later, the mob boss would try cutting a deal with the prosecutors—you know, screw omertà and turn federal informant.

I turned off my pickup's radio as Vira and I were waved past a daunting set of wrought-iron gates by one of SAC Squires's investigators. I steered the F-150 another half mile on the paved road that wound itself toward Druckman Manor. The Kenneth Druckman family lived in a Georgian-style mansion of reddish brick and raked roofs situated on a forty-acre spread along the shore of Lake Michigan. The front of the Druckman estate was a beehive of activity: numerous squad cars from the Glencoe PD, plus a handful of dark sedans, as well as two black panel vans, which I assumed came with SAC Squires, were all parked on one side of an outsized roundabout driveway that encircled a hedge maze. I parked next to one of the forensic vans, leashed Vira, and the two of us loitered about the front walkway. Agent Squires spotted us, nodded our way, but remained standing halfway up a stoop that would look more natural atop the Parthenon in ancient Athens. He was deep in conversation with a bath-robed and clearly shaken Kenneth Druckman.

Any other day and I'd have unleashed Vira and seen how long it would take her to get the two of us to the center of Druckman's maze of hedges. But today, I figured the FBI might frown on that.

Because, today, Calley Kurtz Druckman and her daughter had been kidnapped.

CHAPTER 2

After SAC Squires had instructed me on the phone to make haste to the Druckman estate, he confirmed several of my follow-up queries. Yes, it was *that* Kenneth J. Druckman, the founder and CEO of Druckman Financial Group, a financial planning and asset management firm, and one of the wealthiest people in Chicago, possibly in the United States, maybe even planet Earth. And, yes, I'd probably seen him interviewed a time or two on TV—well, only long enough for me to find the clicker and flip to another channel. CEO Druckman could be found in front of a camera whenever a Windy City business anchor needed a talkative and photogenic financier to discuss upswings or downswings, even minor speed bumps, in the global economy.

Kenneth J. Druckman—with his styled-to-perfection black hair, sparkling blue eyes, and crisp Giorgio Armani suits—served that purpose well.

However, the real reason I knew about Druckman was because of the celebrity whom the financier had married . . . Calley Kurtz.

Calley Kurtz had worked as a fashion model during my, shall we say, *formative years*. I might still have that old *Sports Illustrated* Swimsuit Issue on which Calley had graced the cover hidden away in a bottom drawer somewhere back at my trailer home. CEO Druckman had met the supermodel when she'd come to Chicago for some photoshoot or another, nature took its course, and the two were married in the Crystal Ballroom at the Millennium Knickerbocker Hotel on New Year's Eve a half-dozen or so years ago.

You'd have had to be blind and deaf to live in Chicago and not have heard about the event at the time. Everyone who was anyone had been there. My invite must have gotten lost in the mail, but I saw the pictures in the newspaper, and Calley Kurtz did not appear to have aged a day since the week I blew my allowance springing for that now dog-eared issue of *Sports Illustrated*. The papers also highlighted the engagement ring Druckman bought Calley: a rock the size of Mount St. Helens.

SAC Len Squires patted financier Druckman on the forearm, and stepped down our way.

"Thanks for driving out, Mace," Squires said. The head of the FBI's field office in Chicago fit central casting to a T, that is, if you subtracted half a foot in height. Square-jawed and hawk-nosed, Agent Squires may have topped five-six if he stretched or got measured first thing in the morning. But based on the way he'd pulled our chestnuts out of the fire during those most-unpleasant circumstances last May, in my book Len Squires stood ten-feet tall.

"So the poor guy's wife and daughter were taken, huh?"

Squires nodded. "Two white males and a Hispanic, early to mid-twenties, broke into the house around 3:00 a.m. They knocked Mr. Druckman around a little bit—broke his eyeglasses—and stuck a steak knife to his wife's throat so he'd open their jewelry safe. They also took whatever cash they found lying about, plus watches and rings and other miscellaneous stuff."

"It started as a home invasion?"

Squires nodded again. "They were expecting more cash—as though rich people don't keep their money in banks like the rest of us—and got all bent out of shape at their de minimis haul. Druckman tried educating them on the value of fine art, the paintings and sculptures about the house, but got punched in the face for his effort."

"Not exactly art buffs."

"I doubt this bunch would have a clue about unloading stolen paintings, much less whatever treasures they got out of the wall safe," Squires replied. "Instead, they went postal. Grabbed Druckman's wife and daughter, and told Druckman he'd better pony up ten million in cash apiece if he ever wanted to see them alive again."

"Aw, jeez."

"Anyway, Druckman's going to scrape together the money for when they phone with instructions, but the man's scared to death. He said all three of the assailants kept smacking him in the back of the head at random moments, just out of spite. He thinks they were on drugs and they weren't only looking for cash but painkillers and maybe rec drugs—amphetamines or coke or whatever. They did ransack the medicine cabinets and tear through drawers."

"They get anything?"

"Ambien and some brand of valium Mrs. Druckman had tucked away," he said. "Druckman's terrified the assailants will come to realize how stupid it is to try and collect ransom in this day and age. And when they do, maybe they'll *hurt* his family—maybe do things to his wife—maybe kill both the wife and daughter so they won't be able to ID anyone. That's why he called the cops and then the Bureau."

Behind Druckman's mansion lay several acres of brush and wetland. "You want me and Vira to check the backwoods, right?"

"That'd be great, Mace," Squires said. "It's about a half mile of trees and marsh and muck before it hits a public road on the far side."

"And we're positive they left that way?" According to my earlier call with Squires, the kidnappers had cut through the back mire in the wee hours of the morning.

"They half-assed tied Druckman to the staircase railing in the front entryway. He didn't hear a car start or anything in the five minutes it took him to jiggle free and call 911. And the gates were shut when Glencoe PD showed up." Squires added, "The Druckmans got home late last night from some charity banquet downtown, and he thinks his wife may not have reset the security system after they came in."

Evidently, the Druckmans had originally planned on staying overnight in the city. A reservation for a top-floor suite had been made at the Langham. As such, house staff and security personnel had been given the night off. However, a wave of nausea had swept through Calley during the event's dinner, and the allure of recuperating on the Egyptian cotton sheets at Casa de Druckman proved too attractive to resist. The Druckmans grabbed their daughter, treated their nanny to the penthouse suite for the rest of the evening, and hightailed it back here to Glencoe with Eleanor in tow.

"Eleanor?"

"That's their daughter," Squires said. "She's five years old." He must have read the look on my face, because he followed with, "I know."

The only staff on-site had been the gardener, but he'd been sound asleep in the servants' cottage a hundred yards away when the police arrived. The gardener said he'd been awake, watching TV, and heard when the Druckmans pulled in a little before eleven, but he hadn't seen nor heard any other vehicles before he dropped off to sleep an hour later. This supported the general consensus that the unknown subjects, or *unsubs* as Squires termed the home invaders, must have approached Druckman Manor from the rear, passing through the ravine and the muck.

"Mind if I borrow a few of your guys? There might be some trails back there, and several of us could cover the ground a lot more quickly."

"Of course," Squires said. "We've got you here to cover all bases, Mace. But I hope to hell you don't find anything."

CHAPTER 3

Three of Squires's agents and I fanned out, letting Vira plunge into the woods ahead of us. Human remains detection dogs are trained to identify the distinct odor of decomposing human flesh and then alert their handlers. If there's anyone deceased in the marsh and the woodlands, Vira will find them—with or without that *special thing* she's got going. Dogs kick our asses in the olfactory department. Canines have three hundred million scent receptors, as opposed to the paltry five million divvied out to mere humans. As scents exist for a chunk of time after they've been laid, sniffing, for my pups, is like streaming a National Geographic documentary on things that may have occurred in a particular spot. That said, Kippy and I had always struggled to define Vira's *special thing*. The easiest analogy might be that for every fifty million of us dunderheads ambling about with a finger in our nose and wondering what's for dinner, there's an Albert Einstein or a Thomas Edison or a Marie Curie hidden in the mix.

Why should it be any different for dogs?

When we're at a murder scene—where Vira has discovered human remains—she has the briefest of episodes, the shortest of spells or seizures or whatever the hell you want to call them. And, afterward, my golden retriever comes away having made . . . *connections*.

Now, before you contact the authorities and have me committed to Chicago Lakeshore Hospital, please hear me out.

Murder's an intimate act, right? And we all know, at least from years spent watching the nightly news or true crime shows on cable, that murderers leave behind a mountain of physical evidence. All sorts of DNA for the CSI teams and medical examiners to ferret through—fingerprints, footprints, hair, skin under fingernails, saliva, blood, semen, you name it.

So why couldn't there be scent DNA—some kind of scent aura or chemical signature—left at crime scenes as well?

Vira, and perhaps all HRD dogs, receive this tidal wave of stimulus, this tsunami of scent data, and my golden retriever then takes the art of human remains detection to the next level . . . to the Albert Einstein or Thomas Edison or Marie Curie level. When Vira discovers a body or visits a crime scene, she attempts to process this data, to perform some kind of forensic analysis on the various smells and odors—the scent DNA—in order to decipher their meaning.

I mentioned canine scent receptors, which are for all practical purposes supernatural to begin with as they enable dogs to identify thousands and thousands of different odors. And in Vira's case, she attempts to interpret these odors.

Vira makes links, she makes relationships . . . *connections* . . . Vira connects the unseen dots.

If you'd still feel safer with me eating Jell-O in a rubber room at Chicago Lakeshore, let me bend your ear a moment longer. Let's say I'm a serial killer who—aw hell, I don't know—has it in for the local Tiddlywinks champions. I really hate them disc-flipping bastards, so I'll grab one, take him or her—why do I think they'd mostly be male?—to my hidden lair, where I'd mess with them for weeks before, eventually, jamming a cup full of winks down their throats and watching as they slowly asphyxiate. Later, under the cover of darkness, I'd dump their bodies near playgrounds at public parks.

Perhaps I'd leave behind some blood or hair, saliva or footprints, or even fibers from my clothing for the crime scene investigators to rummage through. Knowing me, I'd make a helluva mess out of being the *Tiddlywink Killer*. I'd likely leave my fingerprints all over the winks for the CSI agents to discover. Anyway, all of this forensic evidence would point in my direction. Similarly, if Vira came across the body of one of my Tiddlywinks victims, she'd do her damnedest to piece together whatever forensic scent or aura exists at the scene . . . up to and including the tiniest trace of the murderer.

In other words, Vira'd sniff out my fingerprints on the Tiddlywinks.

And I'm positive she'd stare at me in a most-peculiar manner right before she ran to Kippy to tattle.

It hadn't rained much in weeks. The ponds on Druckman's back property were shallow, the soil dry, and the brush gnarled and thick. Five minutes in, Vira barked. I cut left to follow the sound, jogged along the gulch until I spotted my golden retriever—dead silent now and quivering as though a million beetles stirred beneath her fur.

Vira was having one of her episodes.

It was then I spotted the small foot jutting out from behind a boulder.

I knelt down, placed a hand on Vira's back, hoping to calm her, hoping she could sense I was there, hoping to snap her out of the spell she was in. I clipped the leash to the back of her harness and wondered for the hundredth time what happens during these episodes of hers. Is the act of murder so intense, so extreme, that some chemical signature lingers in the place where a life has been taken?

But lingers for how long—a day, weeks, a month?

A thousand years?

I followed Vira's gaze to the body. What I saw turned my stomach, and I quickly looked away. Someone had smashed Supermodel Calley Kurtz Druckman's once-stunning face against the boulder. Smashed it repeatedly. Again. And again. Leaving poor Calley lying out here alone in the darkness, alone in the cold . . . never again to grace the cover of any magazine.

Suddenly, Vira sprang to life, back in the here and now. She knocked hard against my chest, caught my eye for the briefest of seconds, jumped around me, and pointed herself back toward the Druckman mansion, tugging hard at the leash.

Vira could not have been clearer had she spoken English with closed captioning on display for the hard of hearing, but I held firm, needing a minute to absorb everything, to sort out what my golden retriever was telling me.

A flash of movement, and I spotted the agent who'd flagged me past the entry gates cutting into the ravine from the opposite side of the thicket, slowly approaching, his eyes focused at the base of the boulder—on what had once been Calley Kurtz. He was one of the agents who'd been helping us search the brush and the muck at the back of the Druckman estate. I tried recalling his name but came up blank.

"A horrible sight," the agent said after a long moment and lifted his head toward me. "I called Squires and he's on his way." The nameless agent held a cell phone in one hand. "I'm going to go wave him and the others over, try and keep them off to the side, off whatever path those bastards took."

"I'll go get him," I said, standing. "You should probably stay here; secure the scene or whatever it is you need to do."

"Okay," the agent agreed. "But keep to the side—by the bushes—and stay off anything that looks like shoeprints or any other tracks they may have left."

Vira and I kept to the side, as instructed, as we threaded our way back toward Druckman's manor. I thought hard about Kenneth J. Druckman . . . and I wondered if he'd concocted his tale of a home invasion turned kidnapping before or after he'd murdered his wife.

You see, if Vira's peeked into your soul—if she's captured your chemical signature at a murder site—she gets aggressive. Some golden retrievers have it in them to be aggressive, especially if they've experienced abuse or neglect at an early age. But I believe it's Vira's street smarts—her awareness on some base level of the evil that men do, plus her having connected the brutality of murder to whom she believes to be responsible—that triggers her aggression.

Sure, Vira's playful, gentle around children, a loving spirit, but if she finds out you've hurt someone . . . or killed them . . . you'd best be on the next train out of Dodge.

And she'd had plenty of time to latch on to Druckman's chemical signature—gotten a big trace off him—as we stood at the bottom of the steps while he interacted with SAC Squires.

"It can never be easy," I said, absorbed in how best to sway Squires away from CEO Druckman's narrative regarding a random band of home invaders. Perhaps tell him Vira followed the killer's scent back to the mansion, which, in a manner, she had. Perhaps suggest they scour the ravine to see if there truly were multiple footprints left by multiple assailants. Perhaps I could bring up domestic abuse or crimes of passion or ask him if they still looked at the spouse first.

Not overkill, not anything to make it weird with the special agent in charge. Just enough to plant the seed—a notion—in order to point Len Squires in the right direction.

Suddenly, another thought occurred to me—what the hell had become of Kenneth J. Druckman's daughter?

I stared at my golden retriever. "It can never be easy, can it, girl?"

Vira barked once and strained hard against the leash.

CHAPTER 4

FOUR WEEKS AGO

The Belgian sat upright on the masculine side—the segment with a male hand and wristwatch engraved in the endcap—of his black Vis-à-vis de Gala. The Salvador Dalí–inspired piece of furniture had been centered in the music appreciation room, and the Belgian expat sat perfectly still, hands cupped on his lap, his eyes shut, as he listened to Wolfgang Amadeus Mozart. His speaker system currently played *Sinfonia Concertante for Violin, Viola and Orchestra*—not one of Mozart's most-celebrated works, nevertheless one of his best.

Though the Belgian played not a note of piano, a meticulously restored 1904 Steinway baby grand—all genuine action parts—dominated the southwest corner of his music appreciation room. In the opposite corner, the northeast corner, stood a six-foot vintage Lyon & Healy Model G, even though he also didn't play the harp. In the northwest corner sat a late nineteenth-century Husson Buthod double bass by Charles Jacquot. Again, the estate's proprietor played not a note of double bass music. And filling out the southeast corner of the music room was a 1720 Red Mendelssohn Stradivarius in a wooden holder lined in black velvet, surrounded by several antique woodwinds—a clarinet, oboe, and flute—on their respective stands. Again, not a note.

When Mozart's *Sinfonia Concertante* came to an end, the Belgian opened his eyes. A second later the door to the music appreciation room swung open—his staff knew better than to interrupt anything by Wolfgang Amadeus—and there stood his caretaker.

"The financials have arrived, sir," the caretaker said softly. "I've placed them in your study."

The Belgian took a sip from his tumbler of Caribbean Cask from Balvenie—a single malt matured in rum casks. The cherry and brown sugar flavor was certainly not for everyone's palate, but he enjoyed it. The Belgian leaned back from his computer, then swiveled about in his leather desk chair and stared out the bay window of his office into the bluish-green waters of Geneva Lake and off into the horizon.

Truth be told, he would give up each and every one of his real estate investments before he'd ever contemplate selling this place. Ultimately, this was his home and, of course, there was that *other* reason he couldn't sell.

Plus, the Belgian had more than a small amount of business in Chicago—ninety minutes by car, much less by air. And there was always the Chicago Symphony, of which he served on the board of trustees, as well as the Lyric Opera, of which he was a patron and also served on their board of directors.

The family's Queen Anne sat on an eighty-acre spread—twenty of which stood atop a hillside overlooking the lake—situated across nearly eight miles of fresh water from the City of Lake Geneva. The mansion—over twelve thousand square feet and twenty rooms—had originally been built as a summer cottage in 1890. Not counting the attic, it stood two stories tall, revealing a roofline of gabled dormers and stone chimneys. His mother had grown up here—back in its heyday, when she'd once attended a performance by the great Louis Armstrong at the Riviera in Lake Geneva—before she ventured off to Chicago, ostensibly for university, but, instead, fell head over heels for his father, a devil-may-care Belgian steel tycoon who was in town on business.

The two were married in record time.

The Belgian loved his summers here with his mother and her

family—great memories; plenty of Rosebuds, though not sleds—much more than the remainder of the year, which the two spent with his father's clan in Antwerp. His father, as it turned out—when his mask slipped, and his father's mask slipped often and without warning—was more devil than devil-may-care.

Six months after his mother's suicide—when he was in his mid-teens—the Belgian dealt with his father and, after the inquiries had concluded, and though he'd traveled all over Europe, he'd never set foot in Antwerp or any other part of Belgium ever again.

The Belgian expat's thoughts returned to the present.

He spent a day each month auditing how the funds from his various financial planning and asset management firms—an extended array of stocks and bonds, derivatives and commodities, currency funds and ETFs, options and futures—were being utilized, as well as what financial returns had been yielded in the latest cycle, what, if any, additional wealth had accrued. His review was a tedious monthly task as he seemed to have amassed more investment advisors than the Hydra had heads.

That's where the scotch whisky came into play.

It had been an *okay* month, a little better than expected and, considering the ways of the world lately, certainly not as bad as it could have been. However, there was a favorable rate of return from a financial group he'd recently begun investing with . . . a most promising RoR at that.

The Belgian swiveled back to his desktop and thought about returning to his music appreciation room. Perhaps a little Beethoven to unwind to after what had seemed an eternity staring at long columns of numerals on printouts. He took another sip from his tumbler of Caribbean Cask, and then pressed the pager to summon his assistant.

Within seconds, the caretaker appeared in the office doorway. "Is there something I can get for you, sir?"

"How is our patient doing today?"

"About the same."

"Still using the eye gel?"

"Four times a day, sir."

"Excellent," the Belgian said. "It's imperative we keep his vision in tiptop condition." He glanced at the financial documents that lay on his desk. "I need you to arrange for travel, my friend. It appears we'll be spending a little time in Chicago."

CHAPTER 5

"I've never known you to be subtle, Mace," Kippy said.

"I couldn't run to Squires screaming, 'Druckman killed his wife! My golden retriever says so!'" I added, "So I went subtle, and we locked eyes."

"You *locked eyes*?"

"I told him Vira was dragging me back to Druckman's house and, yes, Squires and I *locked eyes*." I felt I had pushed him in Kenneth J. Druckman's direction as far as I dare, lest the special agent in charge start looking at me with a suspicion commonly reserved for certain shows appearing on the midway at the state fair.

"Did he say anything?"

I shrugged. "He said they'd already searched the premises and that he wanted me to run Vira around the rest of the woods in case, you know, she caught onto *another* scent."

"The daughter?"

"Yeah, Squires most immediate concern was getting us back out there to search for Druckman's missing daughter. And I couldn't argue with that."

"But he caught the point of what you were saying with the *locked eyes* thing, right?" she asked. "People can lock eyes over anything. Maybe he thought you were asking him out for dinner."

"I wasn't asking him out for dinner. Look, I'll text the guy and spell it out—something like: *I think Vira followed the murderer's trail back to Druckman's house.*"

"Good idea. Much better than locking eyes." Kippy made air quotes over her last two words.

The two of us sat at the picnic table in my backyard, chomping beer brats, corn on the cob, and—courtesy of Kippy—homemade deviled eggs potato salad. I glanced at Kippy out of both habit and hobby. After four months of dating, I'd memorized her features: an athlete's build (Kip kicks my ass in basketball); a silky mane of black hair, medium cut; high cheekbones and sharp angles; a slender neck; and a couple of deep brown eyes that could almost make me crack open a volume of sonnets.

Her potato salad wasn't bad either.

The dogs had all been fed. Vira lay at Kippy's feet. Sue had done his business near a pine tree, and then sauntered back through the open screen door, no doubt returning to his papal throne upon the sofa as there was more TV for him to monitor. Delta Dawn and Maggie May flittered about on the lawn while Billie Joe pressed his luck near the tree line. My bloodhound puppy would be about to step into the woods on the periphery of my property but would then peek back at me, knowing full well what was coming. I'd shake my head, and he'd mosey back to the yard, but, five minutes later, he'd again be edging toward the tree line to test my resolve.

I'd called Kippy on the drive home from Glencoe to ask if she could run a quick check on Druckman. "And don't say anything to anyone," I had instructed her.

"Why?"

"I'll determine by dinnertime whether you're to be trusted or not."

I felt a tinge of treachery as SAC Squires had cautioned me against talking with anybody about my morning in Glencoe. He wanted to contain the day's events and planned to implement a news blackout until the kidnapping played itself out. Before I left, Squires was conferring with the detectives from Glencoe PD about sending Calley Kurtz Druckman to the medical examiner's office as a Jane Doe.

But Vira's verdict in the ravine behind Druckman's mansion had kicked things to the next level . . . the Kippy Gimm level as we tried to figure out what, if anything, she or I could do. Plus, there was no way in hell that Kippy would break radio silence or run to the media.

Ten seconds later she came back on the phone and informed me the man had never been arrested—no DUI charges, no jay-walking or speeding tickets, not even a parking meter violation. Kenneth J. Druckman was squeaky clean; he'd never done a nanosecond behind bars. Once home, I googled *Druckman Financial Group.* It came back with a million hits, brimming with Wharton School mumbo jumbo. I couldn't make it three paragraphs into any of the articles before drifting into a coma. No allegations on how Druckman's investment firm was secretly funding an overthrow of the United States government; no exposés on the financial group's involvement in arms, drugs, or sex trafficking; no claims of tax evasion or price fixing . . . not so much as even breaking the curfew.

Nothing.

"I'm thinking crime of passion, not money, because Druckman's already super rich," I said. "Either he was cheating on Calley, or Calley was cheating on him and he found out, or he's a closet psycho and finally snapped."

"Could be worse, though. It could be intentional and premeditated—first-degree murder." Kippy shook her head. "That poor little girl."

"Eleanor?"

"Yeah—if she's not already dead, he'd have her stashed some-where while this hoax of his plays itself out. All Druckman has to do is dance through today's farce before he kicks everything over to his attorneys."

We sat a moment in silence, lost in thought, and it dawned on me how neither Kippy nor I had weighed the possibility that our golden retriever had been mistaken in the woodland behind

Druckman Manor. We'd been down this road a handful of times, enough to have excised all incredulity about Vira's sleuthing ability.

"So how was your day, *Copper*?" I said, changing the subject. Those old VHS movies of James Cagney and Edward G. Robinson in my dad's collection hadn't completely gone to waste.

"Clearly a bit more subdued than yours, *Dogger*," Kippy replied, and I wondered which of us had procured the better nickname. "Just another day watching my new partner's shoulder blades keep his head from stretching farther up his rump."

Kippy had graduated top of her class at the police academy, had killed it on both CPD's written and physical exams, and had shown up at the table with a bachelor's degree in criminal justice. Kippy had also served as a police officer out of the 17th District—Albany Park—for two and a half years. After the events of last spring, the Chicago Police Department was left with a swollen, shiny, and watery black eye that the press dissected from each and every possible angle. However, in the midst of all this horse manure, CPD's acting superintendent discovered a pony—a pony to feed the media—said pony being young, female, and a photogenic police officer by the name of Kippy Gimm, the cop who'd worked hand-in-hand with the FBI to not only take down the corrupt police superintendent, but Chicago's sitting mayor as well. Kippy found herself cast as the fashionable cosmetic concealer used to mask over CPD's black eye.

With great fanfare and headlines, Kippy was transferred from her station in Albany Park to the Bureau of Detectives and assigned as an investigator inside the Area North Detective Division. Kippy didn't care for the attention and had quietly turned down CPD's initial offer of working for BIA—the Bureau of Internal Affairs. As a result, the acting superintendent went with Plan B, something more in line with Kippy's career goals, and she was assigned to the Violent Crimes section inside Area North.

Unfortunately, something not envisioned in CPD's face-saving maneuver was how Kippy's new colleagues and fellow detectives might take to the news of her advancement through the ranks.

Into the mix walked Detective Trevor Ames—Kippy's new partner. Detective Ames, with his perfectly formed brown beard and mustache, looked as though he'd stepped out from a grooming infomercial on late night TV, only without the pitchman's charisma. And if you're around Detective Ames for any length of time, a beard comb will work its way out from his breast pocket and begin raking away at his face. Kippy once caught him doing so over a bowl of soup at lunch.

But it wasn't her assigned partner's appearance that irked Kippy. It was Ames's condescending attitude . . . and his dismissive treatment of her.

When Detective Ames wasn't outright patronizing, reciting such sage advice as "Murderers must be caught, and not simply because murder is wrong, but to keep them from killing again," he was either rambling on about the perfect barbecue sauce or ignoring Kippy altogether. While operating in condescension mode, Detective Ames tended to drizzle these nuggets of wisdom atop Kippy slowly, overpronouncing each and every syllable, often in front of her fellow investigators, as though he were mentoring a very slow special ed student. It was like she was being shown the ropes by a malignant Mr. Rogers.

"I can't even look at him anymore."

"You're just miffed because we didn't make the cut for his stupid picnic," I replied. Detective Ames fancies himself some kind of virtuoso in front of the backyard grill; he's even submitted his homemade rubs to a few of the Windy City's renowned BBQ contests. And Ames celebrates the arrival of fall by inviting colleagues over for grilled chicken and ribs and shish kebabs on the season's first weekend. And though Kippy was his new partner—someone he should be bonding with as well as mentoring—she'd yet to receive an invite.

"Oh please," Kippy shot back. "I'd have snuck into his bathroom and picked hairs off his brush to wedge under the fingernails of our next homicide vic. See if they let Ames flip burgers while doing thirty at Stateville."

It was good to see Kippy hadn't lost her sense of humor, but

I knew that, internally, it gnawed at her gut like one of my dogs on a chew toy. And I suspected Detective Ames knew exactly what he was doing. Ames wasn't happy about being paired with Kippy—felt she didn't measure up, didn't deserve to be a detective in Violent Crimes, that her promotion was unearned, just public relations BS, and that she was *unworthy* of working cases with him. The man was doing his damnedest to discourage Kippy, to kill her self-confidence, make her second-guess herself, alienate her from the others in their unit . . . and, ultimately, make her quit. I also knew Ames wasn't the only one who believed Kippy's meteoric rise to be the result of favoritism, but despite being her partner—her freaking partner—Ames had no interest in giving Kippy even the tiniest of chances to prove herself.

What Ames didn't know—what he was too lazy and dim to realize—is that Kippy was scrappy as hell. She'd give as good as she got, and a sixth ice age would come and pass before she'd let this pissant excuse for a detective dampen her spirit.

Kippy took off shortly after dinner, heading back to her apartment in Irving Park where she'd continue her efforts late into the evening: verifying case records are as detailed as possible; prepping court papers, search warrants or subpoenas or summonses; contacting witnesses with additional questions; calling the victim or their family; even touching base with other law enforcement agencies or the district attorney's office. Then, after a short night's snooze, Kippy would be up by five and at work an hour or two before Detective Ames or any of her other colleagues came straggling in.

Here's what I know for a fact about Kippy—she'd be putting in these same long hours, day and night, regardless of whether her partner and his acolytes flung shit her way or not.

Her DNA demanded it.

And if the Area North Detective Division inside CPD's Bureau of Detectives didn't appreciate Kippy Gimm . . . I certainly did.

CHAPTER 6

You know Vira—truncated from "Elvira," named after the song made famous by the Oak Ridge Boys—so let me tell you about the other kids. My brood or pack or tribe or den of canines also consists of Maggie May, a short-haired farm collie named after the Rod Stewart gem; Delta Dawn, Maggie's sister, named after the 1970s hit; Sue, our ten-year-old German shepherd and fiery patriarch, named, of course, after the Johnny Cash song; and now Billie Joe, my half-year-old bloodhound, named after Bobbie Lee Gentry's "Ode to Billie Joe."

In case it escaped your notice, I tend to christen my dogs after country or country rock songs.

Billie Joe the bloodhound, however, is also known as Bill the Roller due to this fetish of his I've been working with him to overcome. Instinctually—to hunt successfully—dogs roll in pungent-smelling substances so their prey will be unable to detect their presence; unfortunately, Bill takes all this to the next level. My trailer sits on a two-acre spread in Lansing, Illinois, a village about seven miles south of Chicago's city limits, and if Lansing's Water and Sewer Department ever decided they were going to dump the contents of the porta potties from the local high school's football stadium onto my backyard, Billie Joe would be in seventh heaven. And I'd be in a hell of a bind. Although I've been working with him on this obsession as well as other obedience skills, I suspect Bill's inner kamikaze would seize control and let the frolic begin.

It's hard keeping a house full of hounds clean when one of the little rascals likes to push the envelope. There's a Costco-sized bottle of dog shampoo with Bill's name on it sitting next to the garden hose.

My other male dog, Sue, is a stickler for rules and regulations. He has, shall we say, a zealot-like passion that those with whom he allows to share his domestic empire must conform . . . a protocol . . . Sue's protocol. There is no gray area in the world according to Sue and, if he ever figures out how to dial a cell phone, I'll be in a world of hurt. He'd no doubt turn me in for violating a series of OSHA standards, as well as local zoning laws. Just last night he let me know in real time, with a mid-sized growl, that I'd breached his canons of etiquette by bringing the TV clicker into the kitchen with me instead of leaving it atop the sofa's armrest.

I knew immediately what Sue meant and returned the clicker to its designated home at once, even mumbled a heartfelt apology.

Maggie May had taken to mothering Billie Joe, just as she'd done with Vira. Delta Dawn is the know-it-all aunt, always ready with an unprompted parenting tip or snippy critique, just as she'd been with Vira. My farm collies are unnervingly in tune with each other as only sisters can be. Whereas Bill's greatest affectation is rolling about in the most nauseating pile of gunk he might trip across, Maggie and Delta are heavily into gaslighting. Their favorite hobby involves not only making me question my memory, perception, or judgment, but my very sanity. The two will stare at me for several seconds, and then share a knowing glance and nod before staring back my way.

"What?" I'll say as I begin patting down my pockets in case I've misplaced my car keys, wallet, or cell phone. I'm sad to say they get me nearly every time, and I can't calculate how many times I've trekked out to the backyard to verify that I had indeed turned off the grill. How many times I've trekked outside late at night to confirm that, yes, I'd shut the sprinklers down hours earlier. How many times I'd trekked out to the bed of my truck because they had me convinced I'd been dull-witted enough to forget a bag of groceries. The two were certainly in top form last week as I raced from my spot on the couch, where I'd been peacefully watching ESPN with Sue, to whipping open the laundry closet to confirm that a cascade of soapy water was not, in fact, leaking onto the floor.

I can't blame them, though. If I were a dog, I'd probably do the same.

Maggie, heartbreakingly—having had her right front leg amputated in the grim unpleasantness of last spring—is a tripod dog. She lost a leg but saved my life. And Sue took early retirement last year due to his medical disability. My German shepherd had also saved my life—by taking several stab wounds that were meant for yours truly.

So guess what?

I bought a gun.

First I got an Illinois State Police–issued FOID: Firearm Owners Identification Card. Then I completed five hours of a firearms safety course. After that I applied for a Chicago Firearms Permit. And after that arrived, Kippy and I went to Pete's Gun Shop & Pistol Range in the south suburb of Riverdale as gun purchases are banned in the Windy City itself. Kippy is partial to Berettas, so, with her tutorage, I picked up an APX Compact semiautomatic pistol, 9mm, which, according to the literature, is concealed-carry-friendly. I had Kippy do most of the talking and handling of the merchandise at Pete's so I wouldn't sound like an idiot or inadvertently pop a cap in the proprietor's—quite possibly Pete's—derriere. Finally, after all of this running around, I registered the APX Compact.

Kippy talked me into applying to the Illinois State Police for a concealed carry permit, requiring more rigmarole, money, and time. But what red-blooded American male doesn't want to mosey about town sporting a hidden holster as though he were James Bond or Dirty Harry?

In reality, however, I'm terrified of handguns. I almost wore Depends for the gun range portion of the firearms safety course.

Kippy's taken me to an indoor shooting range a handful of times—not so much to improve my aim as to get me over the heebie-jeebies of handling a firearm. It turns out I'm Wyatt Earp when the target's set in its nearest position—seven yards or less—but anything beyond that reach and I morph into Barney Fife, can't even graze the paper sheet. After our last outing, we went to The Scout, a sports bar on South Wabash, for an early dinner. We got seated at a table about fifteen yards from the bar, and I informed Kippy of how I could empty both magazines that came with my APX at the bartender and he'd have nothing to fear except for maybe slicing open a finger as he mopped up all the spent booze and broken glass.

Kippy, on the other hand, is like Mel Gibson in one of those Lethal Weapon movies where he sends the paper target off into the horizon, to its farthest setting, and then shoots a smiley face into the sheet.

Kippy's so cool.

You may ask why I'm doing all of this—buying a pistol, target shooting, applying for a concealed carry permit.

Have I lost my mind?

I may well have lost my mind, but the bottom line is that my beautiful, sweet, gaslighting little Maggie May might still be bouncing about on all four of her legs had I been—what's the correct phrase I'm looking for?—*packing heat* last spring. And my mildly irritable and considerably imperious alpha male of a German shepherd may not have been forced into early retirement had I also been—how would you call it?—*strapped* last fall.

On a distinctly personal level, I got shot. I am beyond lucky the bullet only grazed my armpit. This past year has also seen me stabbed, something I'd not recommend—do not do this at home, kids—as well as pummeled about the head and torso as though I were a tetherball. Each one of these new *life experiences* of mine came along with its own concentrated allocation of discomfort and pain. And *pain tends to really hurt* as Kippy's new partner, Detective Ames, would no doubt pontificate. Perhaps I would never have had to plumb the length and depth of my health care policy had I been able to—what is it they say in those Westerns my father so loves?—*slap leather.*

It was almost ten, so I took the kids out for their final sniff and pee of the evening. I sat at the picnic table and wolfed down the last of the glazed donuts I'd picked up for dessert. Billie Joe had learned not to leap up on folks; instead, he sat on the lawn next to me and stared up with pleading eyes.

I glanced down at my bloodhound, remembered what my father used to say whenever one of us kids begged for something sweet to eat, and informed Bill, "You'll get nothing and you'll like it."

I stared off into the darkness, beyond the edge covered by my yard light. My thoughts returned to a missing five-year-old girl whose mother had been brutally murdered. I wiped my fingers on my shirt and texted the following message to SAC Len Squires's iPhone: *I think Vira followed the trail of Calley's killer back to the house.*

There, I'd done it—no mushiness. I'd stated it as directly as possible. Squires would likely read the text first thing in the morning, and he could do with it what he may. But as I ushered the kids back into the house, I heard a slight chirp and checked my phone. It was a return text from the special agent in charge of Chicago's Field Office.

Yup, that's exactly what I thought you were driving at today.

Aha!

See, Kippy—it did too work—Squires and I *locked eyes.*

PART TWO

THE GOOSE CHASE

If you don't have a dog—at least one—there is not necessarily anything wrong with you,
but there may be something wrong with your life.
—Vincent van Gogh

CHAPTER 7

"Can I beg a favor, Mace?"

"Sure," I told SAC Squires over my iPhone. "Name it."

We sat parked in my F-150 at a Speedway on White Oak Avenue, about a mile away from the entrance to the Kankakee River State Park Kenneth Druckman had veered off into. I was sipping Mountain Dew and sharing a bag of pretzels with the kids. A couple of empty wrappers sat on the dashboard, waiting to be disposed of on my next supply run. We'd been sitting there nearly ninety minutes, taking sporadic breaks to let Vira and Sue and Delta and Maggie out to lap water from paper bowls and do their business on the grass between the gas station and White Oak as well as venture into the Speedway to purchase additional snacks so the clerks wouldn't feel nervous about the sweaty guy with a band of mongrels camping out in their parking lot.

"Druckman's been in there forever," said Squires. "The trees block us from overhead, so I need your eyes in the park. Play with the dogs by the mouth of the trails, Frisbee or something, and let me know what you see."

I glanced up through the windshield as Squires mentioned *block us from overhead*, figuring helicopters or drones, maybe both. "Won't that tip any watchers off?"

I knew that Squires and company had to take Druckman seriously, had to do the dance and give lip service to the financier's claim about a couple of young white males and a Hispanic man who had invaded his home, murdered his wife, taken his daughter, and, ostensibly, spent this morning bouncing Druckman and his briefcase of cash from Cicero station to Union Station to Navy Pier to Shedd Aquarium to the lobby of Willis Tower and back to Cicero station and finally onward to Kankakee River State Park.

Quite frankly, haven't we seen this bounce around bit done in a few dozen movies? The only difference was Druckman got his marching orders via text messages from a burner phone instead of receiving calls from some dude using one of those voice changers that makes you sound like Darth Vader.

Personally, I'd have gone with the voice changer.

"No offense, but you don't look like one of us, Mace, and that hiker-dog thing you've got going fits in with the park." Squires collected his thoughts and continued, "There are several other cars and a tour bus in the lot, but don't park near Druckman's Porsche. Keep your phone on and toss it in a front pocket. Let me know what you see when you pet Vira; make it seem like you're talking to her."

"Can do," I said, and pulled onto White Oak Avenue.

Easy money, I had thought as I worked my way through a stack of junk food at the Speedway once it'd been determined that the *alleged* kidnappers had sent Druckman deep into the Kankakee River State Park with the admonition, per Squires, that they'd *be watching* Druckman's *every move*. Yup, easy money. I was professional. I didn't rock the boat. And I went along with everything that was requested of me.

But give me a break . . . this whole kabuki dance was such bullshit.

Vira had told me everything I needed to know while we were in the ravine behind the Kenneth J. Druckman manor.

At least I got to skip the part where these *alleged* psychos bounced billionaire Druckman from tourist spot to tourist spot. An obedience class I ran in River Forest ate up most of my morning. I had been loading Vira, Maggie, Delta, and Sue—Billie Joe would have been too much of a handful while I needed to work with the other dogs—into my F-150 when Special Agent Squires called. He informed me that the *alleged* kidnappers had been sending Druckman all over the city and now had him leaving Chi-Town, heading south on I-57. Squires figured they might need some dogs on hand if the meeting—the exchange—was somewhere out in the boonies. I called Dick Weech—a retired railroad engineer, widower, and dog lover who lived up the boulevard—and begged him to let Bill out and maybe take him for a short walk. After I horse-traded Dick down to a bottle of Cuervo Gold and a ten-dollar scratch-off, I beelined for I-57.

I love Kankakee River State Park, not only because I can get the dogs there in under an hour, but because it's one of my favorite HRD training spots. Sure, with four thousand–some acres, Kankakee's got a little of everything for outdoor enthusiasts—fishing and canoeing and hunting and camping and biking—but for me and the kids, it's the hiking. The park's got trails that stretch for miles along each side of the Kankakee River, as well as endless swaths of bluffs and woodlands of white and red oak, hickory and pine, American beech and maples, with wildflowers, shrubs, and an assortment of other brush lining the floor.

Endless space for the kids and me to play our cadaver games in and about and around the nature trails on both sides of the river.

I pulled inside Kankakee's main entrance, spotted Druckman's Porsche 911 sitting at the head of the lot, parked in the first open space, right next to the handicapped spots. So I parked my pickup on the opposite side, near the Smith Cemetery, a family boneyard that sits on a small hill and contains the graves of several Smith family members, most of whom died of yellow fever during the pandemic back at the dawn of the twentieth century.

I led the dogs past Druckman's 911 and onto a patch of grass next to the walkway leading to a log-cabin-style concession stand and restrooms, and from there onward to the various trails and, ultimately, the river. I felt like a fool lugging a bag of dog toys. It didn't help that Sue immediately sat in a sliver of nearby shade and shot me his *What the hell have you got us doing now?* glance, which morphed quickly into his *You've got to be shitting me* glare, as I pulled the chewed-up Frisbee and knotted tug-of-war rope out of the tote bag.

I couldn't blame Sue.

He was absolutely right. This was a sham.

The only thing Druckman getting text messages sending him all over hell meant to me was that he now had an accomplice. Or, likelier yet, he'd always had an accomplice. Hopefully, on the night Druckman murdered his wife and set this charade in motion, his accomplice had his daughter, Eleanor, tucked far away where she was sound asleep. This also meant that Calley's murder wasn't some rash, spur-of-the-moment impulse, a domestic turned deadly.

No, an accomplice meant what happened to Calley Kurtz Druckman was premeditated.

As in *Book 'em, Danno. Murder One.*

Delta Dawn sat in the shade near Sue—canine solidarity, both on strike—and watched as I flipped the Frisbee as far as I could for both Vira and Maggie to retrieve. Vira was being a good sport, giving my collie some downtime between fetches, but I was really tossing it to work with Maggie May on her dexterity. It broke my heart, watching my little girl prance about on her three remaining legs—lopsided and askew and wobbly. Front-leg-amputee tripod dogs have difficulty adjusting as front legs account for the majority of their balance and strength. I've got Maggie on glucosamine for her joints, and the two of us have regular checkups with our infinitely competent veterinarian, Doc Rawson—which isn't terribly unpleasant as the good doctor often tosses my way some unique gadgets and gizmos she gets free from vendors.

Maggie's been a trouper through it all, and I truly believe that, on some level, she realizes that Frisbee and tug-of-war games are a kind of physical therapy.

Otherwise she'd be sitting on the sidelines with Delta, devising ways to make me think I'd dropped my car keys down a nearby sewer drain.

I scratched at Maggie's head, leaned in as though I were telling her how good a girl she was, but, instead, played the game that there were kidnappers in the bushes and spoke into the smartphone in my breast pocket, "His car's still here, but I don't see him. Just a few teenagers hanging around the drinking fountain." There wasn't an immediate reply, so I spoke to my crippled farm collie, "You're doing great, Maggie, you really are. You'd kick my butt in any race."

Squires whispered through the cell phone, "You sure they're teenagers?"

"Yeah, like ninth or tenth grade," I replied. "More are coming out of the shop. I think they're with the bus. Probably leaving soon."

"Okay," he whispered again. "Hang loose with the dogs and let me know if you see anything."

Don't get me wrong. I appreciate being kept on retainer for the FBI—the feebs pay well—but Druckman killed his wife, and today's events at Kankakee Park were not only an exercise in futility, but an exercise meant to buttress Druckman's alibi. I understood that Squires and team had to go through the motions, but I knew where this would end. It would end with Druckman, a steely look on his face and a tearful daughter in his arms, waltzing out from the trails while his accomplice vanishes down one of the opposite trails with the bag of cash. Hell, with Druckman's help, his accomplice had probably dumped the briefcase, along with the handful of crisp bills containing transmitters, in the river and was on his merry way. And Druckman, being a big shot financial guy, would probably get half of the ransom back after he paid off whoever it was he had on the burner phone feeding him bogus directions.

And Druckman—murderer that he is—would probably get away with what he had done to Calley Kurtz.

Squires had mentioned he'd been primarily interacting with one of Druckman's attorneys instead of Kenneth J. Druckman himself. Boy, had Kippy called that one right. The FBI is forced to deal with his mouthpiece while Druckman gets to stand off to one side, like a baboon showing his ass to zoogoers.

So imagine my surprise when Druckman came marching down off the trail, heading my way, still gripping the briefcase in one hand and screaming into a cell phone held in his other.

CHAPTER 8

My dogs found the scent.

I ran after them, pushing through tree branches and thick undergrowth, a good half mile off the river trail. The crowns of the trees, branches, and leaves—the forest canopy—robbed us of the bulk of available light and left us masked in shadows. My heart pounded in my throat, and something ate away at my gut.

I did not want to find the Druckman child—Eleanor—out here in the woods.

Killed and abandoned, exactly as I'd found the poor kid's mother.

The text the kidnappers sent to Druckman's phone, which he held high while cussing saliva about FBI incompetence to SAC Squires, read simply:

You brought the Feds, asshole. Now your daughter pays the price.

It was all Squires could do to keep a red-faced Druckman from jumping into his 911 and gunning it back home to Glencoe. The special agent explained calmly—perhaps hoping his tranquility would be reciprocated—to Druckman and his attorney that the two of them should hang out long enough for my dogs to complete an initial sweep of the section of river trail the kidnappers had directed the financier to. After a few minutes of give-and-take, Druckman and his attorney agreed.

It had been an unpleasant scene, and I was more than happy to hover several car lengths away from it in the parking lot.

I positioned Maggie May about forty yards inland from the Kankakee River. If she got tuckered out, it'd be easy for her to cut over to the trail and rest a spell until we came for her. Fifty yards farther in was Sue. I followed at an even distance behind him and Maggie in case either of my recovering canines needed help. Delta and Vira were, respectively, another fifty and a hundred yards off to my right, and, of course, a good fifty yards ahead of us stragglers.

In fact, I happened to peek their way at the moment they latched on to the scent. A couple of snouts shot up in the air, then the two dogs narrowed the gap between each other, coming together as one, and then they shot forward, a cannonball, racing neck and neck toward the source. Maggie and Sue cut right, picking up their pace, initially caught up in the excitement, but then caught onto the trace themselves. I ran after my kids, keeping them in my line of vision, not sprinting full-bore, as I needed to watch where each step landed so as not to twist an ankle.

The pack came to a stop in a patch of grass and wildflowers. Vira and Delta sat side-by-side, staring at what they'd discovered. I'd kept an eye on my golden retriever in case she suffered through one of her *episodes*, but nothing so far. Being the good sport she is, Vira patted at the ground in front of her. Maggie sat a few feet away, staring down at the find. With only one front leg, Maggie's days as a terrain patter were behind her. Sue had never been one for patting dirt at a discovery site. It was below him. Instead, he turned my way and stared at me with an *I told you not to waste our time on Frisbee* glare.

I couldn't yet spot what lied in the grass and shrubs, and slowed down not only to catch my breath, but to brace myself for what I was about to witness. I walked the final ten yards, glanced at my iPhone to see if I had any bars or if I'd have to trek back to the river trail to contact Squires, took a deep breath, and looked down to see what the forest floor had to offer.

I stepped back in surprise.

It wasn't Eleanor Druckman.

It was some young guy in a blue cycling jersey and bike shorts.

He didn't appear terribly fresh . . . and half of his face had been chewed off.

The main entry to Kankakee River State Park now crawled with investigators from the Illinois State Police, a few squad cars from the Bourbonnais Police Department, and a black panel forensics van from the FBI. My phone call to Agent Squires from the river trail—informing him that we indeed had found a cadaver, but it was definitely not, in fact, Eleanor Druckman—had gotten more than one ball rolling.

Squires was occupied with crime scene logistics and coordinating with the various troops, but he found a moment to let me know I could head home as long as I kept my cell phone handy in case he had any questions. It was now dusk, and as I loaded the kids into my F-150, Vira growled softly. I followed her line of vision, and, sure enough, there he was, across the parking lot, leaning against his 911. I'd spotted Druckman's attorney behind the wheel of a departing white Lexus when I'd brought the dogs off the trail. But even though his lawyer had left already, surprisingly, the financier remained in the park.

Idiot me should have jumped in the F-150 and peeled out of Kankakee, but, instead, I headed over to the investment banker. Druckman looked up as I approached.

"Shame about what happened to your wife?" I said, several feet away, not offering a hand to shake.

He nodded and returned his gaze to his boots.

I followed his gaze and realized he was sporting a new pair of Salomon men's Quest backpacking boots. I knew this because I live in hiking boots and wouldn't mind owning a pair of Salomon's, but they're more than a hundred bucks outside my price range. It was as though Druckman knew he'd be needing something more rugged for today's adventure, so he wouldn't scuff up a nice pair of dress shoes.

Then I wondered what I'd ever hoped to gain by coming over, shrugged, and said, "Don't worry, they're going to catch *whoever* killed her."

He didn't look up from his boots, so I turned to head back to my pickup. I made it all of three steps.

"Hey," Druckman called after me. "You're the dog guy, right?"

"Yeah," I said, turning back, "I'm the dog guy."

Druckman swept a hand in the direction of the trails. "Who the hell did you find out there?"

He seemed genuinely confused.

CHAPTER 9

THREE WEEKS AGO

"Are you sure your man won't sit, Audrick?"

"My friend prefers to stand," the man from Belgium said, and his raven-haired caretaker remained at his perch on one side of the closed office door.

"Well, hell, then," Druckman said. "Can I have Janice get either of you some coffee, tea, or juice, or—since it must be five o'clock somewhere—I've something stronger hidden in the cabinet."

"Don't trouble yourself, Kenneth." Audrick Verlinden sat in a plush leather chair across the desk from the financier and stared out a corner window of Druckman's fortieth-story executive office. They were in the heart of Chicago's Financial District, off LaSalle Street—the LaSalle Canyon—tall buildings and tight lanes. "I must commend you on your view of the Chicago Board of Trade Building."

"It is a thing of beauty," Druckman said, and leaned back in his chair. "Hey, speaking of views—why don't you gentlemen let me take you to LH Rooftop for lunch?"

"Another time perhaps. We came from m.henry, and after the black bean cakes—delicious, of course—I don't think I'll be able to eat until sometime next year. Plus, we fly out of O'Hare by two, and you know how much of a madhouse that will be."

"Let me have our limo run you there."

"That would be most kind."

"Least I could do. I wish you'd let me know you were coming to town, Audrick. I'd have put on the Ritz."

"No worries, Kenneth. We coptered in from Lake Geneva first thing this morning."

"Lake Geneva," Druckman said. "A playground for the rich back in the day."

"That it was."

"Didn't Hefner open a club there?"

Verlinden frowned. "We don't like to be reminded of that."

Druckman laughed and leaned forward in his chair. "What brings you to town—business in Chicago?"

"Yes," Verlinden replied. "With you."

The Belgian and his caretaker had indeed eaten a lengthy breakfast at m.henry before making their way to LaSalle Street. From the security desk on the ground level, the Belgian had contacted the reception desk at the Druckman Financial Group and asked to see the CEO. There was some minor give-and-take about not having an appointment and Mr. Druckman's schedule being booked until the Belgian instructed the receptionist to "Please let Kenneth know that Audrick Verlinden is in the lobby."

A minute later the two men were ushered into a private elevator, which took them directly to the fortieth floor, where—surprise, surprise—Druckman Financial Group's CEO and founder awaited them with a broad smile and an outstretched hand. After a quick tour of the investment firm's office suite, the men were led into Druckman's executive office, a room the size of a tennis court laid out for doubles play.

"Business with me?" Druckman picked a Montblanc pen off the top of his walnut desk and twisted the barrel to make the nib come out.

Verlinden pulled the financial return he'd received from the Druckman Financial Group out from a slim leather briefcase, set it on Druckman's desk, and turned it about so that it faced the financier. Audrick Verlinden then said, "It is quite an honor to meet the Windy City's version of Bernard Lawrence Madoff."

After a long moment, Druckman said, "Mr. Verlinden, sir,

please. Even in jest, I'm not sure you know the weight of those words?"

The Belgian ignored Druckman, removed a second stack of clipped pages out from his briefcase, and set it in front of the financier. "This is my homework"—he pointed at the papers he'd just set on Druckman's desk—"and it indicates how the figures in your return should appear."

Silence encompassed the room.

Then the financier opened a drawer, took out an eyeglass case, flicked it open, and put on a pair of readers. Druckman lifted the Belgian's stack of *homework* and made a show of running a forefinger down columns before flipping pages. He opened the corresponding return from his financial group, turned to a page, scanned it, and then looked at what the Belgian took to be the same page from his financial report.

Verlinden glanced at his watch, sighed, crossed a leg, and returned to gazing out Druckman's corner office window. His caretaker remained standing next to the door, staring blankly across the room.

Another minute passed before the CEO of Druckman Financial Group set both reports back down on the desk in front of him. He took his eyeglasses off and placed them on top of the financial return from his group. "I must apologize, Audrick," he said. "I have no idea how Gipp's team dropped the ball on this— some kind of glitch or processing error—but I assure you I will have answers by the end of business today."

"Don't insult my intelligence, Kenneth." Verlinden smiled. "I doubt you even have someone named *Gipp* on the payroll."

"I'll make this right, Audrick. You have my word."

"I know you'll make this right." Verlinden smiled again. "In fact, that's why I'm here. I shall be made whole within the next half hour."

"Half hour? What are you talking about?"

"Where to begin. The SEC? The Commodity Futures Trading Commission? The IRS has a Criminal Investigation Division; the Treasury Department has something similar? I don't know, perhaps the U.S. Postal Inspection Service?" Verlinden shrugged. "A logical first step would be to contact the FBI's Field Office—they must have some kind of financial crimes unit to get the ball rolling."

Druckman squinted at his client from across the table. "You can't be serious."

"I believe their field office is on West Roosevelt Road." Verlinden turned to his caretaker and added, "You may need to fly back ahead of me, my friend."

The caretaker nodded once.

Druckman again picked up his Montblanc pen. This time he twisted the barrel a half dozen times—nib out, nib in—and finally said, "What did you mean about making you *whole* in a half hour?"

"There is an eight-bedroom, six-bathroom chalet in Barboleuse I've got my heart set on—a breathtaking view of both the Swiss and the French Alps," Verlinden said. "Alas, it's owned by a South African named Nickus Fourie."

Druckman dropped his Montblanc. "What the hell is going on here?!"

At Druckman's raised voice, the caretaker crossed the room and stood behind his employer. He spoke for the first time. "Anything required of me, sir?"

Verlinden glanced over a shoulder. "He's just blowing off steam." He turned back to the financier. "I have *friends* in Taiwan who can do in a week what would take the financial crime unit at the FBI a half year to accomplish, as they have no pesky red tape to cut through. And I assume *Mr. Nickus Fourie* in the Alps is just a *temporary* oasis you'd be parking in—when the balls can no longer be kept in the air—before you move on to someplace entirely off radar."

"I have no idea what you're talking about."

"I trust you're well versed in *clawback* provisions?"

Druckman nodded slowly. He wiped at his forehead with a sleeve of his Brioni suit jacket and stared down at his desk.

"Then you know the U.S. can seize bank accounts and assets in foreign countries. The IRS will go after whatever accounts you've squirreled your money into—named or numbered." Verlinden glanced about Druckman's office and continued, "They'll levy any bank with a branch in the U.S.—a few taps on a keyboard and the funds go bye-bye."

"I have no idea what you're talking about," Druckman said again—more flat tire than earnest protester.

"I've already asked you once not to insult my intelligence, Kenneth," Verlinden said. "I won't be asking again . . . and the clock's begun ticking on the thirty minutes we've discussed."

Druckman looked up from his desk. "What do you want from me?"

"I'm not sure you've been listening, Kenneth. I've got my heart set on a certain ski chalet in Barboleuse. I'd like *Mr. Fourie* to sell it to me."

Druckman processed Verlinden's request. He nearly smiled in the realization he'd caught a lifeline. "Of course that can be done, Audrick."

"You don't think I'm too old to take up skiing?"

"One is never too old to take up something new," Druckman answered. "And we'll get you that chalet for a steal."

"Absolutely not," Verlinden said. "I insist on fair market value. Everything must be done on the up-and-up." He removed a set of forms from his briefcase and handed them to Druckman. "Especially since you'll be purchasing it for me from *Mr. Fourie.*"

Druckman realized his lifeline was a fifty-ton anchor. "But I can't move—"

"No," Verlinden interrupted, "but *Nickus Fourie* has the funds in hand—more than enough Swiss francs in his account—so, a couple of transfers will meet your obligation of making me whole again."

Druckman shuffled through the forms. "The chalet in exchange for keeping your investments funds?"

"I will be made whole again." Verlinden knocked lightly on the desk between them with a knuckle. "I have a representative in Barboleuse, at this very moment, in fact, and he's ready to file the closing documentation."

"Done." The CEO of Druckman Financial Group reached across the table to shake hands, but Verlinden didn't reciprocate.

"You have fifteen minutes to complete those transfers, Kenneth . . . or perhaps I should call you *Mr. Fourie.*"

The transaction was made with a little over two minutes to spare. Funds were transferred about, and the Belgian's on-site representative had all the required materials. The chalet was mortgage free and now in Audrick Verlinden's name. Regrettably, most of the francs in Mr. Fourie's account had vanished.

Druckman looked at his client hesitantly and said, "Are we good?"

"Indeed, we are," Verlinden replied. "But now we must talk about the penalty, Kenneth, because, quite frankly, in a situation such as this, it can be quite steep."

"What penalty?" Druckman said in little more than a whisper.

The Belgian looked surprised at the financier's question. "Why, the penalty for early withdrawal, of course."

CHAPTER 10

Supermodel Calley Kurtz Druckman Murdered, Daughter Kidnapped

By Nicole Pepin, Chicago Tribune

Supermodel Calley Kurtz Druckman, 39, was brutally murdered and her daughter, Eleanor Scarf Druckman, 5, kidnapped in a home invasion turned deadly at their Glencoe residence in the early morning hours of Tuesday, September 8th. Calley's husband, eminent Investment Advisor Kenneth J. Druckman, 47, had been left beaten, bloodied, and bound to a staircase railing. An undisclosed amount of jewelry and cash had also been taken.

Mr. and Mrs. Druckman and their daughter had returned from an American Heart Association charity event thrown at the Langham Hotel in downtown Chicago late Monday evening and retired immediately to bed. According to Kenneth Druckman, his family was briskly awakened at three a.m. and herded into the great room by what appeared to be two white males and a third man of Hispanic descent; all three men appeared to be in their early to mid-twenties.

"The last four days have been a living hell," Kenneth Druckman told the Chicago Tribune. "They killed my sweet and lovely wife. They later texted me that they hadn't wanted to do it, but Calley put up a massive fight—biting and kick-ing at them—which I believe because that's exactly what my wonderfully courageous Calley would have done for our little Elle."

When asked what course the investigation has taken, Druck-man informed the Chicago Tribune that "I've been working hand-in-hand with the FBI on the ransom exchange for my beautiful baby girl, but the kidnappers texted me after I'd ar-rived at the money drop and told me they knew I'd been collab-orating with federal agents. This nightmare won't end . . . and with Calley gone, I can't imagine it ever will."

Although there's been a media blackout on both his wife's murder and his daughter's kidnapping for much of this past week, Druckman approached us and agreed to sit for an ex-clusive interview in order to reach out to the men who might still be holding his daughter. "Please don't hurt my Elle. I'll give you what you want—anything you want—just please don't hurt my little girl. She's all I have left. Please, I beg of you."

The article went on in that mode for a dozen more paragraphs. A tearjerker that soon went viral. Within an hour of the story breaking, newspapers around the country, as well as cable and online news, ran with it. After all, if it bleeds it leads. And this one not only bled, but tugged at your heartstrings.

How truly tragic, you might say. What a poor man, you'd point out. I hope it all works out for the best, you'd pray.

Unless, of course, if you knew what I knew . . .

Then you realized it was Druckman laying down the narrative— fake news—the murderer himself setting the morning's headline in 72-point, bold font.

"Give me a break," I said, and walked away from the kitchen table, surrendering my laptop to Kippy so she wouldn't have to read over my shoulder. "So he dumps the FBI and whatever in hell Glencoe PD was doing, runs to the press, and paints this self-serving portrait of himself."

It was Saturday morning and—lucky me—Kippy had stayed over. We'd had a slumber party with the pups. Well, that is, except for Sue. Sue doesn't do slumber parties.

"I know that name," Kippy said.

"What?"

"Nicole Pepin—the *Tribune* reporter—she normally writes for the Style and Fashion pages."

"Of course," I replied, wondering if I'd ever tripped across that section. Maybe those pages were hidden somewhere between the sports and the comics. "I bet she's done articles on Calley and that's how Druckman knows her."

"So he runs to Pepin with *his story* because he knows she's not a real reporter and that she'll lob softballs at him that he can knock out of the ballpark." Kippy looked up from the laptop. "Which casts himself as a loving, heartbroken husband."

"Like the early days of O.J."

"Tell me again about the nanny."

Okay, I admit it—this is starting to make me look like a bit of a blabbermouth. Perhaps I shouldn't be trusted with the nuclear codes, but I'd only share them with Kippy . . . and maybe Vira.

As the pups and I had sat in the background at Kankakee River State Park, waiting for SAC Squires to send us home or have us search another section or trail, I overheard one of his agents report that they'd *not heard back from the ex-nanny*. Evidently, Squires had his men checking into all of Druckman's employees, including his home staff, as well as any other individuals the Druckmans came into contact with on a day-to-day basis.

"Not much to tell," I said. "Eleanor's first nanny was let go almost two years back, and they're trying to get in touch with her."

"Why was she *let go*?"

I shrugged. "I only heard the agent tell Squires her parents said she'd gone camping but they weren't sure where. He couldn't reach her by phone, left a couple of messages, but suspects she's in some out-of-service area."

Kippy smiled and I read her mind.

"Yeah, I know—nannies are right up there with the farmer's daughter."

"If we ever have kids, Mace, and we get a nanny—she's going to be seventy."

"You and I aren't nanny people, Kip." A thought occurred to me. "At Glencoe that first morning, they had the staff moved off to one side, and there was this older, matronly woman who was standing there all teary-eyed. At first I thought she was the cook, but then there was this other guy in one of them Gordon Ramsay outfits."

"So the Druckmans canned a nanny who's young enough that she lets her parents know when she goes out of town, then they turned around and replaced her with an older woman," Kippy said. "Hmm."

"Could be, or could be she was an idiot around kids." I shrugged again. "The bigger mystery is the dead guy at Kankakee. Steve Andreen, an independent IT contractor and avid bike rider, with no apparent connection to Druckman whatsoever. Dead nine days and no one reported him missing."

"He was single and worked from home. I read he missed some conference calls and didn't return email, but his clients figured he was nose down in programming."

"But nine days?"

"You'd be amazed at how often that happens." Kippy added, "Plus, if you and the pups started doing that thing you do in all the state parks in Illinois, you'd probably dig up another dozen Steve Andreens."

Sue barked once and I turned to the living room. "Oh no."

Billie Joe was all frenzied up and licking at the carpet as if he were starring in a more animated version of *The Walking Dead*, like those movies where the zombies tear ass after you. He worked his way toward the kitchen, now manically licking at the vinyl tile. I should have squirted floor wax in his pathway to get that all-around shine, but instead grabbed his collar and led him into the backyard where he could go after grass.

If you take what most puppies get into and then times that by pi, you get Bill. In fact, Bill the Roller could also be known as Bill the Nibbler. Hell, as far as I know, he nibbles at what he rolls in. This means that occasionally his stomach hurts, at which time he'll gnaw on grass, or, if inside, he'll lick at the floor, and within a half hour—*voilà*—there'll be an interesting puddle of barf.

I joined Bill in the yard. Vira strolled out to keep me company and watch the matinee. At least my bloodhound focused on the taller grass around the legs of my barbecue. I mow in a timely fashion but tend to limit clipping or weed whacking to maybe twice a summer on account of hating every second of it. In a way, Bill was doing me a solid.

"I wonder what Druckman's going to do with all that jewelry?"

I turned back from surveilling Bill. "What?"

Kippy had followed us out and stood on my pip-squeak of a backyard deck, sipping coffee and staring my way. "Part of Druckman's alibi is this jewelry heist thing he's got going, right? The intruders got away with a big bag of bling, gold necklaces, and that huge rock of Calley's."

"He's already super rich," I said. "I'm sure he's chucked them in Lake Michigan."

"I'm not so sure about that," Kippy replied. "They're not the Crown Jewels, but they are worth a small fortune. They can be taken apart and made into other pieces of jewelry."

I chewed on that until Vira nudged my leg with her nose. Bill had vomited, and I cut in front of him so he wouldn't make it his second breakfast. "Now if only I knew a cop who could get us in touch with a fence."

CHAPTER 11

Unbelievable.

The blond finished reading Druckman's account of his wife's death and daughter's kidnapping in the *Chicago Tribune*. Then she started once more at the beginning and read the article a second time. Her heart raced; the lump in her throat solidified. She looked across the tiny living room of the rental cabin toward the door leading into the single bedroom where Eleanor lay sleeping.

The two of them had recently returned from a Casey's General Store, off the main road, where the reception was better for using the burner phones and where an increasingly distraught Elle spoke with her father. The blond had run inside Casey's to purchase a twelve pack of 7Up and an array of snacks that might help in keeping the little girl more tranquil, and that's when she spotted the headline in the row of newspapers near the cashier's station.

The blond flew out of the gas station with only the newspaper hidden in a plastic bag.

She stood outside her vehicle, tapping a foot and waiting for Druckman to finish comforting his daughter. Once done, Elle handed her the phone. The blond shut the car door and walked to the edge of the boulevard.

"You fucking son of a bitch," she had said into the phone. "You murdered her. You killed your wife."

"It wasn't supposed to be that way," he had replied before the blond clicked off and shut down the burner.

The blond sat at the card table in the middle of the living room and blinked back tears. *He'd murdered Calley.* Just the thought of it shattered reality, but there it was on the table in front of her, above the fold in Chicago's largest newspaper. The cabin had no television or radio, and the cell phone reception was shit unless you climbed one of the taller trees—not happening—or ventured up to the main road. And when the two of them had plotted the farce of her bouncing Druckman all over Chicago via burner texts before finally sending him off to Kankakee River State Park, the fucking son of a bitch had kept his mouth shut as to what had become of his wife.

The blond knew this whole thing had been a mistake from the get-go. She should have turned and walked away, or, better yet, walked away and called the cops. Instead, she was in deep shit. Worse yet, she was the only one who could tie Druckman to the murder of his wife, to the diamond heist . . . to his daughter's kidnapping.

The fucking son of a bitch was a murderer.

Scratch being in deep shit. The blond was in deep, deep shit.

"I need help," Druckman had broached the subject right after they'd made love in a hotel room at the Sofitel off East Chestnut, near Chicago's famed Magnificent Mile.

"That's insane," she had responded after he'd laid out what he needed from her. *"I'm not going to kidnap your daughter."*

"It's not a real kidnapping," he had said, and informed her he was being extorted and needed to come up with bucketsful of cash.

"Go to the police," she had suggested.

He had shrugged. "My industry is heavily regulated. They can nail you to the cross for practically anything."

She had found that fishy. "You're guilty of what they're blackmailing you over?"

He had shrugged again. "Everyone in my profession is guilty of something or other."

Later, after another round of lovemaking, he had said, "I can set you up with a million dollars, stick it in a mutual fund or some-place."

"A million dollars . . ."

But now, here she sat sipping at cold coffee in a dilapidated backwoods cabin several miles outside of Galena, Illinois—an accomplice to first-degree murder and a myriad of other offenses. She wiped at her tears with a Casey's General Store napkin.

"It'll only be a few days," he had assured her. *"And I've got a cabin where you'll never have to see anyone, not a single soul until it's over."*

"But your daughter will be terrified," she had countered. *"How can you do that to her?"*

"I'll talk to Elle every day. We'll have to use burner phones and nothing else, but it'll be like an adventure for her." He told her she could crush up half an Ambien and stir it into Elle's tomato soup—Elle loved tomato soup.

"I don't know if that's a good idea."

"Perhaps Benadryl will keep her groggy."

"Nobody's going to get hurt, right?" she had said.

"Of course not," he had replied. *"I promise."*

The blond walked over to the bedroom door and leaned an ear against it. Even though it was time for Eleanor's afternoon nap, and even though Eleanor had eaten half a bowl of tomato soup laced with Benadryl, the blond could hear the little girl quietly sobbing.

It tore at her heart.

The blond walked into the bathroom, stood on the toilet lid, lifted the ceiling tile she'd jiggled loose the first night she was there, slipped a hand inside, and removed the handbag Druckman had given her, the one with a dozen jewelry bags stuffed inside, the one he'd told her to guard with her life.

At the time he'd said it with a wink, but, even then, she knew he had been serious.

The blond walked back to her station at the dining room table, pushed aside the newspaper—which she'd soon burn in the grill out front before Eleanor spotted her parents' pictures—and opened the handbag. She had seen the slip of paper when she'd first peeked inside, before hiding the bag in the ceiling tiles. It wasn't on top like it'd been before, her eyes widened, but then she realized it had fallen between the individual velvet bags. The blond fished a hand through the purse until she felt the small slip of paper, pulled it out, and placed it on the table in front of herself.

It was about the size of a business card. The name and phone number written on it were in Druckman's handwriting. The number had a Chicago area code, but the name looked foreign.

Armen Kuznetsov.

CHAPTER 12

"Unlike the crap you see in the movies, pawn shops aren't run by criminals, nor are they set up to fence stolen merchandise," said Curt Banick, the proprietor of Banick Pawners, which sat off Fullerton Avenue in Chicago's west side. Banick was a small man, fifty-something with graying hair and thick wire rim glasses, which he likely needed because he spent fifty hours a week pricing rings or coins or bullion or watches or computers or TVs or mink coats or any of the hundreds of other items I saw on display in his shop.

"We're small businesses, absurdly regulated, and licensed by both state and city, and, as you know," Banick looked toward Kippy, "we value our relationship with the Chicago Police Department."

Kippy had met Banick last year—back in her uniformed patrol days—when jewelry from a string of Albany Park burglaries began showing up in Banick's store. The young guy dropping off the loot came across as sketchy, red flags went up, so Banick called the police as soon as the man exited the pawn shop, described the items that had been brought in, and an hour later Kippy showed up with an itemized list of what had been stolen from various homes in Albany Park, and darned if not all of the five pieces the sketchy guy had left at Banick Pawners were a perfect match.

The blossoming career of a young housebreaker had been nipped in the bud.

"Most stolen objects get sold on the street or, in the case of jewelry, sold to gold buyers. Pawners like me are required to hold items for fifteen days and send you," he looked to Kippy again, "descriptions and serial numbers. And, as you know firsthand, if some clown comes in here with stolen items, he's going to get caught."

I leaned gently against the glass countertop, listened as Banick and Kippy discussed his life as a pawnbroker, and glanced about at all Banick's shop had to offer. Guitars must be huge as Banick had over a dozen hanging from a line off the ceiling with even more sitting in a row of stands, plus a cabinet of watches, rings displayed under glass, computers and cameras and smartphones, signed baseballs in cases, sport jerseys, necklaces hanging off hooks—you name it, Banick's got it. I began thinking about my wedding ring, sliding about somewhere in the bottom of a sock drawer ever since the divorce, and thought maybe I'd be making a return visit to Banick's shop in the near future.

Kippy said, "But what if some perp had really high-end jewelry—gold and silver necklaces, fancy bracelets, big diamond rings—and he knew the stuff was first class, bought at the places rich people buy their stuff. If he had more than a handful of brain cells, where would he go to unload them?"

Banick looked at Kippy a long moment. "Are you talking about what I've been reading in the paper? That Druckman thing?"

"Hypothetically speaking, yes—but I'm trying to get the sense of where a perp would go if he knew he had something really pricey," Kippy tapped a finger against what appeared to be Banick's space-age version of a cash register, "instead of trying to get a couple hundred bucks on the street corner."

"Well, I mentioned gold buyers before because they're not as heavily regulated, but I don't know—what happened at Druckman's is about as high a profile as you can get, with a murder and kidnapping tagged on." He shook his head. "Who'd want a piece of that pie?"

Banick had no problem with us bringing Vira into his shop— he was a dog person himself—but he might rethink that policy were he to peek our way as Vira's snout was pressed against the ring display, leaving a murky smear on the glass. I didn't have the heart to tell her that none of the items would fit; plus, as far as I could see, nothing on display went with her eyes. I glanced about the store to see if they sold dog collars, but then remembered I got those free from my veterinarian.

"Let's take the Druckman situation out of it, Curt, and say you fell into something big—a bag full of gems—and you'd misplaced your scruples. Where would you go?"

Banick glanced around his shop. There was currently one customer, and he was busy browsing through the NFL jerseys. Another employee—I assumed Banick's son as he seemed a duplicate of the pawnbroker, only twenty years younger—fiddled about at the far end of the counter. Banick's youthful clone had silver watches on a velvet pad next to him, his nose glued to his laptop.

Even though the shop was nearly empty, Banick waved us over.

"Look," he whispered, "I'm just talking here, right? I don't know anything and I'm not making any allegations. I'm just answering your question, like a librarian pointing you toward a book."

Kippy said, "Understood."

"I don't want this to come back at me, okay?"

"We won't say a thing."

Banick looked my way.

I shook my head. "You're just a librarian. I never caught your name."

He took a heavy breath and began, "There is a Russian by the name of Armen Kuznetsov who might, and I stress *might*, fit what you're asking about. Kuznetsov's been in Chicago a little over a decade now, and he owns a pawn shop in River North and an antique store in Wicker Park."

"What do you know about him?"

"Just some talk from my pawner friends, you know, things they've heard . . . mainly rumors. Like Kuznetsov's got connections with whomever one might think Russians could be connected with."

"The Russian mob?"

Banick shrugged. "Ties to his old country—Bratva or whatever they're called over there, or ties to Little Odessa, you know, Brighton Beach in New York City. Hell, I don't know, maybe both are part of the same soup." Banick shrugged again. "It could be true; it could be bullshit. Like I said, just rumors . . . a lot of rumors from my fellow pawners."

"So he's a fence?"

"Again, just more talk, or whispers in Kuznetsov's case. But if they're true, he could take that bag of high-priced gems and get it over to Eastern Europe or someplace, and cut and melt or whatever, and then sell off the pieces."

"You ever meet him?" I piped in, my first question of the day.

"My wife's a hard-core antiquer and she dragged me to his shop in Wicker Park last year." Banick glanced around his shop again. A female customer had wandered in and was showing some earrings to his replica-son. "Kuznetsov was there—he's a big guy, hard to miss—talking to a customer. He had his back to us and, since I'd heard all these rumors about him, I think my eyes lingered on him a second too long—must have sent off a vibe or something—because he turned around and caught me staring at him." Banick took a breath and continued, "He immediately comes over and asks if he could help us, but he didn't ask in a customer-friendly manner, if you know what I mean. Intimidating, in my proximity, glaring at me."

"Did he threaten you?"

"Nothing I could call the cops about," Banick replied, "just got all up in my grill. Fortunately, my wife had some questions for him about a rocking chair she'd been looking at, so he backed off a little." Banick looked from me to Kippy. "When we left, I had us get ice cream from a shop down the street and take our sweet time because I didn't want Kuznetsov to follow us out and get the license plate off our car."

"All this because he caught you staring at him?"

Banick nodded. "It was an *unpleasant* moment. My wife even brought it up later—wondered why he'd acted like such an asshole—and she loves everyone." Banick then shuddered. "I didn't even look at him that long, but somehow he knew I was staring. Like the man has eyes in the back of his head or something."

CHAPTER 13

"It kills me to pay one dime before having all the *pieces* in my hand."

"You've seen what you're getting," Druckman said to the tall man on the park bench next to him. "You've run the assessment— weights, carats, spot prices—all of that. Gold and silver and the engagement ring is in Liz Taylor territory." Druckman crossed a leg. "You'll never get a better deal than this—thirty cents on the dollar for this level of quality—even if you have to recut or sell in Europe or Asia or wherever."

The two men were in Millennium Park, not far from AT&T Plaza, and for all intents and purposes appeared as just a couple of businessmen soaking in the midday sun before heading back to the office. Any person in the know, however, would be astonished to see the most renowned investment advisor in the Midwest sharing a park bench with Armen Kuznetsov, a first-generation Russian, and, arguably, one of the leading movers— fences, that is—also in the Midwest.

"But a man of your *stature* coming to me with this kind of proposal makes me start thinking my thoughts."

"Quite frankly, this is chump change."

"Not to me." Kuznetsov not only was tall, but stocky, wide-shouldered. And though he wore a tailored gray suit and expensive dress shoes, his face screamed longshoreman.

Druckman shrugged. "Consider it a bridge loan. I could go other routes, but that would take more time."

Kuznetsov took the briefcase from between his legs, placed it on his lap, and set his hand atop it. "Divorce can be expensive." He looked at the financier a long moment. "Are you getting one?"

Druckman remained silent, but something flashed across his features.

"I've had two." The Russian smiled. "She won't get her baubles, and I bet the insurance is conveniently in your name." He set the briefcase on the bench between them. "It pains me to hand this over. I'd better have all the pieces in ten days."

"You know who I am," Druckman said. "You have no need to worry."

"And you know who I am," Kuznetsov replied and stood up from the bench. "More importantly, you know *who* I represent. I would not be pleased if ten days came and went without com- pensation, but I assure you *they* would be beside themselves . . . and there would be repercussions." Before he turned and left, Kuznetsov added, "Ten days and I'd better have the pieces."

Fuck.

Druckman grabbed Kuznetsov's briefcase and headed back to work.

That goddamned Verlinden—pompous, better-than-thou Belgian prick, with his fifty-million-dollar *penalty for early withdrawal*— had him stuffed inside a box. Druckman felt as though he couldn't breathe, as though he were being squeezed to death, a giant py- thon wrapped about his chest. And he'd felt this way since Verlin- den and that odd duck of a butler or chauffeur or whatever in hell that threatening son of a bitch was had showed up at his office unannounced, specifically since the wealthy bastard had cut the song and dance and accused him of being Bernard Madoff.

It would have been an outrage—a massive slander, an immense defamation of Druckman's character—had it not also happened to be true.

The first body blow had been Verlinden's knowledge of Druckman's exit strategy: his secret identity as a South African named Nickus Fourie as well as Fourie's ownership of a ski lodge in the Swiss Alps. Jesus Christ—the Nickus Fourie identity had taken him nearly two years to cultivate.

Okay, Druckman thought, you roll with the punches, and that's what Druckman had done. Surrendering the chalet in Barboleuse was no great shakes as Druckman had indeed planned on utilizing that residence only as a stopover until he got all his cards in a row, until he severed any trace-backs—however veiled or numbered—of wire transfers between Druckman Financial Group and good, old Nick Fourie's Swiss account.

He'd bounce accounts from the Caymans to Bermuda and back to Switzerland in a manner that'd take the FBI a hundred years to sort out.

Which is why Druckman had never bought the chalet outright, just the bare minimum.

But that blew up in his face with Verlinden's second body blow, with Verlinden's *I've got my heart set on owning a chalet,* thus forcing Druckman to complete the purchase of the goddamned lodge for him with much of the funds from Nick Fourie's bank account. It was another punch Druckman had been forced to roll with.

Sure, why not? Enjoy yourself, Druckman had internally steamed. I hope you ski off a fucking cliff.

Druckman had no choice but to empty Nickus Fourie's nest egg and, sure, those funds had been Druckman's get-away-free card in case the feds ever came sniffing about. But those funds could easily be replenished. After all, Druckman had always known he'd be going out with a bang. At some future date he'd planned on informing his staff and immediate client base that he and his daughter were going to Spain for a month; only Kenneth J. and Eleanor Scarf Druckman would never make it to Spain; the two would hit a dead end in Australia just as Nickus Fourie and his daughter, Amahle, would be beginning their journey . . . on their way to Switzerland via Italy.

Before he and Elle disappeared into the mist, there'd be a whirlwind of wire transfers at Druckman Financial Group . . . an untraceable whirlwind.

Dammit. He needed that chalet in Barboleuse, less for wire transfers and severing his trail, as he could do that anywhere, and more for doting on Elle, helping her adjust to a new norm with as little trauma as humanly possible. It would be difficult for a month or two, but kids are resilient and, within a year, she'd have trouble telling memories from dreams.

There'd be no golden parachute arranged for Elle's mother as Nickus Fourie, the poor man, was a widower. It was all for the best as Calley was never going to let it go or let them get on with life. Calley was never going to forgive what had occurred with Britt. Yes, Druckman knew that nannies were off limits, and, yes, the two of them should never have made love in the master bedroom while Calley was at lunch with a friend and Elle was napping, especially since Britt left her thong in the bedsheets as they panic-dressed when Elle began crying . . . but the heart wants what the heart wants.

Druckman had apologized like the proverbial madman the instant Calley found the thong. He'd immediately fired Britt and hired an old prude—Berta or Hilda or whatever her name was—in Britt's stead. He'd taken all of the blame in the endless rounds of marriage counseling Calley had insisted upon. He'd said all the right things, had sprung for island getaways for just the two of them, had pampered Calley with flowers and the finest of chocolates and jewelry; nevertheless—nearly two years onward—they still slept in separate rooms and, for all practical purposes, lived separate lives.

Calley's mother, Lucinda—tough broad that she was—had raised Calley singlehandedly after jettisoning her abusive drunk of a husband. A *boozehound* Calley called her father—who could be counted on being three sheets to the wind each and every night of the week. The boozehound had made Calley's early childhood a living hell and, after she and Lucinda fled the inebriated lush on the day Calley turned seven, she'd not seen or talked to the piece of shit ever since, nor wanted to. *Good riddance* had been her philosophy when it came to the man who had sired her; however, Calley loved her mother deeply, endlessly—as the two had been through so much together.

Druckman had always gotten on just fine with Lucinda, and she'd found it in her heart to forgive him, at least to some degree; regrettably, most of their recent interactions had been medical in nature, finding the poor woman the best possible health care money could buy for her deteriorating condition. His mother-in-law suffered from Parkinson's disease. Though Lucinda's most-recent diagnosis found her PD on the cusp of stage 4, the poor woman was usually able to walk as well as stand unassisted—remarkably, the shakes and tremors of the first three stages had become less frequent—but she'd begun using a cane for balance.

Yes, Lucinda forgave him his sins . . . but Calley never would.

Sex was all but forgotten, and what had begun as a light-hearted fairy tale had turned into Brothers Grimm. Frankly, Calley would have already vamoosed had it not been for her mother's failing health. Alas, she was now vying for divorce—it was in the cards—but Druckman had been dragging his feet. *Can we see where we're at after the holidays, hon,* he'd begged her. *Can we give Elle one last Thanksgiving and Christmas together as a family?* And while slow-walking the inevitable divorce, Druckman had spent the time getting his ducks in a row. And the last thing he needed at this juncture was to have Calley's team of attorneys start poking about his finances as that might not end well.

Druckman had been setting up his exit strategy—his Nickus and Amahle Fourie escape pod—since the era of the misplaced thong so that when the time came, he and Elle could vanish into the ether.

But Audrick Verlinden—that goddamned Belgian bastard—had somehow plucked Druckman's escape pod out of the ether and dangled it in front of him. And as if that wasn't bad enough, if those weren't enough body blows for Druckman to roll with, there was Verlinden's final touch—*the penalty for early with-drawal.*

That Belgian had smiled the entire time he'd laid down the law.

And fifty million dollars was one massive penalty to pay for an early withdrawal.

But Verlinden wasn't trying to rub it in. No, far from it, the Belgian had declared; he was being the epitome of reason. Why, he'd graciously accept *Druckman's penalty* in two simple pay-ments of twenty-five million dollars as though it were a simple layaway plan. The first twenty-five mil was due later this after-noon and the second twenty-five in two weeks.

Piece of cake—after all, who amongst us doesn't have scores of millions in greenbacks floating about, perhaps hidden under the couch cushions. Except for Druckman. Druckman was already seriously overextended and strapped for cash. He already had too many balls in the air, not to mention an eternally pissed-off wife as well as a pyramid of early investors he needed to keep quiet until he had the chance to implement his exit strategy.

The Belgian had made no additional threats; nothing had been stated out loud. It didn't have to be as it went without say-ing that failure to pay Verlinden's *penalty* would result in an im-mediate string of acronyms knocking down his door, beginning with the FBI, followed by the SEC, and, of course, the IRS and the CFTC, even the USPS—the fucking post office. Druckman would, of course, be considered a flight risk—no shit, there— and he would clearly be denied bail. Funds frozen, passport seized. Druckman's trial would be a mere formality, and then he'd be tossed into a federal pen to rot for the next five decades or longer.

That Belgian bastard had him hopping about like a god-damned Mexican jumping bean, unloading properties as though Druckman himself were a fire sale, digging into accounts he sure as hell should not be touching, and, now—most humiliat-ing of all—being forced to deal with the likes of some low-rent

Russian hoodlum like Armen Kuznetsov and his thinly veiled threats.

Good Christ—both a Belgian and a Russian on his ass.

Druckman clenched the handle of Kuznetsov's briefcase full of cash and put on his game face.

CHAPTER 14

"With a baseball bat?"

"Yeah," I said. Squires had called to update me that afternoon, and then I'd caught a blip on the radio on the drive over to Kippy's apartment. She'd made a pan of lasagna and I planned on eating half of it. "Evidently, three sixteen-year-olds—guys who'd played JV baseball at the local high school—were playing catch at Kankakee State Park and decided to hike the trails. They claimed the bike guy, Steve Andreen, screamed at them as he flew past, and one of them, the pitcher, tossed the ball and hit Andreen in the back."

"Right—I'm sure he just *tossed* the ball."

"With Andreen dead and unable to give his side, I'd take everything with a grain of salt. They say he got off his bike and charged them. I'm sure it started like some stupid road rage thing, but there were three of them against one of him, and those teens brought the bat into play. Andreen died from epidural hematoma—you know, where your brain swells up. A trauma center might have saved him if his attackers had gone that route, but they thought he was already dead, got scared, and dragged him off the path."

"Vira didn't get a read at the scene?"

I shrugged. "At first I thought she might be accepting it now—you know, the death or murder thing—without having one of her fits. But Andreen had been out there for over a week; there'd been rain, and coyotes or birds or something got at the poor guy's face. Plus he'd been dragged a couple hundred yards from the murder or assault site, so I'm thinking Vira didn't get a read to begin with." My golden retriever sat under Kippy's glass-top kitchen table and stared up at the sound of her name being bandied about. "Yeah," I said to Vira, "we're talking about you, girl, in front of your back, aren't we?"

Once I'd brought all five dogs to Casa de Kippy, but her apartment landlord spotted us on the lawn and got seriously bent out of shape. You'd have thought he caught me strangling his mother. Though her landlord despises dogs, he sure likes Kippy—and loves having a cop in the building—however, the jury is still out on me. He's a Jackie Gleason–looking coot who lives in powder-blue overalls and recently got in my face when I parked in an area reserved for renters as opposed to visitors. In my defense, there were only about two cars in the restricted lot at the time of my capital offense.

I did feel his threats of calling a tow truck were a bit out of proportion.

Nonetheless, I am now trained. It will never happen again.

Kippy jokes that Powder-Blue Gleason owns me. It doesn't help that I've taken to calling her when I'm a few minutes out and have her peek in the hallway, atrium, and over her balcony just in case he's hanging about hassling visitors. Allied spies in Nazi-occupied Europe felt less apprehension than I do whenever I sneak Vira up to Kip's apartment. I also live in constant fear of Powder-Blue finding an errant dog turd on what he considers his lawn. If any of the twenty thousand dogs in Irving Park commit that misdeed, he'll assume it was me and the droppings will likely wind up in the cargo bed of my F-150.

"How'd they get caught?" Kippy asked about the teenagers at Kankakee.

"One of the kids grabbed Andreen's wallet and used his credit card to order a dozen StubHub tickets to last night's Cubbies game. Squires said the teen didn't think the body would ever be found, plus the kid did that electronic thing and had the tickets sent to a fake email address he'd set up." I reached under the table and scratched at the back of Vira's ears. "So imagine his surprise when the cops pulled all twelve attendees out of their seats and cuffed them. Seven other friends and the two parents that drove didn't know what the hell was going on."

"We got lucky then." Kippy set our plates down. "If the kid hadn't gotten greedy, and left the wallet well enough alone, Andreen's death would have gone unsolved."

We ate lasagna, sipped wine, talked more about the day's events, and, as I was about to beg another slab of lasagna, Kippy said, "About Armen Kuznetsov."

"Yes," I replied. "About Armen Kuznetsov."

Kippy carried her plate to the sink and returned with a notebook, a manila folder, as well as a couple images printed in color on copy paper. "I ran a background check."

"Of course you did."

In one way I found myself relieved that—as opposed to work as a patrol officer where you never knew what might occur when you pulled someone over to the curb or answered a domestic dispute—Kippy was out of harm's way, at least in the physical sense of the word. But emotionally . . . a homicide detective in a city like Chicago gets recurrent glimpses of mankind at its worst, its most vile. I worried about the toll that might take on her. And it certainly didn't help that Kippy had been paired on this foreboding journey with a living, breathing sneeze-fart such as Detective Ames. Since Kip could count on zilch, nada, diddly-squat from her partner, it was fortunate the bulk of homicides didn't occur at some byzantine Sherlock Holmes level, where you have no clues and a half-dozen Professor Moriartys at play.

For the most part, witnesses at the scene or nearby cameras or blood trails often lead to immediate arrests, which, I figured, is ultimately what Ames had been skating by on for the bulk of an undistinguished detecting career.

"Turns out Banick was right. Kuznetsov has been in Chicago for ten years. He lives in Wicker Park, not far from his antique store, also not far from Ukrainian Village."

"In case he gets a hankering for borscht."

Kippy ignored me, flipped open her notebook, and continued, "Kuznetsov, who is fifty-one, came over from Minsk, the capital city of Belarus. He arrived in New York City in 1998 where he took up residence in—Banick was right again—Brighton Beach. In February of 2000, Kuznetsov was picked up for possession of a weapon, a handgun, but that got chipped down to a misdemeanor and a minor fine. In 2003, he'd been charged with trafficking stolen goods."

"Bingo."

"The stolen goods included large quantities of cigarettes and, in this case, about five tons of chocolate confections."

"He stole candy bars?"

"I don't know the specifics, but five tons would be a few dump trucks full of Hershey bars. Either way, he squirmed out of this one, too, as one of his *comrades* took the hit, admitted to everything, confessed he did it alone—and the charges against Kuznetsov were ultimately dropped."

"So Kuznetsov knows firearms and moves more chocolate than Willy Wonka."

"It gets better."

"Do tell."

"In 2008 Kuznetsov got arrested and charged by the FBI and NYPD for extortion and racketeering. He pleaded out on extortion, did a two-year stint at Dannemora followed by two years of probation." Kippy handed me one of the pictures. "Here's his mugshot from that arrest."

Kuznetsov had thick features and a brown beard. He didn't look happy. In fact, he glared straight into the camera as though he'd like to rip the photographer limb from limb.

"That brings us to 2012, when Kuznetsov decides to migrate here," Kippy continued, "figuring he'll have a better run at it in Chicago."

"Lucky us."

Kippy handed me the second image. "Here's Kuznetsov's photograph from his current driver's license."

There were a few more lines about his face and more gray in his beard. At least the DMV photographer wouldn't feel the need to file a restraining order against the antiquer from Little Odessa.

"There's even more." Kippy flipped to the next page. "I called a detective in NYPD's Organized Crime Control Bureau and—yes—Armen Kuznetsov had been on their radar. Not a *pakhan*—a boss—but," she looked at her notes, "an *avtoritet* or *patsan* because he's smart, he brought value. Long story short, Kuznetsov was the Bratva or Russian Mafia equivalent of a made man. He had originally been a *vor*, meaning some kind of soldier—what with the gun charge—but quickly worked his way up the hierarchy. In fact, my contact at the OCCB said Kuznetsov, quote, 'knew the worth of things,' unquote."

"That would make sense as an antique dealer or pawnbroker . . . or fence."

Kippy nodded and continued, "My guy said they were happy when Kuznetsov left New York. Happy enough to have thrown him a going-away party. In all that time, he'd only had three run-ins with the police, the first two he walked away from. But according to the OCCB, Kuznetsov was hip deep in the narcotic trafficking, heists, and extortion rackets coming out of Little Odessa during those years."

"Did your guy say if Kuznetsov is in Chicago to branch out or carry on his wicked ways?" I said, bringing my plate toward the sink but pivoting toward the pan of lasagna at the last second.

"He put it at fifty-fifty. Fifty percent Kuznetsov's gone straight with the antiques and the pawnbroking, and fifty percent he's got his fingers into other pieces of the pie."

I scooped a hefty slab of lasagna onto my plate. "Well, there's money to be made in antiques as well as running a pawn shop—just ask Banick."

"True, but my guy told me one last thing," Kippy said. "He made it very clear—if you desire longevity, you do not cross the Russian mob."

I sat back down at the table, picked up my fork, and pointed it at the manila folder. "What've you got there?"

Kippy shrugged. "Nothing."

I reached for it with my free hand right as she said, "Don't Mace," but by then it was too late and I'd flipped the folder open. The top picture was an extreme close-up of a man's face. Evidently, he'd been in bed as his head was on a pillow. His throat had been cut.

"Sorry," she said, taking the folder off the table. "These are pictures of people suspected of having crossed the Russian mob."

I put my fork back down. "Jesus."

Kippy and I sipped at our wine in silence while Vira chewed on a handful of pretzels. I no longer had an appetite and returned my slab of Italian cuisine to its rightful place. I figured Kippy would Tupperware it for me before I headed out. I'd snarf it down later at home, after the image had faded into the darker recesses of my mind.

Kippy got me talking about the dogs I had as a child—hoping that switching to a gentler topic would return my appetite so I'd be able to gobble down a piece of her blueberry pie.

"I can't remember what godawful thing my parents had done—likely screwed me over on the Pudding Pops allotment and left me with no other option but to leave home."

"How old were you?"

"Maybe six at the time," I said. "I still recall sitting on the back porch with some toys and cookies tied up in my nighty-night blankie—like a hobo from the Great Depression—getting ready to head out when my mom stopped by and asked if I'd be heading to California or Alaska."

"Why those states?"

"They were like the only ones I knew about outside of Illinois. But there was this park with a playground a few blocks away, and I told her me and Bagel were going to live in the woods."

"Bagel?"

"Bagel the beagle, a happy galoot. I loved that dog. He slept at the foot of my bed every night," I said. "Anyway, Mom informed me—very gently, gingerly—that Bagel the beagle was their dog, that he was getting up in years, and that he needed to stay at home with them."

"So the trip got canceled?"

"I must have had quite the look on my face, thinking about how dark those nights in the woods would be without Bagel. I wouldn't last ten minutes—the monsters would get me. Fortunately, Mom asked if I'd rather continue living with them awhile longer until I got a dog of my own."

"She gave you an out."

"Thank God. I chewed that over for about a tenth of a second and nodded. I brought my blankie back to my room, put away the toys, ate the cookies, of course, and prayed Mom would never bring the topic up again."

"Aren't beagles great sniffer dogs?"

"Yup—Bagel would have kicked ass as a finder. And if we helped the cops catch anyone, I'd have the added pleasure of letting them know they'd been bested by the beast named Bagel. Let them think about that in stir."

I chuckled and got moist eyes at the remembrance of good, old Bagel when my iPhone vibrated. I saw who it was on caller ID, got surprised he'd be calling me twice in one day, shrugged at Kippy, and walked out onto her third-story balcony.

"This is Mace," I spoke into my cell and listened for several seconds. "Just had dinner." I continued listening as Vira moseyed out to join me on the deck. She peeked down at the strip of grass between the apartment buildings, her muzzle between the railing supports. "Yeah, I can be home in an hour and have the dogs ready. Then, if you call, we can take off from there." As SAC Squires resumed bringing me up to date, Vira nudged my leg with her nose. I glanced down, spotted Kippy's landlord marching between the two apartment buildings as though he were a prison warden—his head down, clenched fists on his hips—no doubt dismayed at the lackluster job the lawn maintenance service had provided. "That shouldn't be a problem," I said into the phone. Knowing Powder-Blue Gleason would eventually look up, I took a step backward. Vira followed suit a heartbeat later; she was none too keen on the old coot, either. "You're shitting me," I replied to Squires, phone glued to my ear as I listened for another minute. "Okay. Talk to you later."

I slid my iPhone back into my pocket and looked at Kippy. She stood in the living room, staring my way.

"What's up?"

"It's Druckman," I said. "He's gone missing."

CHAPTER 15

Armen Kuznetsov leaned back against the countertop, his arms folded together, looking relaxed, as though he hadn't a care in the world. After all, Kuznetsov had just unloaded a hundred-year-old brass bed for perhaps twice what it was worth. But looks could be deceiving, and though Kuznetsov was whiling away the hours in his stylish antique store in Wicker Park, he burned in hell.

Even if he took his readers out from his breast pocket and put them on, Kuznetsov was too angry to see straight.

Druckman, the financier, had screwed him.

The jewelry Kuznetsov was set to receive was too hot for him, or any mover, to handle. The merchandise, as it were, was now tied directly to a high-profile homicide as well as the most note-worthy kidnapping in history since the Lindbergh baby. Yup, Druckman had screwed him, big time, and in ways unforeseen. Once delivered, Kuznetsov would have to sit on the gems a long while, melt the gold, and rework the other pieces before he even thought of sending them off to buyers on other continents.

Druckman would need to return the money Kuznetsov had paid in advance for his wife's jewelry. And Kuznetsov would need to send those funds back east to his Little Odessa sponsors. Kuznetsov cursed himself. He should never have brought in his old associates—friends or not, they played for keeps—but the venture with the investment advisor seemed like a stroll in the park on a sunny afternoon.

Besides—what could possibly go wrong? He'd moved some similar objects of interest for his New York associates over his years in Chicago—fewer and fewer as the days peeled past—after he'd ascertained there'd be little or no risk, of course.

Quite frankly, he'd leapt at Druckman's offer.

Kuznetsov realized now the entire undertaking had been an ill-advised ego trip on his part, to reap glory or at least stay relevant in an ever-changing world. But the last thing he'd intended to do was double-cross his own people over an *ill-advised ego trip*.

That's not something many walk away from.

Unlike several of his fellow inmates, Kuznetsov had not found God in prison. As far as he was concerned, God had not put in a single appearance at Dannemora. Not even on family day. No, Kuznetsov had not found religion; he—or, more accurately, the medical staff at Dannemora—had discovered that Kuznetsov suffered from stage 2 hypertension, more commonly known as high blood pressure. And every time they measured his blood pressure, the doctor with the obnoxious comb-over would cackle and state, "You need to choose a different line of work."

Kuznetsov's hypertension hadn't stemmed from his distress over being imprisoned. Bratva had a presence at Dannemora, and no one so much as sneezed in his direction. Doctor Comb-Over had even gotten Kuznetsov onto the correct dose of Prinivil—some kind of angiotensin-converting enzyme inhibitors, whatever in hell that meant—that he used to this day. And, as much as it pained Kuznetsov, he'd cut back on salt and sugar, caffeine and alcohol.

In fact, he'd taken his blood pressure earlier this morning.

Druckman had certainly done him no favors on the hypertension front.

Kuznetsov had called Druckman—burner to burner—the morning the story about Calley Kurtz's murder broke and been surprised when the financier picked up the phone. No names, events, or context had been brought up, and Kuznetsov's message had been ambiguously worded in case of any prying ears, yet Kuznetsov remained deeply dismayed over Druckman's one-sentence response.

"I understand your concerns, but I need more time."

Kuznetsov *knew* Druckman needed *more time*—he got that—but what the financier didn't realize, and what Kuznetsov knew for certain, was that Druckman himself was indeed running out of time. It had been in the cards since Druckman tainted the gems, since he'd drawn an unsuspecting Kuznetsov into this murder-kidnapping scheme of his as an accessory before the fact.

Druckman would pay what he now owed. That Kuznetsov also knew for certain. But Kuznetsov was not about to live out his days in fear of Druckman taking him down when the investment banker got caught, as he inevitably would. Sure, Druckman was a smart man—smart enough to pull off a little insurance fraud and middle-finger fuck you with his soon-to-be ex-wife's jewels . . . but murder and kidnapping?

What the hell was the dumbass thinking?

Kuznetsov had moved to the Windy City in large part to follow Doctor Comb-Over's advice of getting into a different line of work. Sure, he'd convinced his New York City *associates* that he'd be their eyes and ears in Chicago, and, sure, over the decade there'd been a handful of mutually advantageous opportunities, but time had moved on, and as the saying goes—out of sight, out of mind.

So what the hell had Kuznetsov himself been thinking? Sucking his old associates into a golden opportunity with a big-shot investment banker who had literally shown up on his doorstep with a once-in-a-lifetime offer?

He should have his head examined.

The situation forced him to, yet again, contact an old friend from Little Odessa—a *pakhan*, one of the bosses. Kuznetsov had been careful in his wording, even as the two chatted over burner phones, but straightforward about what had occurred. Anything but candor would be a huge mistake. He informed his *pakhan* that, as matters currently stood, they would be getting both their initial investment back, as well as the promised gems.

There'd been a lengthy silence over the phone—he had to remind himself to breathe—before Kuznetsov was informed that a *torpedo*, a Russian hitter, would soon be on a plane to Chicago, and that Kuznetsov would be picking him up as well as paying for his unique services once the job was complete.

Kuznetsov agreed immediately. To contradict would be suicidal.

Druckman had brought all this down upon himself and, within a day or two after Druckman paid in full what he owed them, the man flying in from New York City would pull up next to Druckman at a red light . . . and then the crisis would be over.

After all, Chicago is the mecca of drive-by shootings.

CHAPTER 16

Before prettying himself up for the American Heart Association event at the Langham Hotel that evening, Druckman spent Tuesday afternoon hiking the half mile of woodlands from the back of his manor to where it connected with a public access road on the opposite side. His gardener was off farting around elsewhere, Elle was napping, and Calley hadn't been on the back veranda in God knows how long. In his first trek, Druckman plotted his course for maximum speed; he wanted to find the most direct, as-the-bird-flies route. As such, he entered the tree line at the corner of his backyard.

However, the dense brush did not permit Druckman that courtesy.

So he curved left and right as the thickets allowed. At one point he came to trees and dirt, which made travel good, but it turned gnarly again the final hundred yards. His task was made all the more difficult due to the size twelve work boots he wore. The new boots were two sizes bigger than his normal size ten. And, to be honest, Druckman wasn't sure if he was creating much of a trail. The soil was dry, and it was difficult to see if his boots were leaving much of an imprint. On the way back, he took the same path, stomping over bushes that allowed it, stepping around ones that didn't.

Druckman's second trek through the woods was with a pair of size eleven work boots, which felt a bit more natural. He'd also uncovered a garden rake in the shed and used that as though it were a machete. If the authorities had a team of *Dexters* for blood spatter, the last thing Druckman needed was some kind of Dexter savant for shoe prints not finding a footpath. Three grown men were going to accost Druckman that night—according to script—and, by God, it was going to appear as though they had marched up through the back coppice. He made the trudge two more times, and if *Boot Dexter* counted more than five tracks in and out of the woodland, well, that would only mean the home invaders had been casing the Druckman estate before the invasion.

He was so lost in thought on his final hike back to the house that Druckman damn near leapt when he spotted the doe. Druckman froze, and the two of them stared at each other a long moment, motionless, no more than fifteen feet apart, before he continued forward and the female deer darted off in the opposite direction.

Druckman had been thinking about leaving a handful of cigarettes at the site where the home invader's car would sit during the robbery and kidnapping. Leave a few on the driver's side, Marlboro or Salem, to make the police think there was a fourth person involved—a getaway driver—left with the automobile so it could be easily moved in case a neighbor drove past and got suspicious. Druckman knew he'd have to do it in such a manner that there would be no fingerprints or saliva for a *Fingerprint* or *DNA Dexter* to discover.

Best not to get too cute. If you get too cute, they'll start looking your way.

When Druckman was finished, he put the pair of smaller work boots in a garbage bag and shoved them in his office closet. He would need those for tonight, for the final trek.

The legs of his jeans were covered in dirt, and those goddamned burrs that prick your fingers when you pull at them were stuck in patches on both his pants and jacket. Druckman glanced at his watch. Plenty of time. He changed into clean clothes, found a heavyset pair of scissors in the kitchen, cut apart his dirtied-up wardrobe, and then stuffed the cut rags into separate garbage bags and went for an hour drive.

Ten miles out of Glencoe, Druckman began dropping individual bags in garbage bins outside fast-food restaurants. He went obsessive-compulsive on the size twelve boots, scrubbing them down with half a roll of paper towels and Windex. He then dropped the new pair of size twelves next to a dumpster at an apartment complex. The boots looked first class; someone would grab them.

When he got home, Druckman took a lengthy shower.

It was going to be a long night.

"Where's Elle?" Calley said.

Druckman damn near jumped out of his skin, like earlier in the ravine when he'd come across that doe. He turned around and caught sight of his wife in the office doorway.

"What are you doing up?" he asked. It was half past one in the morning.

"Couldn't sleep," she said. "Where's Elle?"

"She not in her room?"

His wife shook her head.

"Probably fell asleep in front of Nickelodeon downstairs. I'll go and get her." He set the jewelry trays down on his desk with an air of nonchalance. From where she stood, Calley couldn't see the trays were empty. He hoped she wouldn't step toward him, spot the unfilled trays, and demand answers, but his wife had not been in a *stepping-toward-him* mood for quite some time. "You should go back to bed and try to get some sleep."

Calley lingered in the doorframe before saying, "What are you doing?"

"Putting my cufflinks away." Admittedly, a lame excuse—his cufflinks were certainly top of the line, but they didn't merit a spot in the fire-resistant in-wall safe hidden behind a four-drawer file cabinet in the office closet. The file cabinet looked bulky—the damned thing *was* bulky—but it sat on sliders and didn't take much to pull it across the hardwood floor in order to get at the digital keypad.

THE LOST ··· 95

"Why'd you take out my trays?"

Druckman thought for a moment. "Just looking at the different pieces," he said, hoping she'd stay her distance. "They bring back memories."

With a roll of her eyes, Calley turned and left.

Druckman cut across his office and peeked down the hallway. Good, his wife was headed back in the direction of the master bedroom. He kicked himself for not plotting the evening's events to occur when his mother-in-law suffered a particularly harsh Parkinson's day, which would have forced Calley to stay with her overnight, but that would have been all but impossible to gauge. Tonight could still be salvaged—had to be as he had no time to postpone. *I went down to get Elle,* he could tell Calley and the police, *and these men jumped me. They hit me in the face and punched me in the gut so hard I almost puked. Then they threatened to kill Elle and go upstairs and . . . do things to Calley . . . if I didn't get them money, and the only thing I could think of was the jewelry. I thought that would buy them off. But even after that, they took Elle anyway and said they'd be in touch.*

Calley's jewelry trays were bare and Elle was not asleep in her bedroom because Druckman had made his final trek through the woodland. In fact, if his wife had entered his office, she'd not only notice the trays were empty but, if she came around the desk and looked down, she'd also notice him sporting a new pair of size eleven work boots, which wouldn't make a lick of sense at this time of night.

Elle had been dead tired upon their return, but she'd been a good sport and stayed up another ten minutes to drink a cup of 7Up—never that oversweet Sprite for Elle—while Daddy sipped a cup of ginger ale to help his upset tummy. Druckman had crushed up half an Ambien—one of Calley's—and stirred it into Elle's 7Up. There'd been a minor complaint about an odd taste, but when asked if he should throw it out and grab Elle a Sprite instead, she stuck to her guns, chugged it down, and ran up to bed where Mom waited to tuck her in.

Two hours later, after confirming the door to *Calley's* master bedroom was shut and likely locked, Druckman slipped the straps of Elle's pink butterfly backpack—already filled with her favorite stuffed monkey, security blanket, some clothes, tennis shoes, a coloring book and crayons, and a couple of snacks— over one arm and then, as gently and quietly as possible, picked up his sleeping daughter, cradled her in his arms, stepped softly down the stairs, then on to the rear of his house, and finally out into his backyard. In his left hand, a Maglite Industrial flashlight, and in his right, a handbag stuffed with a dozen velvet jewelry bags containing his wife's collection.

That had been the tricky part, but the Maglite displayed in maximum lumens the trail he'd spent the previous afternoon blazing. Elle squirmed and once lifted droopy lids, mumbled something incomprehensible, and settled back in her daddy's arms. It was not unlike the nights he'd carried her out of Epcot at Disney World.

This final trek gave Druckman time to think, and he thought about his parents—something he rarely did—and how it'd been one of the best days of his life when he'd purchased that three-bedroom in the Florida Panhandle for them, how he was able to get those two out of Chicago and exile them to the Sunshine State where they'd only exist as a monthly phone call, which he'd generally pan off on Elle. His father, Larry Druckman, had sold furniture. Or a more apt description would be that Larry had spent fifty-hour weeks staggering around discounted sofas, cut-rate recliners, cheap mattresses, and bargain-basement table sets until some proletarian flagged him down. His mother had worked part-time at a fabric store, cutting yarn or God knows what—he'd never had the curiosity to ask.

Pathetic.

Humiliating.

A couple of losers from a long line of loser stock. It was in his parents' blood; it pumped through their veins.

Everything Druckman had done since junior high was to break from the pitiful mold of his parents' existence. He was the first one in his family to get a college degree: a bachelor's in finance from Northwestern University. And then the MBA, also at Northwestern, before founding Druckman Financial Group.

And he'd been on a roller-coaster ride of success ever since.

But tonight he felt pathetic, bumbling about the woods like dear old Dad bumbling about second-rate home furnishings in the hope that some other loser would flag him down and ask if they had an installment plan on the armchair recliners. Druckman figured his lineage must be calling out to him in the night—mocking him for trying to break the family curse—and for the first time, Druckman felt like a failure . . . an embarrassing joke of a man . . . a congenital loser, just like his father.

Suddenly, Druckman wanted to cry—no, not cry . . . Druckman wanted to weep. He wanted to plop down on his ass, hug his daughter to his chest, and sob until the morning sun began to rise. Sure, he had taken certain *shortcuts* to get where he was, and he'd known exactly what he was doing each and every step of the way, but his eye had always been on the prize. And the prize had not been some half-assed dream of striking it rich. Nope, not for Kenneth J. Druckman. He had dreams of striking it super-rich—like Audrick Verlinden—and Druckman had done his damnedest to appear as though he was already part of *that club*, and appearances counted more than reality on the crazed merry-go-round he rode.

Druckman spotted the light up ahead, a flashlight sweeping across the trees and brush. It was the woman helping him—his junior partner in crime—signaling him from the edge of the road.

Once the handoff had been completed, and Elle was near-comatose in the back of his accomplice's vehicle, Druckman headed back home to set the stage.

"I can't find her." Calley again stood in the doorway of his office, eyes wide, landline clutched in her left hand.

Though his wife had made as much noise as a cat in her approach, Druckman had not been surprised this time. He'd finished staging his office—the site of the jewelry heist—with empty trays littered about the floor, scattered about as if haphazardly tossed aside after being emptied. Druckman had even stepped on one with his size eleven for good measure. And he'd been heading out to check on Calley, to make sure she'd fallen back asleep or, if not, let her know he'd brought Elle back to her bed, tucked her in, and was heading off to sleep himself.

"I thought you were going back to bed?" Druckman stood in front of her, hoping to keep her from peeking about the office.

"Enough with me going back to bed," Calley said. "I'm calling the police."

"Let me check first."

"I have checked, Ken. The main level, the lower level—which you know she's afraid to go to unless one of us is with her—the kitchen, all the guest rooms."

"You know how Elle likes a good game of hide-and-seek."

Calley raised her voice. "At two in the morning?"

"Calm down."

"Don't tell me to calm down. My daughter's missing, you idiot, and it's two o'clock in the fucking morning."

"Don't call me an idiot," Druckman said, and stepped into her proximity, but she held her ground and glared back at him. "All I'm saying is let me look for her before you go calling 911."

"I've already looked everywhere," she said, and peeked around him as if he'd been hiding their daughter from her in his home office.

"I know you did, but it'll be pretty embarrassing if a bunch of squad cars show up and she pops out of a lower cupboard or some hiding place."

Calley stood at her full five-eleven and looked her estranged husband in the eyes. "Why are my jewelry trays all over the floor?"

Druckman said nothing.

"What the hell have you done now, Ken?"

Druckman remained silent.

Calley stepped back, flipped the phone to her ear, and began punching in numbers.

Druckman was calmer than he would have thought. He'd been pressed mercilessly these past few weeks, like carbon into diamond, by that goddamned Audrick Verlinden. And before the bastard showed up unexpectedly in his office, Druckman dealt with the day-to-day pressure of what he'd been accomplishing at Druckman Financial Group—of keeping those balls in the air. But, were he to be honest, it hadn't been Verlinden that triggered Druckman's nightmare. Druckman's descent into madness stemmed from Calley's absolute refusal to *let it go*—to forgive him these past two years—and she'd made his life miserable every single day since.

And there wasn't a goddamned thing Druckman could do about it, couldn't kick her to the curb, because he'd been a fucking idiot and not insisted she sign a prenup—why bother, he'd thought at the time; Calley was already rich—but if her divorce lawyers started poking and prying about in his finances . . . that could spell disaster.

And so the stalemate dragged on . . . and on . . . and on.

Druckman's fist hammered into Calley's jaw before she hit a second digit on the landline phone. Her head snapped backward, colliding hard with the mahogany wood of the hallway wall, and then she dropped like a rag doll to the floor.

Druckman's reptilian brain must have taken charge as he found himself making yet another trek into the woodlands, this trip unplanned. As Druckman cradled his wife's body in his arms, he had yet to feel his blood pressure rise, and his heart only beat faster due to his current physical exertion. Druckman mumbled as he walked—perhaps it was gibberish, perhaps he was deciphering the secrets of the universe—his Maglite pointing the way. But Druckman's lizard brain steered him along the path, taking the financier away from the trail to the access road and toward the boulder in the ravine he and Elle had found when they'd gone exploring one spring day.

Calley wasn't dead. In fact, she started coming to, but Druckman's reptilian brain knew what had to be done. Calley began thrashing about, even got off a stunted half-scream before

Druckman had her by fistfuls of her beautiful golden hair and began smashing her face into the unforgiving surface of the massive stone. Druckman wasn't sure if his mumblings continued as he smashed her face again into the rock and then again.

But when Druckman was done, his lizard brain had him cut across the ravine and into the brush, heading toward a woodland path he'd made what seemed like eons ago.

CHAPTER 17

"We don't have chocolate milk," the waitress-slash-stripper told the young man with the buzz cut.

"You got milk?" Buzz Cut asked in some kind of accent the waitress-slash-stripper couldn't place—Europe somewhere.

"Yes."

"They use chocolate syrup on stage?" He waved an arm across the gentlemen's club, toward the stations where the house dancers performed their solo acts.

"Now and again."

"Mix syrup with milk," he said. "And tell Skye that Dima is here."

"What do you want Skye for?"

"Not your business," he said. "Your business is syrup and milk." His eyes challenged her to dispute this basic premise. When the waitress-slash-stripper didn't respond, he added, "Get Skye first, before milk."

It was early afternoon, and Skye—the only name Dima had been given, likely a fake stripper name—managed the Flaps Lounge first shift, and, though at forty she might be past her sell-by date, Skye performed the occasional striptease herself whenever one of her girls called in sick, took care of a pregnancy, or ceased coming in at all.

Dima had flown in from LaGuardia to Chicago O'Hare. He then took a taxi to Flaps Lounge, which took all of five minutes

as the gentlemen's club was just off Lawrence Avenue. Dima figured the name of the club referred to the flaps used to slow an
airplane for landing. In fact, an aircraft flew overhead in Dima's
short walk from the cab to the club.

Dima wasn't certain, but perhaps the club's name was a double entendre, like Hooters.

He had never met Skye, but a sexy redhead in a mini skirt
and V-neck crop top stood next to the bar, staring his way, a hint
of trepidation in her stance. Dima knew immediately it was Skye
as the aging stripper clung to a black shoebox.

He beckoned her over.

Skye slid into the booth across from him. "I didn't look inside,"
she said softly as she pushed the shoebox across the table.

Dima chuckled, brought the box down to his lap, and slid a finger under the lid, along all four sides in order to pop the strips of
tape that kept the shoebox closed. He lifted the cover and peered
down in the darkened haze of the gentlemen's lounge.

The black shoebox contained an MP-443 Grach pistol—a stan-
dard Russian military issue sidearm. The box also contained an
extra magazine along with a box of 9x19mm Parabellum cartridges.

Dima loved guns.

He was naked without one, which is why Flaps Lounge had
been his first stop immediately upon touchdown at O'Hare.

The MP-443 Grach was a good gun.

He'd used one before.

It would more than suffice.

Dima dismissed Skye with a twist of his head—a dismissal
the strip club proprietor complied with in great haste. He took
out his phone as the waitress-slash-stripper set a large glass of
chocolate milk on the table in front of him.

"I poured in a ton of syrup and stirred it real well," she said,
her voice more enthused than it had been earlier. "Let me know
if you need anything else . . . anything at all."

Dima gave her a fifty-dollar bill and told her he looked forward
to seeing her perform.

In a few minutes he'd call Armen Kuznetsov to come pick him up, but Dima was in no hurry.

First, he'd drink his chocolate milk.

And watch the show.

CHAPTER 18

Last night had been a bust.

Instead of snuggling in front of the television with Kippy, I raced home and eventually wound up nodding off on the couch next to Sue. Squires hadn't called back, so there'd been no mad dash with the pups to some tangled, overgrown jungle or God knows where in search of the missing Kenneth J. Druckman—affluent financier, Chi-Town celebrity . . . wife killer.

I woke to the morning news. My German shepherd was already up and monitoring the television, so I cranked the volume and we both waited for any updates on Druckman's disappearance. The talking heads chattered about Calley's death and Eleanor's kidnapping—the story had remained the talk of the town—but all of their babble was just a repackaging of what they'd been broadcasting since the story had broken.

There was nothing on how the investment advisor had vanished into thin air.

As I left the tribe outside to do their business and then began setting up their morning buffet of dry dog food and water, I formulated my own theory. Druckman's attorney, the one liaising with Squires—some Ivy Leaguer with the Roman numeral IV after his last name—had contacted the special agent in charge yesterday evening after Druckman had been a no-show for their morning meeting, had neither responded to his lawyer's repeated phone calls or texts for the entire day nor returned additional calls and messages left at Druckman's office and home numbers. Mr. Ivy League Lawyer IV must have wet his pants, thinking something unkind had occurred to his current cash cow; perhaps those fabled home invaders had sent his client off to some godforsaken place for another ransom exchange, only this time without the FBI in tow.

My personal theory, based on what Vira had signaled to me that first morning, was that there'd be no additional ransom exchange. Nope, Druckman was smart enough to see the writing on the wall: he knew the center wouldn't hold . . . and the financier had run like hell for the hills. End of story. Druckman had money to burn, so he's probably munching spring rolls in Southeast Asia or, better yet, hiding wherever Hitler's officers had fled to in South America.

It was still early, but after a few sips of coffee I got the courage to check in with SAC Squires. Of course he answered on the first ring. Of course the SAC was wide awake, he was even at Druckman's estate, and he informed me that the missing financier had yet to emerge since Squires had contacted me last night. All of Druckman's vehicles, including his Porsche 911, were accounted for. No one had answered the doorbell or heavy knocking late last evening, so they'd snatched the gardener from the servants' cottage—all other household staff were currently on paid leave—and got him to unlatch the front door. Druckman's security system had been turned off, so the FBI hadn't had to deal with alarms or codes or the local PD showing up. The gardener then accompanied Squires and his agents through all levels of Druckman's mansion, into each and every room, bathrooms and closets included, to confirm that no one was at home, injured, incapacitated . . . or deceased.

And this morning, Squires had stopped pussyfooting around. He told me he and his agents were camped out in front of Druckman's estate, waiting on a search warrant.

Squires signed off by telling me he'd call if my services were required.

So, after I'd wrapped up my morning obedience class, which

I constrained myself from rushing through, I drove the pack to Glencoe on the off chance we might be of help. The front gate to Druckman Manor was wide open, unmanned this time round, and I parked the pickup on the far side of the hedge maze. I glanced about the entryway. It was an anthill of dark suits— hopefully, the agents get some kind of volume discount at the Men's Wearhouse. Some agents were heading up the entryway steps while others were heading down, a few more hung by the black vans, deep in conversation, and a few others walked about the periphery—perhaps heading to or from the eight-car garage, the garden shed, or the servants' quarters.

Then it sunk in, and I felt like an ass for showing up at an active FBI investigation, both uninvited and out of the blue. I wondered—sadly, not for the first time—if I were too stupid to realize I'm stupid. As I stepped out from my F-150, an agent hustled over and asked for ID and, after a bit of stammering on my part, went inside Druckman's residence to hunt down SAC Squires.

"Mace?" Squires strode over, shooting question marks my way. Ten minutes had passed. Excruciating minutes. I'd have backed up the pickup and peeled out of Glencoe had the first agent not held onto my driver's license in his quest for the special agent in charge. "You didn't have to drive all the way out here."

"I had obedience training in Northbrook, just down the block. I figured I'd stop by in case you needed the dogs before I headed back home," I over-explained, hoping they'd give my ID back and maybe not haul me away in cuffs.

Squires looked from me to Vira and Bill, both of whom had their heads hanging out the side window of the F-150, and said finally, "We've got a desk drawer stuffed with burners, but nothing yet points to where Druckman could be, so I'm thinking we have you cover Kankakee State Park again as we know that's where the unsubs or whomever had sent him last time." The *whomever* made it sound like SAC Squires had begun discounting Druckman's allegations of two white males and a Hispanic. "Stay here, and I'll send an agent to hit the park with you in case anyone there gives you shit."

"Is it okay if I leak the dogs before the trip?"

"Sure," Squires nodded toward the lawn, "but, you know, pick up anything that needs picking up."

"Of course." I was about to ask if that one guy still had my ID, but Squires turned and headed back toward the anthill.

Depending on traffic, it could take two hours to reach Kankakee from Glencoe. I popped open the side doors, kept Bill on a leash—as I had during the obedience class, since Bill was not to be trusted—and let the others roam Druckman's yard, the portion across from the hedge maze, in order to lift a leg or take a squat. A quick pit stop before the road trip. I set five paper bowls in a perfect line on top of the curb, opened a bottle of water, and splashed a few shots in each. The rest I kept for myself and took a sip from the bottle as Bill yanked at the leash.

"Chill, Bill," I said.

Instead of chilling, Bill let loose with his customary "Roooo."

I turned about to see what had set him off today and caught sight of my other four dogs, tails up and coming together as they jogged toward the rear of Druckman's property, angling toward the tree line. I whistled once, and the four dogs came to an immediate halt. Maggie and Delta faced forward, into the woods, but Vira and Sue turned my way.

Vira's face told me everything I needed to know. Sue, on the other hand, looked as though he were about to roll his eyes, shooting me his *must you always jerk us around* scowl.

"Here's your license," a voice from behind me said. I turned to find the original agent who had absconded with my ID. He did not look pleased. "Looks like you and I are headed to Kankakee State Park."

"Yeah," I said. "Can I speak to Agent Squires again?"

"What now?"

I pointed at my four dogs, standing in a row before the back woodlands, awaiting my command to do what they did best. "They found something."

* * *

I had a distinct feeling of déjà vu as we followed damn near the same trail that Vira had led me down that first day. My golden retriever was in the lead—after all, she'd taken this route before—with Delta and Sue and Maggie hot on her heels. I kept Bill on the leash as he and I jogged after the gang. Bill kept glancing back at me, smiling as only a bloodhound can smile, in sheer amazement at this new game we appeared to be playing. Bill had conquered basic obedience—well, he'd gotten a passing grade—and soon enough I'd be training him as a human remains detection dog.

Too bad Bill didn't have a notebook in which to jot down some observations.

Lagging behind us were Squires and Special Agent Davitt—the agent who'd returned my driver's license and appeared delighted at not having to blow a day or two at Kankakee.

We cut across knotted brush and dry soil, past trees and stumps, as we worked our way down toward the now-familiar ravine. Vira and the others began to bark as Bill and I stepped out from the thicket. Though the remains of Calley Kurtz had long since been removed in a body bag, and the gulch scoured by a team of forensic experts, barricade or police tape—except for one narrow strip—remained in place, circling the crime scene, the site where Calley's life had been cut short. My four dogs, of course, had darted under the yellow tape and now sat in a wide arc around the boulder from where I'd first spotted Calley's foot. Vira and Delta patted at the dirt beneath them while Sue and Maggie sat still.

Bill and I stopped at the police tape a long moment, and then stepped off to the side, out of the way of the incoming investigators. I whistled my dogs over. "You guys are rock stars," I said as they came and sat near Bill. Vira slid about my ankles, and I bent down to scratch her head as she sniffed at imprints in the dirt left by the leg of some piece of forensic equipment. "You're frigging Mick Jagger."

Agent Squires and Agent Davitt approached slowly, came even with the tape, and stared down at what my dogs had discovered.

The FBI had their answer. The reason Kenneth J. Druckman had been incommunicado for the past day and a half was not because he'd been sent traipsing about Kankakee State Park in search of another ransom exchange site. Nor was it due to my personal theory as Druckman had, most certainly, not run for the hills . . . no, far from it.

The reason Kenneth J. Druckman had been incommunicado for the past day and a half was because he now lay dead in front of us, a little round hole in the side of his head. A small pistol rested in the dirt between his right hand and the boulder he'd used to kill his wife.

CHAPTER 19

"Wicker Park Antiques," Kuznetsov said into the shop's landline. "How may I help you?" There was a long pause, and Kuznetsov wondered if it was one of those marketing calls where it takes a second or two of silence before the computerized recording kicks in. "Hello," he said gruffly.

"Hi," a female voice replied. "Is this Armen Kuznetsov?"

"Speaking," he said, still gruff.

"I, um, was given your number by a friend of mine named Kenneth Druckman."

Kuznetsov snapped upright in his chair. It was midafternoon, and he'd been sitting in his backroom office, racking his brain over—with Druckman now dead and the gems missing—how he could possibly pay Little Odessa back their advance, with interest, in a manner that would preclude him from taking two shots to the back of the head. He snatched a pen off his desk and began scribbling the number from his landline's caller ID onto his forearm.

"I don't know of anyone by that name."

Another long pause before she said, "Have you caught the news lately?"

"You mean the dead man whose wife was killed last week?"

"Yes," the female said. "Hadn't he come in recently to see you about the price of diamonds or gold?"

Kuznetsov stood. He glanced at the intense-looking man with

the buzz cut—the torpedo from New York—who'd taken up residence in the corner of his office, drinking chocolate milk and reading comic books. He knew if he called Little Odessa and appraised them of his current situation—no jewels, their money gone, Druckman dead, and no remediation plan—the buzz cut in the corner of his office would receive a phone call half a minute later, and a half minute after that, Kuznetsov would be deceased, his brains blown across his computer monitor.

It was a moot point as, back east, they were no doubt meeting over this very issue.

"I'm sorry, but I've never met the poor guy." Kuznetsov smiled and held up an all-is-good palm when Buzz Cut glanced up from his comic book. "Thank you for calling. I've got a customer waiting."

Kuznetsov set the phone back in its cradle, walked out onto the floor of his shop, nodded at his salesman, and headed out the front door and onto the sidewalk. He pulled a burner out of his suit pocket as he walked south and punched in the number he'd written on his arm. The phone rang for a long time, long enough for Kuznetsov to regret having hung up on the woman.

"Hello," a voice answered finally. Same female, same Midwestern accent—Kuznetsov was good with accents.

"Please don't call my shop," he responded, no longer gruff, now accommodating. "I've done nothing wrong, and I don't want to get into any trouble."

"I understand," she said. "But did that man we talked about stop by?"

Good, Druckman's accomplice—whoever the woman was—wasn't going to be tossing names about over a cell phone. "Yes, he came in a couple weeks ago with some pictures and a list of specifications regarding pieces from his collection, and, though I did not have the items in hand to perform a traditional evaluation, I provided a ballpark estimate of their worth."

Dead air hung between them before she finally replied, "Was he looking to sell *his collection* to you?"

"He asked what I would pay for them." Kuznetsov wanted to

phrase it just right. "I told him he should try other, more appropriate channels in order to get the best deal as I could only provide him a fifth of their estimated value."

"Did you know who he was?"

"Yes."

"Where did it leave off?"

"He wasn't thrilled with my *offer*, but he told me he'd be in touch. I've heard nothing since," Kuznetsov said, adding, "and now I never will."

"Is your offer still on the table?"

"No," he said. "Not after the news of the past week. And, to be frank, you're just a voice on a telephone. For all I know, you're the one who—"

"I had nothing to do with any of that," she interrupted. Kuznetsov heard her voice catch with emotion. After an awkward moment, she added, "Thank you for calling me back."

"Don't hang up."

"What?"

"Twenty percent would be absurd, considering the events of the past week, but—and I should get my head examined—I could go to five percent."

"What would that be?"

"Two million," Kuznetsov said, and heard the woman exhale over the phone.

The two talked another minute, making plans, him bringing the money—something about a public meeting, something about a crowded restaurant.

Tomorrow morning Kuznetsov and the man who'd flown in from New York City would be taking a trip to Galena, Illinois. Not too bad, less than three hours by car. The voice on the phone—Druckman's female accomplice—had a dozen velvet jewelry bags stuffed with diamonds and gold and rubies that she'd hand over to him in return for two million dollars in cash.

But Kuznetsov didn't have two million in cash.

And the voice from the phone would be getting nothing.

CHAPTER 20

"I see it showed up?" Kippy said, stepping into my trailer home with her laptop bag and a six pack of Heineken. It was her night for dinner at my house; reciprocity, I believe it's called.

"Not fair," I protested. "It was supposed to be a surprise."

My concealed carry permit had arrived, so I had my APX Compact semiautomatic pistol tucked in an inside-the-waistband holster clipped to my belt. I had even slipped into my extra-large Bears jersey, but her cop eyes caught the negligible bulge right off the bat.

"Unloaded, right?"

"Of course."

"You'll have to load it someday."

"Baby steps," I said. "I'll ease into it, like putting your toe into a cold pool."

"The dang thing won't do much good if it's not loaded."

"Don't worry—I'll fill the magazine."

"That would behoove you." Kippy headed for the kitchen with a gaggle of pups in tow, all but Sue, who nodded at her once from the couch and then returned his attention to the ballgame. Kippy tore two beers off the six-pack ring, handed me one, tossed the rest in the fridge, sat at my kitchen table, and flipped open her laptop.

"What ya got for me, Copper?"

"Patience, young Jedi." Kippy logged in, brought up Facebook, and then surfed to Britt Egan's home page.

"Oh," I said, looking at Egan's cover photo.

"What?"

"Nothing."

"You think she's good-looking?"

"Hmm, I imagine a case could be made for that," I replied. "You know I never notice that kind of stuff."

"Right."

Druckman's first nanny, as Kippy implied, was not unpleasant on the eyes—light brown hair, a suntanned face, hazel eyes, and the smile of a tomboy turned homecoming queen. Egan looked twenty but was likely five years older. She appeared to be in great physical shape based on Kippy scrolling through one of Egan's photograph albums, which highlighted her hiking somewhere stifling hot as well as working a sailboat with several bikini-clad friends.

"Druckman said they'd not seen Egan since she'd quit to go back to college."

"Squires speak to her?"

"She called Squires's agent back. Said she was out camping before classes kicked in at Northwestern."

"Didn't Druckman attend Northwestern?"

"I imagine a lot of Chicagoans go there." I may have pressed my luck with SAC Squires, querying him about Druckman's ex-nanny. The agent had looked my way a long moment before volunteering additional information. "Egan said she'd not seen the Druckmans since she'd quit to go back to school."

"Wow, it's almost as though Egan and Druckman were reading off the same script."

I took a sip of Heineken and said, "I see what you did there."

Kippy opened her beer. "Don't you have steaks to put on?"

Kippy was kind enough to take over as head chef. It had been a crazy couple of days, and I lay in my backyard lounger, sipped at my beer, and tried to shake the image of Kenneth J. Druckman prone in the muck of the ravine, lying before the boulder as though worshipping at some kind of hallowed altar. I set the lounger at the furthest level, 180-degree angle, lay back, and shut my eyes against the evening sun.

That must have served as an invitation as my bloodhound was on me a second later, licking and slobbering at my face.

"No, Kippy, not now," I called out to the yard. "Let's wait till after the dogs are down." I did my best fending off an overly enthusiastic puppy as I sat back up. "Oh my God, it wasn't Kippy after all. It's Bill."

Kippy stared at me from the grill, holding a plate of steaks covered in aluminum foil. Vira sat by her feet, also staring my way. Maggie and Delta were next to the picnic table; both looked on in surprise, and then glanced at each other as though to confirm I'd finally lost my marbles. Sue even marched out onto the deck to see what the ruckus was all about, barked once in my direction, and, with that pronouncement out of the way, did an about-face and returned inside.

Kippy set the plate of sirloins on the picnic table. "So Bill's kisses are just like mine, huh?"

"It seemed a lot funnier in my head before I said it."

"Are you done now?"

"Yes, let's never bring it up again."

"Good, because I want to talk to you about Druckman's death."

"That Beretta 950 he used was listed as stolen in a burglary in Hinsdale thirty years ago."

The steak was medium rare, delicious—setting it in tinfoil a few minutes before eating is the key—and I swallowed what I'd gnawed on before replying. "Looks like Druckman was into all sorts of shit."

"He'd have been in junior high back then, Mace. I don't picture him riding his bike a bunch of suburbs over to break into a random house."

"No, but don't stolen guns wind up on the black market and, you know, get sold on the street?"

"So Druckman's going to buy that pocket pistol from God knows where while he's in ninth grade?"

"A few years later, maybe. Stolen guns probably get sold and sold again."

Kippy shrugged and cut at her sirloin. "Druckman already had two pistols, both registered and stored in a gun safe in his bedroom."

"You know how some folks get—they got a couple in reserve in case the gub'ment comes collecting."

Kippy shrugged again. "If we ever have a kid, Mace, and I decide to take you out, but later the guilt becomes too much—I'd be sure to get our kid back to our parents before I grab the pills or head out to the boulder or whatever. I wouldn't leave our child in the wind. You know what I mean?"

"Yeah, but Druckman was inebriated. There were bottles everywhere." My female dogs pranced about the yard, but Bill never left the foot of the picnic table, staring from Kippy to me as we nibbled our dinner. I shook my head at him. He took the hint and walked over to sniff around the grill. "Squires said the guy's blood alcohol content was off the charts."

"Wouldn't it have been a hell of a lot easier to pop himself in the house?" Kippy said. "How'd he even manage to stumble out there in the dark by himself?"

"He's depressed, the alcohol adds to his melancholia, and going to the ravine to take care of business is symbolic, I guess." I savored my last piece of sirloin, and then said, "The note was in his handwriting. You know that, right?"

Kippy nodded slowly.

"But you think someone else was there? That Druckman was killed?"

She shrugged a final time. "It's not beyond the realm of possibility."

CHAPTER 21

This was no longer "fun" or "a big adventure" as her father kept telling her over the cell phone. He sounded more like one of those parrots she'd seen at the zoo than her dad—"It's a big adventure, Elle" and "Think of it as fun, Elle."

And now her father wasn't even answering their phone calls anymore, and Eleanor didn't believe for a minute it was because of a *bad signal* or they'd used up their *minutes*, no matter what the blond lady kept insisting.

Eleanor missed her mother so much. She wanted to crawl inside her mom's arms and disappear.

It had been the strangest week of Elle's life, beginning with a dream of her father carrying her through some kind of darkened swamp, a place where all sorts of monsters lurked. The next day it took forever to wake up. Elle lay motionless on the bed, staring up at the ceiling, so tired and groggy it took her a full hour to realize it wasn't even her ceiling, that she wasn't in her bedroom at home. When she was finally able to sit up, she found a bag stuffed with her clothes lying next to her on the bed as well as her favorite blanket and Mr. Monkey.

First she thought her parents had taken her on a surprise vacation, a final summer trip before school starts, maybe to celebrate her *half-birthday,* as her dad joked about, so she grabbed Mr. Monkey and galloped out of the bedroom only to find some strange blond lady sitting alone at the kitchen table—in some kind of cabin that old pioneers must have lived in—reading a magazine.

The blond lady smiled at her and acted nice and all, and she spoke in that funny accent, like the way people in London, where Mom had taken her last Christmas, talked. And the blond lady told her she was there to watch Eleanor for a few days, and that the pioneer cabin was stocked with all the food Elle loved, and that Elle would get a chance to talk to her father each and every day.

And Eleanor was really excited at first, and she gobbled up the nummies when she was able to eat, but she thought she must be *coming down with something,* as Grandma Lucy liked to say, because Eleanor felt so darned sleepy all the time. But when Elle was awake, the blond lady would talk to her as if she were a big girl, and ask her all sorts of questions, like if she was ready for kindergarten, and what was her favorite ride at the amusement park, and what kind of food would she eat if she was stranded on a deserted island.

But as the days passed, Elle began to think there was something a little odd about the blond lady.

Like when she'd get her daily phone call from her father, the blond lady would disappear inside the gas station and come out with an armful of treats, and even though Eleanor liked the snacks, she never got to go inside the gas station herself to pick out her own goodies. Even once when Elle had to go potty and asked if she could go inside and use their bathroom, the blond lady told her the bathroom was dirty and she needed to hold it until they got back to their pioneer house.

And Elle would watch the blond lady talk to her father after he'd finished talking to her—after he'd got done telling Elle to have fun and that it was all a big adventure—and though Elle couldn't hear what was being said, the blond lady acted all frustrated and angry with him, much like her mother had been around Dad for quite some time, which is probably why she and her mom and Grandma Lucy had flown over the ocean to London without him to celebrate Christmas.

Elle thought she must be getting over her cold as she wasn't so darned drowsy anymore. It helped Elle think her thoughts. She'd been so scared since her last chat with her father . . . he didn't sound like himself at all. And it wasn't the slightly goofy-silly way he'd act whenever he had a glass or two of that yucky stuff that smelled like gasoline.

It was as though a ghost or something had taken him over.

Something was wrong.

And they'd not been able to contact him in two whole days.

Something was very wrong.

Elle was certain of that and scared to death.

She needed to get home so she could hug her mother and disappear into her arms.

She needed to get home so she could save her father.

So Eleanor decided to escape.

She knew where the flashlight sat on the wall shelf next to the cabin door. The blond lady had let her play with it once, to shine it in the darkness under her bedcovers. Elle thought she could reach the flashlight if she stepped high up on her tiptoes. And she'd played around with the lock on the door earlier that evening, when the blond lady was busy making dinner. All it took was a quick twist to unlock the door, but that wasn't what frightened Elle.

What frightened Elle was the noise the door would make as it opened.

She would have to be as sneaky and as quiet as she possibly could, as though she were playing a championship game of hide-and-seek.

Eleanor was a big girl; she was only *halfway* afraid of the dark, unlike some of her friends who were *all-the-way* afraid of it. In fact, whenever she had a sleepover, she loved it when her mom and dad would sit on the terrace as the sun set and watch as she and her friends played night games in the darkness of the backyard.

She would be afraid all right—halfway afraid . . . but she could do this.

And Elle knew her left from her right. She'd watched as they drove back from their daily visits to the gas station. Even though the pioneer cabins were spaced far apart, there were four driveways—she'd counted them—before the blond lady turned onto the one leading down to where they were staying.

So once she slipped outside the cabin, if Elle turned right and kept walking, the flashlight leading her way, she'd eventually bump into another pioneer cabin. And then Eleanor would ring the doorbell and tell whoever answered who she was, and tell them she wanted to go home to hug her mommy . . . and to save her daddy . . . and maybe have them call the police.

It was almost impossible for Elle to keep from falling asleep. She finally sat upright next to the bedroom door and did her best to keep from crying or slipping down to the floor. She caught herself sliding at one point, jolted awake, stood up and shook her head, and then very slowly opened the bedroom door.

The blond lady sat on the sofa, her head to the side, her eyes closed.

She was asleep.

Eleanor tiptoed toward the cabin door.

CHAPTER 22

The blond woke with a start.

She'd been sitting on the couch, wishing for the thousandth time she'd never been sucked into this insanity by that lying, cheating, wife-murdering scumbag. Wishing she'd blown him off, simply not shown up in the tree line off the access road by Druckman's property at midnight last week. The blond somehow knew, somewhere deep inside, that she was never going to get the million dollars Druckman had promised her. He was never going to set seven figures aside in a mutual or trust fund, in stocks or bonds, in Treasury notes or, hell, stuffed inside a piggy bank.

And barring some Lazarus-like miracle, Druckman certainly wouldn't be doing anything now.

At some point the blond must have nodded off, her head lolling alongside the back cushion.

The only light was a bulb over the kitchen sink. She blinked her eyes, rolled her head against a kink in her neck, and glanced down at her watch. It wasn't yet midnight, but the blond was dead tired. She looked about the cabin. The door to Eleanor's bedroom remained shut. The poor kid had cried herself to sleep.

For better or worse, the blond was done drugging the child. She had flushed the Ambien and Benadryl first thing this morning.

She couldn't do it anymore.

All of this insanity had to stop.

After she met with the Russian—after picking up the two

million in cash—she would load Eleanor Druckman into the back of her Honda Civic, drive the kid back to Chicago, park a block away from Northwestern Memorial so her license plate wouldn't get picked up by the hospital's security cameras, and send Elle into the hospital lobby, up to the front desk, and have her tell them who she was.

What an unmitigated shit show this past week had become.

The blond didn't think too highly of Calley Kurtz, but that woman deserved better, much better, than being beaten to death by her lying, cheating, scumbag of a husband. And now that same lying, cheating, scumbag of a husband had very likely offed himself.

The articles she had brought up on her smartphone in the candy aisle of Casey's General Store—as she sank quietly into shock—kept mum on the exact cause of Druckman's demise. The articles only mentioned that he had been *found dead.*

Druckman had done something terrible, something unforgivable—amongst other terrible, unforgivable things—and the guilt had to be overwhelming. Even for a lying, cheating, murdering scumbag. So she guessed at suicide. Druckman couldn't live with himself anymore and, quite frankly, had finally done the right thing, even if that left the blond all on her own, even if it left her holding the bag.

Since hearing about Calley Kurtz's death, the blond worried for her own safety as Druckman most certainly would feel the need to tie up loose ends. And if he could do what he did to his wife—the woman he'd not that long ago promised to love, cherish, and obey, the mother of his child—then God knows what he'd do to her.

But what if she was mistaken?

What if the lying, cheating, murdering scumbag did not commit suicide?

Then who would have killed him?

Not the Russian who owned the antique store. Kuznetsov's only interest lay in the dozen bags of jewelry she had stashed inside the bathroom ceiling tiles. She had given Elle ice cream, told her the cashier inside the gas station said the phone service was often hit and miss, also told her she'd forgotten her purse inside the store, and went into the station's restroom and somehow got her shit together long enough to call the number Druckman had left inside the handbag of jewelry.

If Druckman was murdered, it would most likely be by the individual who was extorting money from him. *His blackmailer.* But was that person even real? Or was that just something the lying, cheating scumbag had told her to make himself sound more sympathetic? If an extortionist or blackmailer truly existed, why would he kill Druckman when Druckman was in the process of getting him the money?

It made no sense.

None of the past week made any sense.

Two days ago Eleanor had had her final conversation with her father as she sat in the back of the blond's Honda—Elle's entire life for the past week had been either the cabin or the backseat of the Civic—while the blond picked up sugary and salty snacks at the gas station. She liked their daily venture out from the cabin in the woods. She liked how Druckman took a full half hour over the burner phone to calm his daughter down, to soothe Elle, to tell her how much he loved her, and that he'd be seeing her soon—*in just two shakes of a lamb's tail*—as it made Elle more *pliable* for the remainder of the day. Those father-daughter chats kept the little girl as happy as could be expected under the circumstances. And the ground-up Ambien in her tomato soup kept the little girl sedate, groggy, and less prone to tantrums, tears, or questions . . . and more prone to a deep and, hopefully, dreamless sleep.

After Eleanor handed the cell phone back to her at the end of their father-daughter chat, Druckman had informed the blond that the nightmare was coming to an end and that she would be bringing Elle home tomorrow evening. Druckman said he would make it appear as though he'd come to an agreement with the kidnappers, that an exchange had been made, and he'd finally gotten his daughter back. Druckman told her to wipe down the cabin as best she could and to have the car packed and everything ready to go as he'd give her any final instructions when they talked again the next day.

And though Druckman had sounded more than a little buzzed over the phone, the news that they'd finally be able to bid adios to the cabin in the woods left the blond with an enormous sense of relief.

But the *next day*—yesterday—with the car packed and everything ready to go, she made the call to Druckman, burner to burner, and it rang and rang and rang and rang. She checked the cell to see if she'd somehow misdialed, but she'd gotten the number right. The blond dialed again and got more of the same.

She'd glanced in the backseat at Eleanor—who reached out a small hand in the hope of speaking with her father—and said, "I'm not getting any signal."

She figured there was only one thing that would keep Druckman from taking the prearranged call with his daughter.

The blond went into Casey's General Store and glanced at the headlines from their rack of daily newspapers. There was nothing about Druckman having been arrested. She picked up the *Chicago Tribune* and thumbed through the news section. The only story she'd spotted basically existed to state that there were no new developments in the case that had *shocked the nation.*

She took out her personal smartphone, turned it on, and browsed through a handful of news sites.

Still nothing.

Then why was the lying, cheating, murdering scumbag not answering the daily phone call from them? Screw her—how could he do this to Eleanor? And how could she risk driving Elle back to Chicago if Druckman was incommunicado? She needed to be clued in on Druckman's plan before the two of them ventured out onto the highway.

The only thing the blond could think of was that Druckman was in an unexpected meeting with the police.

Or possibly the FBI.

She shut down her smartphone and picked up an ice cream

cone for Elle. And as Elle half-heartedly attacked her ice cream, the blond used her burner to call Druckman's burner several more times.

No answer.

And as for today's call—things had gotten worse. Much worse. No answer, followed by no answer, followed by, as she was about to hang up, an answer.

"Hello," a voice that wasn't Druckman's answered Druckman's burner phone.

The blond said nothing.

"Hello," the non-Druckman voice said again. "Who's calling, please?"

The blond hung up.

She wanted to cry, she wanted to scream . . . she knew it was some kind of cop on the other end of the line.

"Was that my daddy?" Elle said from the backseat, but she sounded a thousand miles away.

"No," she said, turning off the cell phone and rubbing it with a hand wipe. "It was an operator because we've used up all our minutes."

"Can we get more?"

"I'll be right back," she said, shut Elle in the Civic, and trotted into the gas station to check the headlines again.

And again there was nothing.

However, when she turned on her smartphone and surfed the news sites, she almost collapsed amongst the bags of chips and bars of candy as she scrolled through the late-breaking news. The lying, cheating, murdering scumbag who had sucked her into his madness, who had made her an accomplice to homicide and kidnapping and God knows how many other felonies—jewelry theft being the least of her concerns—had been *found dead* at his Glencoe estate.

She must have been ghost white as a young clerk stopped by to ask if she was okay. The blond nodded and picked up another ice cream treat in order to keep Eleanor occupied while she got up the nerve to contact this Kuznetsov character.

She was numb, hadn't a clue what to tell Eleanor, and decided it'd be best for the little girl to hear the news about her parents from a social worker once they were back in Chicago . . . a social worker and the girl's grandparents.

The blond stood up from the couch, did her best to shake off any heebie-jeebies, and went to turn off the light over the sink when she heard a crackling sound coming from outside. It'd been a warm night, so she'd left the windows open but drapes drawn so no prying eyes could peer inside. She stood frozen at the kitchen sink—there it came again, dry sticks cracking.

Someone was outside the cabin at an hour when they shouldn't be.

Had that been what woke her? Someone out there poking about?

Then she noticed the cabin door was no longer shut. It was ajar, open a full inch. And she knew damn well she'd shut and locked it hours ago. She stood like a sculpture, afraid to even breathe as she now heard light running sounds fading off into the distance.

A thought cut through the fright that'd kept her motionless. What if she'd not been woken by someone trying to get in . . . rather by someone trying to get out?

The blond cut across to the bedroom door, grasped the handle, flung it open, and turned on the light.

The bed was empty.

Eleanor was gone.

CHAPTER 23

"Eleanor!" the blond woman shouted, chasing the pinprick of light that danced in the darkness a good fifty yards ahead of her. The Druckman girl must have lifted the flashlight off the wall cubby near the cabin door on her way out. "Come back!" she screamed; the nearest cabin was a half mile away.

It had to have been Eleanor stepping down a creaky and rotting front stoop that snapped the blond back into consciousness. The girl must have crossed the living room, silent as a cat, and been bright enough to take the flashlight before easing open the door. Elle didn't want to risk more noise by shutting it, but the front steps had betrayed her.

Elle must have frozen up on the grass right outside the front window, the blond woman thought as she sprinted after the swaying light, ginning up her courage to run, and taking off as soon as Elle heard her heading toward the sink.

The poor little girl, taken in the middle of the night—even if she'd slept through most of her abduction—and waking up in an antiquated cabin in the middle of nowhere with a strange woman who looked as though she'd won last place in some cheesy Marilyn Monroe look-alike contest. Elle gets to talk to her father every day, and he reassures her that all is well, and the blond lady buys her treats and cooks for her and appears pleasant enough, albeit distant, as she reads her stacks of magazines, but then

Eleanor gets so very tired in the early evening and remains a bit groggy until lunch the following day.

"Stop running, Elle!" the blond shouted. She was sprinting now, gaining on the flickering light, maybe only forty yards out. Light off the moon was dimmed by a dark landscape of overcast skies and a canopy of overlapping branches and leaves. "I'm bringing you home in the morning."

She was thirty yards out—could now make out Elle's silhouette—when she hit a rut, went down hard, face-first into the gnarled roots of an oak tree. The pain was overwhelming—eyes watering, blood in her mouth, ankle painfully twisted. She wiped a forearm against a fattening lip, spotted crimson in the darkness. A tooth must have cut the inside of her lip. Throbbing now, in pace with her heartbeat.

The blond spit blood and spit again.

Through moist eyes she watched as the flashlight faded in the distance.

If there had ever been a rock bottom . . . she was there.

She tore off her wig with her right hand and lay next to the oak. Through tremors and sobs, she screamed to the treetops, "Scarf! Come back!" She pulled off the wig cap and threw it aside. "It's Britt Egan, Scarf! It's Britt—I know you remember me." Egan took a deep breath and said in a murmur, more to herself than to the night, "It's Britt."

After a long minute, the now-brunette shuffled up against the oak, back to the tree, her tongue tenderly probing the wound inside her mouth, as she rubbed the ankle she'd twisted in her collision with terra firma. Egan placed her arms across her raised knees, leaned forward, and set her forehead against them. She opened her mouth and let a string of blood and saliva worm its way to the forest floor.

It was done.

She was done.

In a manner she was relieved, and if she'd ever stop bleeding, she'd get up, limp back to the cabin, grab the keys to the Honda Civic, and go turn herself in to the Galena Police.

"Britt?"

"Scarf?" Egan slowly lifted her head, and then cupped a hand against the light shining in her eyes. "I wasn't sure you'd remember me."

"You were my nanny from way before—the one that started calling me 'Scarf.'"

"Once I found out it was your middle name, it was so cool I couldn't resist." Egan wiped at her mouth. "I'm sorry, Scarf." Egan began to weep. "I am so, so sorry."

Eleanor Scarf Druckman ran to her old nanny, arms held wide.

Britt Egan hugged the little girl, and then hugged her some more.

PART THREE

THE NANNY

*Histories are more full of examples of the
fidelity of dogs than of friends.*
—Alexander Pope

CHAPTER 24

TWO NIGHTS AGO

"How did you get here?" Druckman swayed in the front doorway as he peered over the night visitor's shoulder. He spotted no car in the lots on either side of the roundabout.

"I cut through your neighbor's lot, along the stables," the new arrival said. "I may have stepped in something."

"Why'd you do that?"

"There's an SUV at the mouth of your driveway." The visitor could smell the alcohol radiating off the financier like steam off a boiler. "I suspect it's the FBI."

"Screw them." Druckman clung to the side of the door as though on a boat in turbulent waters. "If they see your car on the street, they'll run your plate number."

The night visitor stepped back and took in the financier. Druckman was decked out in gray sweat bottoms and a white T-shirt with a mosaic of stains splattered across the front, of which the visitor was able to ascertain tomato sauce, mustard, and perhaps a splash of red wine. "One of your neighbors is throwing a shindig down the road—apparently, you weren't on the guest list—so I parked in a long line of cars and hiked over."

Druckman stared inquisitively as he continued to sway in his entryway but remained silent.

The night visitor sighed. "Aren't you going to invite me in?"

"Why not." Druckman turned and lurched down a marble-tiled

foyer, past the stairwell, and stepped down into a sunken living room. After shutting and locking the front door, the night visitor followed on Druckman's heels.

Druckman plopped into a leather recliner off to the side of an unlit fireplace. A half-empty bottle of Remy Martin and an empty snifter sat on an end table beside him. The financier filled his empty glass with brandy, made no effort to offer a pick-me-up to his guest, and said, "What are you doing here?"

The night visitor looked about the living room; spotted pizza boxes scattered about on the brick in front of the fireplace; noted the hardwood floor was covered in an array of spent wrappers, fast-food bags, and crumpled napkins; and saw that wine bottles stood about the room as if they were glass bowling pins. "Maid's day off, I see?"

"What are you doing here?" Druckman asked again.

The night visitor stepped between wine bottles on the trek to a sofa across from the financier and sat down. "So this is what it's come to, huh?"

"Don't look at me like that." Druckman had been slurring his words, but at least he wasn't so sloshed as to be incoherent. "I don't need your condescension." The financier jerked up his snifter as though to give a wedding toast. Brandy splashed over the edge of his glass. "What do you want from me?" he said, and tossed what remained in the snifter into his mouth.

"Don't you think it's time we had a heart-to-heart?"

"What is there left to say?"

"Well, evidently, the FBI has turned their sights on you."

Druckman's head bobbed as he struggled to maintain eye contact.

"They think you set this up . . . they think you killed Calley."

"I loved her," he said quietly, and then louder, "I loved her so much."

"I know you did, Kenneth," the night visitor said. "I know you did."

An involuntary wail, more animal-like than human, sprang

from deep within the financier's chest as he slid back into his easy chair. The night visitor took it as the sound of unadulterated grief.

"It wasn't supposed to happen like that." The financier wiped a wrist across wet eyes. His shoulders began to shake. "It wasn't."

"I believe you, Kenneth. You may be many things, but you're not a killer. Yet newspapers are stuffed full with stories about how *it wasn't supposed to happen like that.*" The night visitor's voice took a harsh turn, like that of a judge passing sentence. "Nevertheless, things did happen. And underneath this alcoholic haze and sleepless nights, you're a bright enough man to know this can't go on."

Tears poured down his cheeks. "I know."

Silence filled the room a long moment before the night visitor said, "For Christ's sake, Kenneth, what have you done with your daughter?"

Druckman wiped again at his eyes. "She's safe."

"Well, thank God for small favors. Although when she finds out what *happened*," the night visitor replied in a softer tone, "is there enough forgiveness in the world for something like that?"

A faintly lesser wail escaped the financier's throat.

"Where do we go from here, Kenneth? That's the real question, isn't it? I imagine the FBI is tracking your every move. If you tried jumping on a plane, you'd be picked up at the airport."

Druckman leaned forward, his head in his hands.

"Between all that's happened, Kenneth," the nighttime visitor continued, "I don't see how you'll ever see the light of day again. I just don't see how, Kenneth."

The financier's shoulders shuddered as he slowly looked up from the recliner. Druckman's face was deep red; he looked old, he looked spent. "I killed Calley," he said with just the slightest hint of a slur. "I killed her . . . I killed the love of my life."

"I know you did, Kenneth," the visitor said softly and pointed a finger in the direction of Druckman's driveway. "And so do they."

The financier wept a minute, gritted his teeth, and whispered, "I want to die."

"I know you do, Kenneth. I know you do."

"Was it a good note?" Druckman said almost in the voice of a little boy—a man no longer larger than life.

"Under the circumstances, I think it's a great note," the night visitor said, holding a flashlight as the two headed through the brush and dirt on their way toward the back ravine. Druckman still clutched his bottle of Remy Martin. "You confessed, Kenneth. That had to take a mountain of weight off your shoulders."

Druckman shrugged and then took another long sip of brandy.

"You apologized. You told your daughter how much you loved her. That was wonderfully sweet of you to tell Eleanor *Daddy will always love you.*"

"I will always love Elle," he continued in the little voice that appeared to have wrestled control over the financier. "I will."

Something had snapped inside Druckman, and the night visitor figured all the king's horses and all the king's men would never be able to put the investment banker together again.

They came upon the police tape. Druckman yanked a slip of it aside, walked a few more steps, and stood still, his eyes transfixed on the boulder. "Won't they hear the gunshot and come running?"

"The Beretta 950 is fairly peaceful, Kenneth. Not much louder than a pellet gun," the night visitor said, behind him and off to the side, putting on a pair of surgical gloves. "No neighborhood dogs will bark, no police will be summoned, and that agent in your driveway is a few hundred yards away. He won't come running to investigate."

Druckman took a second and then continued in his little voice, "I am so sorry, Calley." He placed a palm atop the boulder. "I am so very, very sorry."

Druckman's body trembled again. He took a final gulp of brandy and placed the nearly empty bottle of Remy Martin on top of the huge rock. "You know I've always hated my father," he said more to the night than to the person behind him. "Not for anything he ever did to me—he was a good man—but because he accepted his lot in life." The financier sunk to his knees in front of the boulder. Without looking back, Druckman said, "Do you think there's a god?"

"I don't know, Kenneth. I just don't know."

Druckman bowed his head as though in prayer, swallowed, and said, "I'm ready."

The night visitor took the small pistol out of a jacket pocket, approached the financier from behind, and handed him the gun.

Druckman held the barrel of the Beretta 950 to his right temple and took a deep breath. What seemed an eternity passed before Druckman's shoulders again began to tremble and shake. He made a nearly inaudible sob and said, "Oh, Jesus."

"What's the matter, Kenneth?"

"I can't do it."

"I know."

In a heartbeat, the night visitor's hand shrouded Druckman's, a forefinger over Druckman's inside the trigger guard, the barrel returned to the man's temple.

A shot rang out.

The financier dropped to the ground.

A second later the Beretta 950 fell to the dirt next to him.

CHAPTER 25

"My God, Kip," I said through barely raised eyelids. It was four-thirty in the a.m. I'd gotten up to use the bathroom, sleepwalked through that affair, returned to bed, and rolled an arm around Kippy only to discover it was the hind end of Maggie May. I pushed myself back out of bed, stumbled past an inert Bill splayed out in the khaki green doggie bed he's laid claim to, past a snoozing Delta Dawn on her memory foam pup rug, and followed the light through the living room. "How long have you been up?"

"Not long." Kippy sat at the kitchen table in cut-off sweats and a V-neck Chicago Cubs T-shirt—her official overnight gear—working her laptop, Vira warming her feet. She glanced at me with fully raised eyelids. "Something occurred to me and I got up to check it out."

"What is it?" I leaned against the sofa and squinted down at Sue, still sound asleep and snoring. His morning shows weren't scheduled to begin for another hour or two.

She flagged me over. "Remember all those pictures on Britt Egan's Facebook page? Typical young girl having the time of her life with her gal pals—hammocking and camping at national parks, days at the beach, concerts, and, you know, endless pictures of partying."

"Yeah," I said, staring over Kippy's shoulder.

"Her most recent posts—the ones from over the past week—lack all of that."

"What do you mean?"

"Check them out. Gone are her friends. Just selfies of Egan in a forest somewhere or eating an ice cream cone at a gas station."

I scanned the page Kippy had pulled up. She was right. Underwhelming images of Egan in a slouchy cap with a noticeable absence of her girlfriend posse. There was even a depressing picture of a two-man tent on a squat of dirt.

"Did she write any posts to go with these pictures?"

"Just generic BS like *I Love Camping* or *Pit Stop* for the one at the gas station. A friend of hers even asked where she was camping at this time," Kippy pointed at the comments under the photo, "but Egan blows her off with a *Nearby as classes start soon.*"

"So you figure she's whipping up a Facebook presence so no one starts wondering where she really is?"

Kippy shrugged.

"What if she's just doing the Henry David Thoreau thing by Walden Pond before school kicks back in?" They'd made us read *Walden* in high school. I got a C minus.

"Not unless Walden Pond has Jell-O shots and margaritas." Kippy scrolled down Egan's site. "It doesn't fit with her history, Mace."

"What are you thinking?"

"I don't know. I called her cell phone, but it rolled over to voicemail."

"Did you leave a message?"

"Real short, you know, blah, blah, blah, Detective Gimm. Blah, blah, blah, call me when you get this."

"I'm sure she's sound asleep," I said. "Or camping in a dead zone." Kippy stared up at me and I recognized the look on her face. "What else?"

"I tracked the plates."

"What plates?"

She pointed at one of Egan's recent Facebook photos, the selfie of her eating ice cream in front of what appeared to be a Casey's General Store. You could see part of Egan's face in the corner foreground, and then a row of gas pumps and a couple of parked cars in the background.

"You tracked the license plates off those parked cars?"

Kippy nodded. "People are creatures of habit, and they usually gas up at the same place near home."

"But those plates are fuzzy."

"I saved the image to my desktop and opened it with software that allowed me to deblur and sharpen. Then I called the plates in."

"Wow," I said, followed by, "And?"

"And both cars are registered to individuals who live in Galena in Jo Daviess County, Illinois—a few hours west of here."

I thought about it for a moment. "Okay, so Egan passed through Galena on her way to pitch her tent at God-knows-where campground."

"I don't think Egan passed through Galena," Kippy said. "I think she's there or holed up someplace nearby."

"How do you figure?"

Kippy pointed again at the laptop monitor. "Look at the gas station picture. Sunny day, no clouds."

"Okay."

Kippy scrolled down a few posts. "Look at this picture from two days earlier. It's overcast, and all clouds. She's smiling, or faking a smile, but look at those trees in the background."

"Yeah."

"Do they look familiar?" Kippy asked and scrolled back up. "Maybe it's a rural gas station, maybe it's a mile out of Galena, but look at those trees in the background."

I did. A moment later Kippy scrolled back down.

"Holy shit," I said. "It's like she walked twenty feet over and snapped the picture—no gas station this time, but the identical tree line."

Kippy stood.

Vira followed suit.

Then Kippy said, "So should we head to Galena now or wait till after breakfast?"

CHAPTER 26

"Why did you talk in that silly voice?"

"You didn't like my Mary Poppins?" Britt said through swollen lips. It was almost sunrise, and the two had somehow snuck in a few hours of sleep, both of them snoozing on the double in the cabin's bedroom, Britt on her back with Scarf snuggled alongside her.

"I love Mary Poppins."

"I played her in a high school skit," Britt said. "I guess my accent could use a little fine-tuning."

"But why did you talk like her?"

"You were never supposed to know it was me, Scarf. That's why the fake voice and the wig and those huge sunglasses, even that awful perfume I wore." Britt took a moment to collect her thoughts, wondering where to begin. "Your father asked me to watch you for a few days, which would normally be a blast, but I wasn't supposed to say anything to your mom about it. It was a stupid and mean thing to do . . . and I wish I could take it back."

"I don't think you're stupid or mean."

"That's because you're sweet."

"Can I ask you something?"

"Of course."

Scarf whispered, "Are my parents getting a divorce?"

Britt stared up at the ceiling. She was navigating a minefield here. The most important thing to her was getting Scarf back to

Chicago, safe and sound, and into the loving arms of her grand-parents as well as into the hands of whatever type of child social worker they have working godawful nightmares such as this. Britt didn't want the brutal truth—that both Scarf's parents were dead—to come from her lips.

She had already done enough damage to the poor kid.

Britt finally asked, "Why do you say that?"

"Because they're never happy."

"Oh, Scarf."

The little girl's voice trembled as she added, "I always sleep with my door open. One night I got up to go potty, and I could hear my dad talking to someone in his office. So I snuck down the hallway and peeked in, but no one else was there," she said. "It was just my daddy sitting there, his head in his hands, talking to himself."

"What was he saying?"

"Something about losing . . . about being a letdown," she said. "And he sounded real sad."

"Oh, Scarf." Britt turned sideways and took the girl into her arms. They lay that way a few minutes until Britt used a slip of bedsheet to wipe at her eyes and then dab at Scarf's face. "I wish we had a big old box of Kleenex."

"I just use my pillowcase."

"I think," Britt said, attempting to smile through fattening lips, "that sounds like a grand idea."

Scarf took one of Britt's hands in hers and said, "Are you going to be in trouble when we get back home?"

Britt pondered that equation a long moment. "You know how you get a time-out when you've been bad, like if you had a tantrum or broke something?"

Scarf nodded.

"I may have a time-out coming my way, Scarf . . . and that's okay," Britt said, and repeated, "That's okay."

"But I don't want you to get in trouble."

Britt choked back a sob. She knew when Scarf was old enough to grasp what had occurred, she would no longer share that sentiment. Quite the opposite, in fact. "Maybe we can go out for pizza after my time-out is over," Britt said, trying to keep things light and upbeat, likely failing.

"With my mommy and daddy?"

"Wouldn't that be nice."

CHAPTER 27

Britt insisted Scarf take the first shower, told her it'd make them both feel better to wash away the dust and grime and dirt and tears, and get squeaky clean for the ride home. Britt even stayed in the cabin's pint-sized bathroom, feeding Scarf shampoo and soap and conditioner, taken from what she told Scarf was her *bag of smell goods*, through the shower curtain. And as Scarf dried off, Britt gargled in front of the mirror with salt water, thinking it'd cleanse the gash along the inside of her upper lip. Instead, it stung as though she'd taken a large chomp out of an active beehive.

Apropos with all the events of the past week.

After Britt brushed out Scarf's hair, got the little girl dressed, and set her up with orange juice and a bowl of Froot Loops, she dive-bombed through her own shower. The cabin didn't have much hot water in reserve, so she lathered and scrubbed and rinsed in lukewarm water, finishing right as the temperature turned frigid. Britt dried herself under the ceiling tile that contained the hidden bags of jewelry. She even glanced up as she worked her hair with a beach towel.

Britt was torn.

The smart thing to do would be to jump in the car with Scarf and head directly back to Chicago, to not stop in Galena . . . and to not collect the two million dollars. That would be the bright thing to do. If she were to call her mother or father, uncle or aunt, or any extended family member, she was positive that's what they would advise.

But Scarf's father had done a number on Britt, sucking her into the insanity of a faux kidnapping yet one hundred percent authentic jewelry-heist-insurance-fraud scheme, and then turning around and blowing up Britt's entire world by murdering his wife, and then, if that weren't enough, the cowardly sack of shit checked himself out . . . leaving Britt holding the bag, scratching at her cheek, and wondering where the hell she could go to get her life back.

Britt had made a horrible decision—shockingly horrible!—and, like quicksand, it kept pulling her down, inch by inch, smothering her, destroying her. She'd already lied through her teeth in a short phone call with a federal agent who'd left a message inquiring about her current whereabouts.

Oh Christ, that call would be coming back to haunt her.

Also coming back to haunt her was how she'd been let go by Calley Kurtz due to her having had an affair with Husband Kenneth Druckman. Also haunting Britt was how she had continued seeing Husband Ken, every so often and mostly in hotel rooms, since her services as Scarf's nanny had been abruptly terminated. Additional haunts would include how Druckman had coughed up tuition payments for her—whenever Britt felt the pinch—as Northwestern was anything but inexpensive.

The final nail in her coffin would be that, yes, Britt had, in fact, been the unknown person on the other end of the burner phone that led Druckman on his wild-goose chase about Chicago and then on to Kankakee River State Park in order to throw the FBI off any trail that might lead the investigation back to its proper target—the poor, grieving financier.

There's no way, Britt thought, that the jury won't view me as the slut who wanted to be the new Mrs. Kenneth J. Druckman. A jury will likely believe Britt had badgered Husband Ken into killing Wife Calley so Britt could take her place.

The prosecutors will throw the book at her.

The press will nail her to the cross.

The jury would likely set a Guinness record for the world's shortest deliberation—ten nanoseconds—before they marched back into the courtroom with a verdict of guilty on all counts. And that's if they even needed to leave the jury box to deliberate.

She was so screwed . . . so very, very screwed.

Facing that, how could she possibly leave all that money sitting on the table?

Britt needed that two million dollars.

She'd need it to pay for some hotshot criminal defense attorney who could explain her side of the story, tell how she'd only signed on as a babysitter, and how, after Calley Kurtz's murder, Britt feared for her own life as she was the only person alive who could tie Ken Druckman to Calley's death. As well as explain how Britt had indeed kept Scarf safe and sound—never in the slightest hint of danger—and had brought the little girl home as soon as she caught wind of Druckman's death.

Britt had no prior record—not even a speeding ticket—and all she had agreed to do was watch Scarf for a few days as though it were some kind of extended slumber party. She'd only agreed to babysit Druckman's daughter in such an *unusual* manner because Druckman never let up; he kept putting the screws to her, time and again. She'd only relented to his sorry-ass plan once he swore to her that no one would get hurt.

And, no, of course she hadn't a clue about the missing jewelry. That was just one of the loose ends that Kenneth J. Druckman took with him to the grave.

There were so many things to think about it made Britt's head pound.

First of all, she'd be meeting with the Russian antique dealer in a public place—in a Galena restaurant at noon. She'd been the one who'd contacted him, not vice versa, and she'd be going in disguise, once again sporting the blond wig and sunglasses. But if anything looked odd, she'd drive on by. If the Russian antique dealer looked in any way hinky, she'd walk away without saying a word.

But, if it went as planned, she'd need to stash the money first before bringing Scarf to the police.

Where?

She thought of her best friend, Jenny.

Jenny, who Britt had known since grade school. Jenny, who had always been there for her. Jenny, who knew Britt—who really knew her—and would see through all the BS.

Jenny, who she could trust with her life.

They could hide the money in Jenny's ancient pop-up camper. When the two of them weren't using it to traipse about campgrounds and national parks, the camper sat folded down in Jenny's uncle's barn.

Nobody would trip over it there.

Another thought flashed through Britt's mind. This was going to be a high-profile case, no doubt about it, based on how the home invasion, Calley's murder, Scarf's kidnapping, and Druckman's subsequent demise had owned all news cycles since the story first broke. Didn't defendants in high-profile or famous criminal cases—like Casey Anthony or Scott Peterson or, good Lord, O. J. Simpson—get big-shot defense attorneys who'd defend their clients for free or, more accurately, do it for the publicity?

Didn't that happen in *notorious* cases?

If that turned out to be the case, then there wouldn't be any raised eyebrows or sideway glances as Jenny doled out hundred-dollar bills to Britt's attorney. If that's the case, Egan figured, then Jenny could use the money to open a shop, invest in a business, or pay off a house so Britt would have someplace to live when she got out of prison.

Conversely, when she got out, Britt could use those funds to get as far away from Chicago as humanly possible.

She needed that two million dollars.

"I have to fill the gas tank and run a couple errands in town before we head out."

"Can I come with you?"

"That's the thing, Scarf, people are looking for you, and it's best to bring you home rather than have someone in town spot you and start jumping up and down."

Scarf giggled. "I can stay in the car so they don't start jumping up and down."

"It's a tourist town, honey, so people walking down the sidewalk will see you sitting in the car alone and get concerned," Britt said. "I won't be long, and we'll still get you home by late afternoon."

Scarf pursed her lips. "But I'll be scared being in the cabin by myself."

"I don't know, kiddo. That was a pretty brave girl I saw in the woods last night."

"You promise me you won't be long?"

"I pinky promise." Britt locked her pinky finger with Scarf's. She knew she'd need to finesse the next part. "But let's have a Plan B."

"A Plan B?"

"Yes, all great thinkers like you and me have a Plan B in case Plan A doesn't work out," Britt said. "Plan B is if I'm not back by two o'clock, you go to the next cabin like you were going to do last night and—"

Scarf cut her off, "I don't want to do that."

"I know you don't, honey, but if there's just the smallest of baby chances that I'm not back when that," Britt pointed at the digital on the kitchen countertop, "reads two o'clock, go to the next cabin over and tell them who you are." Britt added, "And if no one is there, go on to the next cabin until you find someone."

A cloud had fallen across Scarf's features. "But you're coming back for me, for sure, aren't you?"

"Oh, honey," Britt said, kneeling down and holding Scarf's hands in hers. "I will do whatever it takes to be back before two."

CHAPTER 28

"I am ordered to kill you."

Armen Kuznetsov glanced over at the torpedo from Little Odessa—the man who said his name was Dima, not that Kuznetsov believed him—who rode shotgun in the white Econoline cargo van with the swapped-out plates as they cruised west on I-90 at seventy-five miles per hour. "Now would not be the time."

"They want you dead once diamonds are in hand," Dima continued in his thick, Eastern European accent.

"I'm making them millions of dollars and they want me dead?"

The contract killer crushed his empty chocolate milk carton and tossed it rearward into the hold of the van. "You brought them trouble."

"How have I brought them *trouble*?" Kuznetsov played dumb. "I brought them a great opportunity."

Dima laughed. "They are not stupid," he replied. "They know you gave them shit sandwich."

Kuznetsov swerved into the left lane, accelerated the Econoline to eighty miles per hour to pass a lagging Peterbilt, and then returned to the right lane. Though the man was now dead and, hopefully, burning in hell, Kenneth J. Druckman had reached out from the grave and fucked him—fucked him good.

Kuznetsov wouldn't say he loved his life. The antique store brought him a certain degree of contentment, mostly involving the treasure hunt, the exhilaration of the rare find—a vintage gem in a haystack of junk—but he'd be lying if he didn't admit to missing parts of his old life in New York City. The appeal of brokering Druckman's pot of gold had been too much for him to resist.

So he'd let his sense of self-importance—his conceit—get the best of him.

Kuznetsov gave up playing dumb. "The financier is dead," he said. "There is no link to me."

Dima pointed at the freeway ahead of them. "We're on way to meet with link to you—whore of dead man."

"And we are taking care of her. That's why you're here."

Dima shrugged. "The merchandise cannot be hotter. Police have descriptions—weights and shapes, measurements."

"But the stones can be re-polished—disguised—new jewelry from old, and then dumped in Hong Kong or Dubai. And gold can be melted."

"That is much work for high risk. Dead man and wife are in news around world."

"What are you telling me? Our friends from Brighton Beach don't want the jewelry?"

Dima laughed again. "Of course they want jewelry," he answered. "But they want *all* links to jewelry severed."

"Why don't they trust me?" Kuznetsov smacked at the dashboard with the palm of his hand. "I did two years in Dannemora for them."

Dima shook his head as though in sympathy. "Not for something this big, I am afraid."

"So I'm dead?"

The torpedo from Little Odessa took a heavy breath and said, "I tell them no."

"You told them no?" Kuznetsov was confused. These were not the kind of men you said no to.

"See, rich men have pretty mistresses, no? I convince our friends whore of dead man can be used in house in Novosibirsk," he said.

Kuznetsov was skeptical. "That bought my life?"

"No, little girl bought life."

"Little girl?"

"You know black market in Russia? She make new daughter to oligarch whose wife can't make own kid."

"But Druckman's daughter is not a baby. She's five years old."

"You see pictures in paper? She porcelain doll. Lot of demand back home, little supply." Dima added, "After month, she say, 'I love you mommy and daddy.' After two, America forgotten."

"But her pictures are all over the news. They're all over the Internet."

"Ah, we clip her hair." Dima shrugged. "Kids—they grow like radish—I bet even now she not look like photograph." Dima smiled. "Maybe we get more if they know it's her."

Kuznetsov nodded his head as though Dima's arrangement made perfect sense. Except, of course, it didn't. Dima just needed Kuznetsov's help in getting the diamonds as well as both Druckman's daughter and mistress back to Chicago or, more likely, to whatever airfield their *friends* could land a private plane. At that point, Little Odessa would have their bags of high-end jewelry, Druckman's mistress for sex trafficking in Novosibirsk, and Druckman's prize of a daughter to, evidently, be sold to the highest bidder. Also at that point, Kuznetsov would no longer be of service . . . and Dima would put several bullets in the back of his head.

And Little Odessa's link to this entire cancerous Druckman affair will have been severed.

CHAPTER 29

Kippy asked, "You really know a guy named Boone?"

"You think a name like Boone fits with my gig, huh?" We'd written off the first Casey's General Store in Galena—too urban, buildings not trees—and were now in search of Casey's second gas station, this one located on the outskirts of town. I'd been working my cell phone from the passenger seat of Kippy's Chevy Malibu and informed her that my nearby neighbor and all-around good egg, Dick Weech, would watch the dogs later in the day, and that my buddy Boone had agreed to cover my evening obedience class in Clarendon Hills. "Boone's right up there with Joe Bob and Gomer?"

"I plead the fifth," Kippy said as she steered us down Galena's historic Main Street with its redbrick buildings full of local shops, art galleries, restaurants, and bars—a sign referred to this strip as the *Helluva Half Mile*. Hidden in the rolling hills of northwest Illinois, Galena had that small-town nineteenth-century thing going for it, and, if this road trip turns into a bust, I could think of worse ways to while away the hours.

Vira stood in the Malibu's backseat, staring out the rear window, no doubt checking to see if we'd picked up a tail.

"Just so you know, his name is really Taylor Irving, which sounds more professorial than Mayberry R.F.D. He came to a Halloween party a few years back sporting a coonskin cap, and we've called him Boone ever since."

"You dog handlers throw Halloween parties?"

"One of the guys has an old farmhouse, and he and his wife have them most years."

"Did you bring the dogs?"

"A couple of them."

"Did you force them into costumes?"

"My turn to plead the fifth."

"So you did."

I shrugged. "It was a family event. The little kids loved it."

"Did you bring His Highness?"

"Oh God no." I shook my head. "Sue doesn't play dress-up."

Kippy took a right into Casey's General Store, drove past the rows of gas pumps, parked the Malibu on the far side of the lot, and turned off the engine.

The tree line told us everything we needed to know.

We shared a smile.

It was the right gas station.

"We get nonstop traffic in here and a ton of tourists," the clerk said. He had thick white hair, looked to be well past retirement age, and his name badge read *Jerry*. Kippy had waited for a break in Jerry's string of customers before flashing her badge, laying down a blown-up image from Britt Egan's current driver's license along with the two selfies from her Facebook page Egan had taken outside of what we strongly suspected was this Casey's General Store, and asking Jerry if he'd ever seen this woman. "She doesn't look familiar."

"She may have stopped in fairly recently," Kippy probed. "She may also have parked her car and hung around outside a time or two over the past week."

Jerry looked again at the three pictures of Egan and shrugged. "I see so many faces every day, they all meld into one."

"Do customers ever hang out in the lot?" I chimed in, a step back and to the right of Kippy.

"Not adults. Mostly we get kids who ride their bikes here for candy bars or pop, and sometimes they'll sit on the curb or over in the grass," he pointed at the strip of lawn between the gas station and the street, "and eat their goodies."

I was starting to groove on this detective thing and followed up with, "Does Casey's have security cameras?"

"Right up there," Jerry answered, pointing at the ceiling above the registers. "They also have them set to capture plates at the pumps in case someone runs off without paying, but that's never happened in the years I've been here." He scratched at a red blotch on his neck. "Some folks will forget their wallet or purse, but they'll come in and let us know, and then drive home and come straight back."

"Any other employees working we can show these pictures to?" Kippy asked a question she knew the answer to as we'd spotted a younger man tossing bags of ice into the box near the station's entry.

I glanced outside, and the employee now stood petting Vira with one hand and trying to feed her an ice cube with the other. I'd instructed Vira to "stay" on the sidewalk out front as Kippy and I entered the convenience store—with her as sentinel, Casey's had never been safer. In fact, Vira caught my eye through the glass door and I gave a quick nod. A second later and she snarfed the ice from the kid's palm.

"Give me a second," Jerry said, sounding a little peeved as Kippy and I shimmied to the side and let him ring up a woman who'd come in to pay for her gas as well as pick up a pack of gum. After that transaction, Jerry came out from behind the counter, walked to the front entry, opened the door, and called out, "If you're done with the dog, could you come inside a second, Ben?"

Ben came in wearing a smile and looking much the opposite of the cashier—pleasant, thick black hair, and young enough to pass for a high schooler. The older clerk pointed us toward a closed cashier's station and returned to his register.

"I like your golden retriever."

"She's one of a kind," I said, and then found I couldn't resist. "Ben and Jerry?"

The kid nodded. "We get that all the time."

Kippy did the intro thing again—made me long for a badge I could flash around at folks—and spread the images of Britt Egan on the countertop.

It took all of a second for Ben to say, "Oh yes. She's been in every day for the past week or so." He looked up. "Is she in trouble?"

"That's what we're here for," Kippy said. "We just want to make sure she's safe."

He pointed at Egan's driver's license photo. "Weird seeing her with brown hair."

"Her hair's not brown?"

"Must have dyed it—she's a blond or platinum blond now," Ben said, and pointed at the Facebook selfies, "when she's not wearing her slouchy cap."

"What in hell's a slouchy cap?" Jerry appeared on the other side of the closed cashier's station. Good old Jer must have felt left out.

Ben pointed again at the two selfies taken outside their station. "Skully or slouchy beanie or whatever the heck they call them," he said. "My sister's got one just like this."

The older clerk rolled his eyes as though this were yet another in a long line of indictments against today's youth and returned to his station in time to ring up a kid buying a fountain drink the size of Hoover Dam.

Kippy and I exchanged a glance, and, though nothing was said, I'm sure we were on the same wavelength. The last thing Britt Egan wanted on Facebook was for her friends to make a big deal out of or ask questions about her now-blond hair, hence the beanie, slouchy, or skully cap she sported in the photographs.

Kippy asked, "Would you happen to know where she's staying?"

Ben smiled again. "She's gorgeous, but I'm not a stalker." He then noted the no-nonsense look on Kippy's face, lost the grin, and added, "Not in town because she heads out that way." Ben pointed in the opposite direction from where we'd come. "Must have a cabin in one of the valleys that doesn't have the greatest of cell reception."

"Why do you say that?"

"Well, she tends to show up here around three o'clock and then makes a phone call."

"Does she make the call at exactly three, like it's prearranged with whomever she's calling?"

"Could be," he said. "She'll let her kid talk to Dad or the grand-parents or whoever while she comes inside and buys some chips or ice cream."

"*Her kid?*" Kippy said. "Does she have a boy or girl?"

"I don't know." He thought for a moment. "She'll always park her Honda on the far side of the lot, facing the street, and all I can see is the bump of a head in the backseat."

"A red Honda Civic, right?"

"Yes."

"How do you know her kid's on the phone while she comes inside the store?" Kippy said. "Did you ever talk to her about that?"

"No, I never talked to her about her kid—" Ben said, and stopped. He'd gotten flustered at the firm uptick in Kippy's line of questioning. "Look, I'm observant, okay, and, yes, she's kind of good-looking, but I didn't do anything wrong."

"We know you didn't, Ben. We're just trying to find out where she and the child are staying, and we appreciate anything you can tell us."

"She and *the child*," Ben said slowly. A lightbulb had gone off over his head. "Are we talking about what I think we're talking about?" He stared at Kippy and whispered, "The missing Druck-man girl?"

"We're chasing down a series of leads," Kippy said, "and this is likely nothing, but it's very important that you keep this to yourself, Ben, and that you not start any rumors." Kippy added, "Are we clear on that?"

Ben's face paled as he nodded. I glanced over at Jerry and was pleased to find his attention lay in ringing up a mother with a couple spinning toddlers, the woman's hands juggling several small bags of potato chips as well as a twelve-pack of Diet Coke.

"You were saying you saw her child on the phone while she came inside the store?"

"Okay, right," Ben said, and nodded again. "She'd bring treats back to the Civic, pop open the back door, and hand the treats inside. She'd get a cell phone in return. And someone was still on the phone as she'd walk toward the road and talk for a minute or two. I figured it was mommy and daddy stuff she didn't want her kid to hear."

"When was the last time she was here?"

"Today. She stopped by to fill up her tank," Ben said. A little color had returned to his cheeks. "She was all alone this time and paid at the pump, but came inside and asked for directions to a restaurant in town." He thought for a second and continued, "Something must have happened, though—her face was scratched up and she's got a swollen lip."

We let that sink in, and then Kippy asked, "When was that?"

Ben glanced down at his watch. "An hour ago."

CHAPTER 30

Britt could have found Durty Gurt's Burger Joynt without hassling the gas station clerk, but she didn't dare boot up her personal iPhone to use the Maps app lest someone get a bead on her location. Britt wasn't being paranoid as she'd turned on her phone when she was gassing up at Casey's General Store and listened to a message left by a female detective from the Chicago Police Department. The detective left a cell phone number and requested that Britt return her call as soon as possible.

The message had been left earlier that morning, at a time when most people were still asleep, including her and Scarf . . . which meant they knew.

After Britt deleted the message, she broke the speed of light shutting down her iPhone.

Besides, Durty Gurt's Burger Joynt was on Galena's Main Street—the town's Helluva Half Mile. It would be impossible to miss. Not to mention she and the lying scumbag had eaten lunch there less than two weeks earlier when Druckman had driven her to Galena in order to show her where the rental cabin was located as well as stock it full of Scarf's favorite foods.

"Won't they figure out you rented the cabin?" she had asked him.

"It's through a shell company," Druckman had replied. "They'll never tie it back to me."

Druckman telling her about a *shell company* and how *they'll never tie it back to me* should have served as a giant red flag flapping in the breeze—begging Britt to run as far and as fast away from Druckman as humanly possible—but she'd been too big a dope to listen to her instincts.

Britt glanced in the rearview mirror. Not much traffic for a weekday in late summer, and no cars appeared to have been following her from Casey's. Then she caught her own image in the mirror. Good Lord—a blond wig, a fat lip, and an I'm-walking-the-plank gaze in her eyes.

The nineteenth-century buildings of this stretch of Galena made Britt feel as though she'd stepped back in time. She even spotted signs advertising for ghost and trolley tours as well as pub crawls.

Perhaps another time.

Britt stopped at a light, spotted Durty Gurt's in the corner building across the street, hit her signal, and turned right onto a side street, happy to note an abundance of vacant on-street parking spots, which was exactly what she'd been hoping for. No parking garages for her. Not today. Britt wanted to be in full public view of shoppers and diners, tourists and townsfolk, every step of the way. She also wanted the ability to be on Main Street in mere seconds, before heading back to the tiny cabin in the woods to pick up Scarf. Britt took another right onto a back street that ran parallel with Main and, after a couple of city blocks, took two more rights back on the Helluva Half Mile.

Britt turned right again at the side street before Durty Gurt's. This time she cruised slowly, noting the vehicles parked on the left side of the avenue, along the sidewalk outside the restaurant. First there was one of those VW hippie mobiles, then a blue RAV4, followed by a white Econoline. Someone must have recently departed as there was an open space in front of the VW big enough for her Honda. Britt drove a little farther, hung a sharp U-ey at an alleyway, came back up the street, and claimed the open spot next to the burger joint.

This was perfect. Once the *transaction* was complete, she'd be able to walk out of Durty Gurt's with her bag of cash, jump into her Civic, lock the doors, and peel out of this tourist trap.

Britt slipped her arms through her North Face backpack, the one she used to lug her textbooks and laptop all over Northwestern University's campus, but today the backpack was being used for something entirely different. Today, the backpack held Druckman's pouch containing the dozen velvet bags of Calley Kurtz's jewels and gems.

Britt shut the driver's door, locked the car, all the while glancing about the street. She didn't have far to go, maybe ten yards to get inside the restaurant. Easy peasy. Perhaps she was being overly suspicious—certainly not without reason—but Britt wished there were more people moving about the streets and boulevards of Galena.

Her left hand clung to the shoulder strap of her North Face. Britt would not be giving it up without a fight. Her right hand was inside the front pocket of her Levi's, clinging to a canister of pepper spray.

She entered the restaurant, was pleased to see nearly half the tables packed with diners—a jovial atmosphere—much like it had been when she'd eaten here with Druckman, which now seemed like a thousand years ago.

Britt was a half hour early. She spotted no gentleman sitting alone and staring her way.

The sign in front read *Seat Yourself,* so Britt headed toward a table in the far corner and took the chair facing the entryway, her back to the wall. It was about as secluded a spot as the restaurant had to offer. And if no other patrons sat near them, and the waiter kept his or her distance, there would be plenty of privacy to riffle through a couple of satchels containing the most interesting of items.

Britt set her iPhone on the table in front of her. If needed, she'd flip it on for however long she'd need the calculator app as she shuffled through the contents of the bag the antique dealer would be handing her. Hopefully, there'd be rhyme or reason with how he'd have it filled. Britt was good at math and figured if there were bundles of ten thousand dollars or stacks of one hundred hundred-dollar bills, then there would be two hundred stacks. Britt planned on flipping through at least a third of the stacks of cash as well as randomly pulling out and examining several of the bills to make sure she wasn't being ripped off with Monopoly money or carved up newspaper.

She figured the antiquer would be walking away with at least five million dollars in jewelry, maybe even twice that, so there shouldn't be any bullshit. But if there was any bullshit, the man would get his face washed in pepper spray whether they were in a family establishment or not.

That thought almost made Britt chuckle. Her insides quivered like Jell-O, and she felt like bolting for the side entrance, but here she was—*this was happening*—and she'd keep her game face on.

Speaking of the side entrance, Britt was glad she'd been here before and knew about its existence—a single door at the end of the hallway that contained the restrooms. Once Britt ascertained she wasn't being ripped off, that there was two million dollars in the antiquer's bag, she would excuse herself for a second—take her sack of cash, but leave her backpack of jewelry at the table—and head off as though she was on her way to the ladies' room, but would just keep on walking till she was through the side door, a few car lengths up the street, and behind the steering wheel of her Honda Civic.

Britt would be passing Casey's General Store by the time the antique store owner realized she wasn't coming back.

Britt gritted her teeth.

She could do this.

A waitress appeared at her side. "Welcome to Durty Gurt's. Can I get you a drink to get started?"

"Sure," Britt replied. She'd kill for a glass of Merlot—it would probably be her last for a long, long time—but this was not an occasion for her to catch a buzz or get tipsy. "I'm waiting on someone, but I'll have a Coke."

CHAPTER 31

"Look how obvious she acts," Dima observed from the passenger seat in the Ford Econoline parked on the side of the burger place. "She is beauty, though," he added. "I will have her."

Kuznetsov turned toward Dima. "You can't be serious."

"It is, what they say, quality control—make sure she is worthy of Novosibirsk."

Kuznetsov watched a sly smile creep across the Russian's features, and, though he'd not place money on it, figured the man had been joking.

He twisted about and stared into the rear of the cargo van for the hundredth time that morning. The only thing back there— ignoring Dima's handful of spent chocolate milk cartons—was the green duffel bag. It remained zipped shut, stuffed near bursting with old *Antique Trader* magazines, and perched in front of the van's rear doors.

Everything was ready to go.

"Why you not go in restaurant?"

Kuznetsov checked his watch. "I'm going to keep her waiting. Let her sit there by herself and get all antsy."

"What is antsy?"

"Nervous and impatient, so she'll want this over with." He glanced out the side window and continued, "After I go in, give me ten minutes and then go stand in the alleyway as though you're waiting for someone." The alley running along the back of Durty

Gurt's was about ten yards farther down the side street from where they sat. "You'll be the ambush hunter."

Dima shot Kuznetsov an icy glare. "I know what to do."

"Let's go through it a final time for my benefit, okay?" The two had gotten to Galena early as they didn't have to fiddle around withdrawing any funds from a bank or yanking it out of a safety deposit box or whatever Druckman's mistress thought they'd have to do in order to get ahold of two million dollars in cash. "You hide in the alleyway until I get her in the blind spot. I'm going to open both rear doors—right and left—and stand back with my arms folded so I don't appear as a threat, okay?"

Dima nodded along with Kuznetsov's plan, his eyes in perpetual motion—scanning the street, taking a quick gaze into the side view mirror back toward the alley and glimpsing at the exterior of Durty Gurt's, and then back to scanning the street again. The Econoline had been parked there since ten o'clock. Dima had hiked the length of the commercial section of Main Street—peeking in windows, even entering a store or two—but returned through the back alleyway. By contrast, Kuznetsov had stayed in the van. He'd tilted his seat back to make it difficult for any passersby, via foot or automobile, to spot him unless they pressed up against the driver's side window.

And then they'd be in for a surprise.

Kuznetsov finished talking through his strategy. "She'll see the duffel and step in between the back doors—blocking any view of her—and begin unzipping the bag. You come up from behind, quiet as a mouse, and shove her into the van with you as I close the doors." Kuznetsov snapped his fingers. "That quick." He added, "And keep her quiet back there until we get her out of town."

Dima smiled again. "I will keep my girlfriend quiet."

Kuznetsov nodded. He had no doubt the man would do just that. "Then we find out where she's got the kid."

Once they picked up the little girl, and Dima was busy securing the two of them for the ride back to Chicago or wherever Dima would be instructing him to take them, Kuznetsov would have to make his move. He'd have to take out the torpedo from

Little Odessa while Dima was vulnerable—as quick as humanly possible—two shots to the back of the young man's head.

Truth be told, Kuznetsov had never killed before, not even in the early years when he'd been utilized as muscle due to his size, back before he'd proven his worth in areas more cerebral.

But he knew how to use a gun. And he had a Smith & Wesson .38 Special pocket revolver hidden under the driver's seat.

After it was over, and Dima was dead, Kuznetsov would be left with the stash of jewelry, which he could then use to broker some kind of truce with the *pakhans* in New York City.

As for Druckman's mistress and the child . . . Kuznetsov felt his eyes moisten . . . he didn't like to think about that.

Dima—dead inside as were all the killers Kuznetsov had known from his years on the East Coast—may not have had such repulsive ideas, after all. Perhaps Druckman's mistress and daughter could be used as additional bargaining chips in Kuznetsov's quest for a brokered peace.

Kuznetsov stared at the side of Durty Gurt's Burger Joynt . . . and wondered if he, too, were dead inside.

CHAPTER 32

Two Cokes and forty-five minutes later, Britt had passed into the *drop-dead* stage.

She and Jenny had come up with a three-tiered approach for ejecting boys from their lives with great haste. First was the *let-him-down-gently* stage. This was employed on those sweet and gangly boys in class who got all puppy-dog crushing on you and ginned up the nerve to ask you out. In these cases, generous servings of *you're such a great guy* and *can't we just be friends* were ladled over the poor dweebs until they shuffled away, self-esteems mildly bruised but, all in all, thinking good thoughts. Next up was the *be firm* stage. This was strictly aimed at break-ups with boyfriends in which there was zero chance of the relationships ever rekindling. You had to be firm in order to get it through their thick skulls that it was finito—so they could head home for a long cry or to pen poetry, or both—but not so over-the-top rigid that they'd begin plotting how best to boil your pet rabbit.

It was now quarter past twelve and Britt had entered the final stage. It was the *drop-dead* level used mostly on assholes in bars or at school or work who couldn't take "no" for an answer. It was the stage where you cut them off at the knees, where you informed them you'd get the bouncer to toss them out on their ass or, worse yet, a bigger guy to beat them up. At school, you threatened to go to the administration; at work, you threatened a trip to HR.

Britt fumed. Perhaps the antiquer wasn't coming. She had the burner phone she'd used with Kuznetsov on the table in front of her, next to her smartphone, and it had yet to ring.

Britt decided she'd give the man exactly fifteen more minutes, until twelve-thirty, before she'd bail and head back to the cabin, but a second later a tall and thickset gentleman stepped into Durty Gurt's entryway. He appeared to be somewhere in his fifties—pick a number—bearded, with broad features on a wind-battered face. He donned a gray suit over a sweater-vest, and Britt figured the guy could pass for a proprietor of an antique store or perhaps a history professor at some community college.

Britt understood the first half hour of sitting in Gurt's was on her for arriving early, but she didn't appreciate, in a precarious situation such as this, being left to hang in the breeze for over a quarter of an hour. She took a deep breath, exhaled through her nose, and tried to reel it back in from the drop-dead level to be firm. Britt watched as the man dawdled in the restaurant's entrance. He looked down at his watch, then took in the sign instructing patrons to seat themselves, and then began glancing about the half-filled room.

Britt did nothing to flag the man over. Instead, she nudged her backpack under the table. The man's eyes swept through the room and then back again, this time coming to a stop on her.

Britt held his gaze as he headed across the room.

"Where's the bag?" she asked an instant before he countered with, "Are you okay?"

"You should see the other guy," she said as Kuznetsov pulled out the chair across from her and sat down. Britt ran her tongue over the cut on her inner lip and repeated, "Where's the bag?"

"It's locked in the back of my car," he replied. "I don't know about you, but this isn't how I normally spend my workday. I didn't want to get smacked in the head out on the sidewalk."

"You weren't going to get smacked in the head." Britt added, "Go get the bag or we're done here."

Kuznetsov took his time to respond. "It's in a big duffel bag, and I'm not going to be hauling it around until I know this is for real, okay? So far you've just been a voice on a phone promising great fortune."

Brit sighed, and lifted the backpack onto her lap.

"So glad you showed up, hon," Britt's waitress appeared at Kuznetsov's side. "She was starting to look down in the dumps. Can I get you something to drink before you order?"

"What's she drinking?"

"A Coke."

"I will have a shot of your house vodka and a beer chaser," Kuznetsov said. After the waitress left, he added, "I rarely drink, but today—it's for my nerves."

"Is that a Russian Boilermaker?" Britt asked as she pushed a single velvet bag across the table with her left hand, her right hand back inside her front pocket, fingers gripping the canister of pepper spray.

"Yes." Kuznetsov dug into a breast pocket and took out a loupe—a handheld magnifying glass for gemstones—and set it next to the bag. He opened the jewelry bag, peeked inside, and shut it as the waitress set the shot glass and beer in front of him.

"Have you two decided what you'd like to eat?" Gurt's waitress asked. "Or do you need a few more minutes?"

"We're not staying for lunch," Britt said, her eyes not leaving Kuznetsov.

"Okay, then—just give a holler if you need anything."

Kuznetsov tossed back the vodka, glanced behind himself, reopened the jewelry bag, and took out Calley Kurtz's engagement ring. He brought the loupe to his eye with one hand and held the ring up with his other. When Kuznetsov was done, he set the ring back inside the velvet bag and pushed it across the table toward Britt.

"What's the verdict?"

"It's not the Hope Diamond," he said after a long pause, "but it'll do."

Britt spent the next ten minutes feeding the antique shop

owner the remaining individual bags of jewelry. The waitress stopped by long enough to see if either of them wanted another round; both shook their heads. Sometimes Kuznetsov would hold the loupe up to his eye as he examined a piece, but more often than not he didn't.

The two sat in stillness as the antiquer verified the jewelry was authentic, and that the individual pieces matched the list Druckman had provided him weeks earlier. Britt took Kuznetsov's continued silence for affirmation. Though nerve-racking, it was better than having the man screech about *paste* and *glass* and *fool's gold* and then stomp out the door.

Britt kept an eye on the room, more specifically on their waitress, ready to clear her throat if the woman approached their table. At one point, a young guy with a golden retriever came into the restaurant, spotted the *Seat Yourself* sign, and began looking about the room. He caught her staring at him; their eyes lingered a split second before both broke off the gaze. A second later her waitress was in the entryway, talking to the customer— evidently explaining Durty Gurt's policy on dogs not being allowed inside with the dinner guests. The man nodded as if that were expected, asked the waitress a question, and was handed a menu in return. He sat at an empty entryway bench, likely used when Gurt's was hopping with diners, his pooch at his feet, and scanned the menu, apparently content with ordering takeout.

Kuznetsov had been checking off his list of the Druckman jewels as he worked his way through the velvet bags. After looking inside the twelfth bag, he set his pen down on top of his sheet of paper and said, "These are exactly the pieces *that man* had me evaluate."

"So we're good here?"

Kuznetsov finished the last sip of his beer and set the glass down next to the list. He returned the loupe to his suit pocket. At last he said, "I could only put together one million and nine hundred thousand."

"What the hell?" Britt said, edging back into her drop-dead stage. "I fulfilled my end of the bargain."

"I don't know who you think I am," he replied, "but I am not a bank. It was all I could do to scrape these funds together on such short notice." Kuznetsov began folding his itemized list. "Keep the bag of gold bands and we'll call it square."

"I don't want the gold bands." She pointed at her backpack. "I don't want any of this stuff."

"Is the hundred grand a deal breaker?"

She scanned the restaurant. The lunch crowd had begun to thin out. At one table a toddler was screaming bloody murder, at another table an older woman set a credit card down on top of her tab. The dog guy finished handing the waitress the menu along with some cash and headed outside with his golden retriever.

Britt knew this had to end; she needed to get back to Scarf. "Go get the money."

"It's in a huge duffel bag."

"Put it on the floor and I'll thumb through it."

"It's going to look like we're making a drug deal."

"I don't give a flip."

"I do, and I think you should, too," he replied calmly. "We've already given the waitress enough to remember us by. Now my van is outside; it's parked right next to the building."

"Your van?" Britt said. "You told me you had a car."

"It's what I use for my store, to pick up or deliver antiques," he said. "Look, my wife had an appointment with her oncologist today. She took the car because she hates driving the van in the city."

"I'm sorry about your wife, but I don't do vans."

"The cancer's in remission, but she gets checked four times a year." He added, "My van is right next to the building. People are all over the street. I'll open the doors and stand out of the way, okay?"

Britt shook her head. "I don't do vans."

"If you scream, everyone comes running, right?" Kuznetsov said. "And me—I'm just an old man with gout."

She stared at the antique store owner and said nothing.

Kuznetsov's list and pen followed the loupe into the breast pocket of his suit jacket. "I shouldn't be doing this," he said, taking a twenty dollar bill out of his wallet and dropping it on the table. "This was a mistake."

Britt stood, looped her arms through the shoulder straps of her backpack, and said, "Let's go."

"What?"

"Let's go, already."

CHAPTER 33

"What's so interesting in the car?" Kippy asked the man in the leather jacket.

She had followed Ben's directions from Casey's General Store to Durty Gurt's Burger Joynt, dumped Mace and Vira out of the Chevy Malibu in front of the eatery with instructions for Mace to peek in the restaurant and see if he could spot Britt Egan. Nearly as important, though, since the Druckman child had not been in Egan's Honda Civic at Casey's—it'd be insane for Egan to cart the little girl around in public—was one question: Who in the hell was the nanny having lunch with?

Other accomplices?

"Why do you ask?" The man turned his attention from Egan's Honda toward her.

Kippy had worked her way back toward Durty Gurt's, turned left, and immediately spotted what she suspected was Egan's red Civic sitting in the first space outside the restaurant. Kippy swung into the first spot available on the right side of the street and killed the engine. She flipped open her pocket-sized notebook and memorized Egan's plate number. Just as she stepped from her Malibu, she spotted the man in a leather jacket—mid-to-late twenties, a buzz cut—hunched over and peering into the passenger's side window of Egan's vehicle.

Kippy had crossed the street and was now approaching slowly, silently; a quick glance at the license plate confirmed it was Egan's

172 ··· JEFFREY B. BURTON

Honda. Kippy also noted how the man's leather jacket dipped lower on the left-hand side as though that portion was somehow weighted.

Unconsciously, her right hand dipped closer to her own holster.

Kippy took out her badge at the man's query and held it up for him to see. "This is why."

Leather Jacket stepped off the sidewalk, onto the strip of road between Egan's car and a VW van, and examined her ID as though he were studying for a final exam. "What name is *Kippy* for cop? Sounds like poodle. Should have dyke name like Greta or Ruth?"

Kippy stuffed her badge away in a single, fluid motion. She might need both hands free to deal with this creep. Bells had gone off when she'd discerned his Eastern European accent in somewhat broken English. Kippy wasn't one to believe in coincidences, and the inference that Leather Jacket was part of Armen Kuznetsov's entourage didn't seem too big a stretch.

Which meant that Kuznetsov was inside Durty Gurt's with Britt Egan.

"Let me see some ID, please?"

Leather Jacket took another step closer. He was now inside Kippy's personal space, trying to intimidate her, and looking at her as though she were some kind of peculiar specimen under a slide. "Badge says Chicago," he replied. "You have badge say Galena, I show you ID."

"So you're going to make this difficult?"

"No," Leather Jacket said, and shrugged. "I make it proper. You have no, what they call it on TV . . . *jurisdiction* here."

Kippy didn't budge an inch, not for this scuzzbucket, but her mind kicked into overdrive, and she realized the question at hand was—if Leather Jacket is one of Kuznetsov's Russian thugs, should I keep pressing him?

The answer came back a resounding "no."

If I keep pressing, Kippy thought, I give away that the police are onto them, that is, if I've not given it away already. She decided to cut her losses, and, though it went against every fiber in her body, Kippy stepped back. "A lot of cars get stolen in tourist towns."

"That is pity," Leather Jacket replied and took a step back himself. "I'm not in Galena to steal beat-to-shit Honda." He smiled at her. "I'm here for pub crawl."

"I've heard good things about that." Kippy hadn't heard jack shit about it.

"What say you and I go on pub crawl? We start over—maybe I show ID."

"Another time perhaps."

"I pay for drinks," Leather Jacket pushed.

"Another time."

Kippy was on the sidewalk an instant later, and, as she passed Mace and Vira outside the diner, she whispered, "Follow me."

The trio walked four shops down before Kippy knelt to scratch at the back of Vira's ears but continued whispering to Mace, "A punk with a Russian accent was looking into Egan's car, and I was dumb enough to show my hand."

"What do you mean?"

"A cop from Chicago braces him because he's standing next to Egan's car." Kippy shook her head. "Anyway," she nodded back toward Durty Gurt's, "I guess we know who she's in there with."

"What do you want me to do?"

Kippy thought for a moment and said, "Confirm Egan's in there with Kuznetsov and text me, okay? Then we'll sort of know what the hell is going on here."

"What are you going to do?"

"That guy at Egan's car radiates bad news," Kippy said under her breath, "and he's carrying a gun. I'm going to try to keep an eye on him."

Kippy finished petting Vira and stood. Though Vira enjoyed the massage, the golden retriever looked up at Kippy with inquiring eyes. Kippy could tell that Vira knew something was up, that today was no longer a walk in the park.

"One last thing, Mace," Kippy said. "Whatever happens, do not let Egan get in a car with Kuznetsov, okay? If Egan gets into a car with him, she's dead."

Mace lost color but nodded agreement.

Kippy jaywalked Main Street but turned back in the direction of the burger joint, this time on the opposite side of the road. When she hit the intersection, Kippy saw that Egan's Civic was still there, as was Kippy's Malibu on the other side of the street; however, the man in the leather jacket was nowhere to be found.

CHAPTER 34

I set my iPhone on top of Durty Gurt's menu, typed "It's him" in the box, and hit the up arrow to send the text message off to Kippy.

From my vantage point in the entryway, I was able to view a good chunk of the restaurant and, sure enough, there sat Britt Egan—definitely sporting blond hair—and Kuznetsov at a corner table on the far end of the dining room. And though Kuznetsov's back was to me, I caught a few flashes of profile and a full flash of his face as he shot a glance over his shoulder before examining whatever it was that Egan had slipped across the table to him.

The Russian looked exactly like his photo on the Illinois driver's license Kippy had enlarged and printed out.

So Kenneth Druckman is dead and it's been all over the news since shortly after my pack of canines discovered him in his back ravine—Egan would most certainly have heard the news by now—yet somehow she's also wired into Kuznetsov, and, unless I'm very much mistaken, a deal was going down in real time at a back table in Durty Gurt's Burger Joynt while I sat on a bench in the entryway, with Vira at my feet, and ordered takeout.

It was all I could do to keep from gawking at the two lawbreakers as though I were streaming a new show on Netflix. Instead, I busied myself studying Gurt's menu. I remained stuffed from an ill-advised overdose of French toast sticks at a Burger King drive-through a few hours earlier, but I knew Kippy would want to grab Britt Egan, have her immediately take us to Eleanor Druckman, and then either powwow with Galena PD or convoy it straight back to CPD. So, not knowing when we'd get a chance to eat again, I figured I'd pick a little something up for Eleanor and maybe something for whomever else was in need of nibbling.

Plus, it gave me a chance to keep an eye on Egan and Kuznetsov without arousing their suspicion.

"What do you think, Vira?" I said. "A little kid would love a cheeseburger, right?"

Vira looked up at me, her tongue out as if to say *I'd love a cheeseburger.*

That was all the confirmation I needed. I ordered a cheese-burger and potato fries for the Druckman child as well as a ba-con cheeseburger and sweet potato fries for Kippy and myself to split. I toyed with picking up something for Egan but knew she'd soon be losing her appetite. I gave the waitress twenty-five bucks and had her keep the change. She called me "hon" and told me to check back in ten. As Vira and I headed outside, I gave Gurt's a backward glance.

Egan and Kuznetsov were still at the far table. And though I couldn't hear a word they said, their conversation seemed in-tense.

Vira and I loitered about the front walk, watching the traffic, peeking over at Egan's Civic, and glancing about the streets for Kippy. Five minutes later I stepped back inside the restaurant and froze in my tracks. The back table was now vacant. The only sign that Egan and Kuznetsov had been there were a few empty glasses.

"Another five minutes, hon," my waitress said, ten feet away—a pitcher of water in one hand and holding up four fingers and a thumb with the other.

"Have you got a restroom?" I stammered, louder than the ques-tion warranted.

"A right at the hallway," she answered, pointing the way with her free hand, "but you can't bring your dog."

I'd been under the impression there was one entrance to Durty

Gurt's, which also doubled as its exit, and that I'd been monitoring the pinch point, but a thought occurred to me. "Do you guys have a side door?"

The waitress shot me a puzzled look as though I'd soon be demanding the diner's blueprints, so I added, "I'm trying to find my sister."

It wasn't a bald-faced lie. I do, in fact, have an older sister, but the chances of me finding her in Galena, Illinois, on today of all days were slightly below zero.

"Yeah," the waitress replied. "It's by the restrooms."

I darted back outside the entryway, Vira at my heels, cut left and around the restaurant's brick exterior. Sure enough, Kuznetsov stood halfway down the block, on the curb and next to the back of a white van. The Russian was motionless, arms comfortably folded about his chest as though he'd hardly a care in the world. I couldn't spot Egan, or anyone else for that matter, but I could tell the rear doors of the van had been flung wide open.

And I remembered Kippy's warning.

Whatever happens, do not let Egan get in a car with Kuznetsov, okay? If Egan gets into a car with him, she's dead.

Suddenly, a man in a leather jacket appeared as though he'd morphed out from the sidewalk itself. I thought of who Kippy had warned me about as I watched the man take lengthy strides up the sidewalk.

And he was angling toward the rear of the van.

CHAPTER 35

Though Kuznetsov motioned for her to head out in front of him—perhaps being chivalrous—Britt waited long enough for the Russian to shrug his shoulders and venture down the restroom hallway ahead of her. Kuznetsov had said all the right things, he had examined the individual bags of jewelry and checked each piece against the list Druckman had provided him, had even confessed to not being able to come up with the entire two million dollars; nevertheless, something was off about the man.

Britt couldn't put her finger on it, but something was off about him.

However, wasn't something off—as in way, way off—about her?

She should be coasting through her final year at Northwestern; in fact, Britt should be turning cartwheels about graduating this winter, a full quarter early. And, until Druckman had sucked her into this living, breathing nightmare, the only criminal activity Britt had ever been entangled in was shoplifting a Snickers bar back when she was in third grade, and even then her mom had caught her in the act and made her return it to a scowling cashier.

Yet here she was, acting like some dime-store outlaw in a straight-to-video movie.

How could anything not feel *off* about him or this entire meeting?

Britt paused in the doorway, watched as Kuznetsov waved a hand at a white van about twenty feet down from the restaurant's side exit as though to prove he'd not misled her. The antiquer disappeared from sight as he stepped behind the van and opened both rear doors. Kuznetsov then returned to the sidewalk, held his palms up in a *be-my-guest* gesture, crossed his arms, and took another step backward.

Britt walked around the front of Kuznetsov's van so she wouldn't have to pass by him, strode along the driver's side, the street side, and walked several feet beyond the vehicle. She glanced into the cargo hold and noticed there were no lurking strangers. Except for a few pieces of litter and a green duffel bag, the Econoline was empty. The duffel bag sat at the lip of where the van's rear doors opened. The bag looked nine months pregnant, and Britt understood why Kuznetsov didn't want to haul the damned thing inside the diner.

"This old van may not look like much," the Russian said, "but it's been a workhorse for my antique store."

Britt looked at Kuznetsov, and he took another step backward. She pulled the canister of pepper spray out of her pocket, made sure the Russian got a glimpse of it, and then stepped between the rear doors.

Britt lifted the duffel bag by its green handle. Heavy, but doable—she only had to jog up the street with it. She set the duffel back down and pulled at its zipper.

Stuck.

Shit.

Britt set the pepper spray on the floor next to the bag of money, gripped one side of the duffel with her left hand and worked the slider with her right. Still no go. She squinted down at the zipper.

Was that paper caught in the teeth?

"Hurry," Kuznetsov said in a muffled voice.

There was a spark of confusion at Kuznetsov rushing her, but by then Britt had thrown her full weight into the effort, pulling the slider as hard as she could until the zipper broke free, opening the duffel bag . . . and displaying the packs of magazines stuffed inside.

That's when she heard the footsteps.

CHAPTER 36

"Vira," I said, sprinting down the sidewalk.

The man in the leather jacket sped up, but my golden retriever sailed past me. She didn't know what was going on, but the tension in my voice and the man's aggressive movement kicked her into high alert . . . Vira knew something needed to be stopped. She flew down the block, leapt into the air, landed in front of the perceived aggressor, and came down snarling.

The would-be assailant jumped back a yard, then froze to the curb, transfixed by the growling dog before him, wondering if its attack was just starting or completed.

Then I stepped into the mix, squeezing between Kuznetsov and a flung open van door. I stood in the street, halfway between Vira and Druckman's ex-nanny. Up close I could see her face was scratched and her upper lip puffy. "Are you Britt Egan?" I asked as though I hadn't a clue in the world—this was the part where I winged it.

Egan had spun about at the commotion, dumbfounded at Vira's arrival onto the scene, further stunned by the presence of an unknown male who'd been creeping up behind her, and blown away by my appearance and hearing me voice her name. We locked eyes as she snatched something off the floor of the van.

"Your to-go burgers are ready," I said, hoping she could read the look in my gaze or make sense of the desperate expression that had become my face.

"Why your dog jump at me?" the man in the leather jacket demanded as Vira continued facing him, now at a low growl—she'd not left her warning mode.

I turned sideways. "Sorry—strangers make her uncomfortable," I said, making no effort to call her off. I wanted the Russian gangster intimidated, an emotion he likely wasn't used to. I turned back to Egan. "The waitress saw you leave and knew you'd forgotten your burgers," I said, and tried to clue her in. "The hamburgers for you and *your daughter.*"

Like a dead snapping turtle, Egan had her fingers tightly clamped to the shoulder strap of her backpack. In her other hand was what she'd whisked off the floor of the van—a can of mace or pepper spray. I put the odds at all three of us menfolk getting doused at fifty-fifty.

Egan ignored my nonsense about takeout food and glared at Kuznetsov. She had migrated from shock to anger and, if looks could kill, Kuznetsov's family would be scheduling a closed casket.

On Kuznetsov's end, the man stood dumbstruck on the sidewalk—eyes wide, mouth hung open. The antique dealer had not progressed beyond his initial wave of shock. For a moment I thought he was on the verge of a stroke, but then Kuznetsov's eyes broke from Egan, turning to the back of his van. I traced his gaze to an open duffel bag on the lip of the Econoline's floor.

It was filled with magazines—lots and lots of magazines.

I now put the odds at the three of us getting doused in pepper spray at eighty-twenty.

"Take dog and fetch burgers," the man in the leather jacket said, a sturdy suggestion.

"I don't work there," I replied. "The waitress will be out any second."

"Take dog and fetch burgers," he said again, no longer a suggestion.

I stared at the Russian mobster.

He stared back at me.

The only thing keeping him from ripping the skin off my face was Vira. She stood between the two of us, snarling his way.

We were never going to be mates, so I turned again to Egan. "Come on, Britt," I said calmly, nodding. "Let's go get those burgers."

Egan must have caught my drift—that I was tossing her a lifeline—as she began to nod in agreement.

The thug said, "Fuck this."

I turned in time to spot him reaching a hand into his leather jacket, but Kippy grabbed at his arm from behind, her Beretta out, pointed at the ground. She'd snuck up from the alleyway at some point during the chaos Vira and I had created.

"And here I thought we were going on a pub crawl," she said.

Kippy faced Kuznetsov. "I already showed your friend my badge."

The Russian thug was quick to reply, "We have done nothing."

"Then don't start by interfering with an arrest." Kippy released his arm, slipped around the man, moved past Vira, and backed toward Egan and me at the rear of the Econoline.

Her gun hung at her side, still pointing down.

Kuznetsov and his buzz-cut comrade shared a glance, so I lifted my shirt, letting them spot the top of the waistband holster clipped to my belt. I made a Broadway production of sliding my fingers downward. I hoped to come across as Clint Eastwood, but probably struck them more as Ben Stiller.

The thug moved both hands away from his jacket. "We have done nothing," he repeated and shook his head. "And you take guns out."

"Welcome to America." Kippy kept her eye on the two men as she held handcuffs out sideways for me to take. "Cuff her, Mace. And get her the hell out of here." She shot a glance in my direction. "Ben and Jerry's."

"Gotcha," I said. "Vira stays with you."

Vira, like most golden retrievers, is loving, gentle, friendly, and cheerful; eager to please—she boasts an all-around tail-wagging demeanor. However, in Vira's case, if you threaten her pack—the teeth come out.

And Kippy was part of Vira's pack.

I relieved Egan of her pepper spray and escorted her up the street, one hand on her shoulder, leading her to her Honda Civic. I had Egan cough up her car keys before I placed her hands behind her back, put the nickel-plated carbon steel around her wrists, and snapped them shut. Egan was soundlessly compliant in our trek to her vehicle, her eyes moist in what I took to be acceptance, and she didn't say a word as I belted her into the backseat while she still sported the backpack filled with what I assumed to be Calley Kurtz's jewelry.

It would be an uncomfortable ride, but, hopefully, not a lengthy one.

As I slid behind the wheel of Egan's Honda, I heard Kippy ask Kuznetsov, "How do you know this woman?"

"She tell us of ghost tour and trolley car," the Russian gangster answered in lieu of the antique dealer.

It was then I realized who truly ran the show.

By the time I made the left turn onto Main Street, Kippy had backed her way across the street to her Malibu and whistled for Vira to follow. As I passed Durty Gurt's, I shook my head and wondered if the burgers none of us would get to eat were finally ready.

"She doesn't know," Egan said under her breath. We were nearly to Casey's General Store, and Druckman's ex-nanny had been so quiet I'd almost forgotten I had a passenger.

"Know what?" I asked.

"Scarf doesn't know her parents are dead."

CHAPTER 37

"They told stories of you from back in day," Dima said, back in the Econoline's passenger seat, MP-443 Grach pistol atop his lap. "I am not impressed."

"I'm inside the restaurant all of twenty minutes and you get yourself made by a Chicago police detective," Kuznetsov replied, not bothering to conceal his sarcasm. "I am also not impressed."

"Druckman whore tell them who you are, if not already."

Kuznetsov was slow to respond, "What happens now?"

"We can go to dirt path with trees," Dima said, tapping his MP-443, "or we follow cop to Druckman kid."

Kuznetsov tossed a hand in the air. "How do you propose we do that?"

"After cop fuck off," Dima said, "I put GPS tracker on Honda in case plan turns to shit, which plan did."

Kuznetsov turned sideways to face the torpedo from Little Odessa. "You did what?"

"I put tracking device on whore's shit Honda."

"When did you get a tracking device?"

"I put them on your vehicles when I first get to town in case you run. I grabbed one off this morning in case we need it."

"I am becoming impressed," Kuznetsov had to admit. "But they're halfway to the police station by now."

Dima shook his head. "They turn wrong way for police," he said. "They go get Druckman girl."

"You know where the Galena Police Department is?"

"I do homework." Dima took his smartphone out from his jacket. "Not much time—get heap moving," he said, tapping at the screen of his cell phone. "I bring up app."

Kuznetsov hit the left turn signal, pulled onto the street, and headed for the intersection on Main Street.

"You get Druckman whore, little girl, and diamond bag." Dima now laid out his plan. "I shoot dog first, then dog cop, but I have chat with bitch cop before I shoot her in pretty face."

CHAPTER 38

"If you cannot afford an attorney, one will be appointed for you," Kippy finished Mirandizing Britt Egan.

Kippy had pulled into Casey's General Store long enough for us to switch cars as we didn't want any Russians in a white Econoline randomly spotting us at the gas station. Ben stepped out of the store and headed in our direction, but Kippy waved him back. She had taken a circuitous route from Durty Gurt's to Casey's and didn't want that effort to be in vain.

Kippy tore out of Casey's in Egan's Honda while I sped to catch up in her Malibu. A few minutes and two turns later Kippy pulled over, with me following suit, on a gravel road that, per Egan, wound toward a series of old-fashioned cabins. Kippy wanted me to witness the Miranda warning in case there was any lawyerly BS down the road.

"Do you understand these rights as they have been read to you?"

"Yes," Egan replied. She then asked, "Can you move these cuffs to the front? They hurt my arms."

Kippy nodded and said, "What happened to your face?"

"Nothing." Egan noticed us both staring. "Seriously, I tripped over a tree root and fell down."

I watched as Kippy popped off the handcuffs, slid Egan's backpack off her shoulders, and set it onto the gravel. She re-cuffed Egan, arms in front, and belted her into the backseat of the Civic.

Vira ran off into the weeds to take care of business as Kippy knelt and unzipped Egan's backpack.

"Did they say anything after we took off?"

Kippy looked up and held a hand against the afternoon sun. "The younger one asked me out for later on, when we're both back in Chicago."

"Should I be worried?"

"He's probably loaded, but I'm not that into gangsters." She turned her attention to Egan. "You know those men were Russian Mafia, right?"

Egan shook her head. "Druckman left Kuznetsov's name and number in with the packets of jewelry. I thought the two of them had an agreement."

"The younger guy's a killer." Kippy began peeking inside the individual jewelry bags. "If they got you into the van, they'd have taken your backpack and dumped your body on the side of a road like this one."

Egan's face whitened.

"Speaking of that," I said, "what are we going to do about those two?"

"We've got Kuznetsov tied into all of this." Kippy patted Egan's backpack. "We'll pick him up later and, hopefully, his pal, too." She looked back up at me. "There would have been blood in the streets if we tried taking them outside Gurt's. The muscle guy wasn't going anywhere he didn't want to go, and he had a gun. I imagine Kuznetsov did as well."

"Good having Vira knock them back on their heels."

"That's for damn sure." Kippy turned back to Egan. "You know how screwed you are, right?" She held up the backpack. "This ties you to the home invasion and murder of Calley Kurtz."

"There was no home invasion," Egan said, staring at her lap. "And I didn't know he was going to kill Calley." She shook her head. "There's no way I'd have gone for that." Egan glanced up and added, "Druckman told me he was in trouble—that he was being extorted—and that he needed to get his hands on some quick cash."

I got confused. "But wasn't he already super rich?"

Egan shrugged. "He just wanted me to watch Scarf . . . to keep her safe for a few days," she said. "That's all."

"So you kept her safe by leaving her out here alone," Kippy put the backpack into the Honda's front seat, "while you toddled off to town to sell her mother's jewelry to the Russian mob."

Egan's eyes returned to her lap.

Kippy had a simplistic view when it came to child endangerment—one which I tended to share—if a child's in danger, move heaven and earth to get them to safety.

"We should get going," I said. "What's the game plan, Kip?"

"We need to get Eleanor and this charming piece of work," she tossed some fingers toward the backseat of the Civic, "to Galena PD as soon as possible."

CHAPTER 39

"Why are you in handcuffs?"

Egan had convinced Kippy to let her lead the way as we approached the rental cabin so Eleanor wouldn't get alarmed by two unknowns—stranger danger—trudging across the yard and heading her way. The Druckman child must have been watching from a back window as we heard a door shut a second before a little girl came barreling around the side of the small house, sprinting straight to Egan, who, in turn, stooped down to greet her.

Eleanor wrapped her arms around her old nanny.

Egan looked at Eleanor a long moment and said, "Remember when we talked about my getting a time-out?"

The Druckman child nodded, a look of concern crowding out her features.

Egan smiled at the little girl. "This is me getting a time-out."

"But I don't want you to be in trouble."

"It's okay, honey. Really—it's okay." Egan glanced back at us. "I brought along some friends that are going to help get you back home . . . and guess what they have?"

Kippy, Vira, and I—not making any sudden moves—hung by the front bumper of Egan's Honda, giving Eleanor a chance to acclimate to the evolving state of affairs. A gravel driveway led down to a patch of dirt for parking vehicles at the rear of the rental cabin. The cabin itself looked to be at least seventy years old and in need of some mending or—possibly a better investment—being torn down and rebuilt. There was no nearby lake for any boating, fishing, or water fun—just a cabin in the woods, like the kind you'd see in the horror movies on late night TV.

Eleanor peeked our way. Her eyes lit up. "A dog?"

I took my cue and stepped forward. "Hi, Eleanor," I said. "My name is Mace and this is my best friend. She's a golden retriever named Vira."

"Vira?"

"Yeah, it's a bit unique, huh? It's like the name 'Ira,' only with a 'V' in front."

"My friends call me Scarf."

"So I've heard," I said. "That's a unique name, too." I knelt down to her level. The girl was slim, had wavy brown hair down below her shoulders, a thin face, blue eyes, and a freckled nose. She could be a model like her mother. "Can I call you Scarf?"

She nodded slowly and asked, "Can I pet Vira?"

"Of course you can."

"My parents don't let me play with dogs."

"That's a pretty good idea if you don't know the dog, but Vira's a sweetie pie. And she likes getting scratched behind her ears or under her chin." I smiled at the little girl. "Who am I kidding, Scarf? Vira likes getting petted everywhere."

Scarf looked at Vira as though she were an alien that had crash-landed on Earth and then began petting the top of her head. A grin stretched across Eleanor's face as she started scratching behind Vira's ears—itty-bitty scratches—and then migrated south and began scratching Vira's neck and underneath her mouth.

Vira, in turn, began licking at Eleanor's fingertips, which caused her to giggle and move back.

Kippy stepped to the plate, introduced herself to Eleanor, shook the little girl's hand as though she were meeting with a local dignitary, and then said to me, "How about if you and Scarf play with Vira, Mace, while Britt and I get everything into the car?"

"Sounds like a plan."

Scarf asked me, "Does Vira chase after sticks?"

"Hmm," I replied. "Good question. She goes after Frisbees and tennis balls, but sticks—should we find out?"

Scarf got excited, and while she and I debated where we'd find the best type of stick for Vira, I heard Kippy say, "I get no reception out here."

"I know," Egan confirmed. "It sucks."

"Have you got a landline inside?"

"No."

"Then let's hurry." Kippy glanced at her watch. "We need to get the hell out of here."

CHAPTER 40

It was a damn shame the antiquated cabin lacked a basic land-line phone.

The owners likely jumped with joy on the two or three occasions a year they were able to pan the place off on anyone interested in hanging about rural Galena for a week or two. Sure, Kippy had sent Mace off to have Scarf play with Vira—the little girl was certainly in need of a therapy dog, however briefly, as the poor kid had a river of tears in store for her. Moreover, Kippy wanted Scarf out of earshot when she contacted Galena PD.

Damn, Kippy'd cursed under her breath as she tried again for cell reception. She couldn't get a bar on her iPhone, which explained why Egan made the daily trek down to Casey's General Store to contact Druckman. She needed to prep Galena PD for what was heading their way, something a tad bigger than the occasional shoplifter or trolley-jumping tourist they normally contended with.

This case would put Galena on the map.

Kippy wanted a child welfare worker on hand for when they arrived.

Kippy also wanted answers. And she couldn't wait until they got to the station. "Even if he was being blackmailed," she said to Egan, both hands clutching luggage as the two women walked along the side of the cabin, heading for their cars, "faking a kidnapping, insurance fraud, cutting deals with the Russian

Mafia—why would someone of Druckman's stature go that far off the deep end?"

"Ken was full of shit." Hands still cuffed in front of her, Egan carried Scarf's stuffed monkey and security blanket. "Maybe there is no blackmailer—maybe it was all about killing Calley."

"But if Druckman rigs his wife's death to point away from himself," Kippy thought out loud, not so sure *it was all about killing Calley*, "why does he drag a man who fences stolen jewelry into the equation? That's just dumb as hell. It wouldn't make sense to—"

Kippy didn't complete her sentence as Kuznetsov and Leather Jacket stepped out from behind the cabin's corner and blocked her and Egan's path. Leather Jacket had his arm extended, his pistol pointed at the center of Kippy's forehead.

He smiled and said, "This last stop on pub crawl."

Kippy wasn't exactly sure how . . . but she knew she'd screwed up bad.

Vira wasn't much in the stick chasing department, but we had a few minutes to kill, and I figured I'd let Scarf find that out on her own. We strolled about the woods and got nearly a football field beyond the rental cabin before she spotted a stick the size of a crescent wrench. She handed it to me for further inspection. I turned it about in my hands as though I ran quality control at the local lumber yard before nodding my approval and returning it to her.

Then Scarf threw it as far as she could, a pretty good toss for a five-year-old, and said, "Go get it, Vira."

Vira ran over to where the stick landed, nudged at it with her nose, and then looked our way as if to say, "Yup, it landed here."

"Is she going to bring it back?"

"I'm thinking no."

"Should I say 'fetch'?"

I shrugged. "Vira's more of a finder than a bring-it-backer. Now, if we only had a Frisbee or a tennis ball, whoa, we'd be out here all day."

The two of us meandered in Vira's direction when Scarf stopped and pointed at the base of an oak tree. "That's where Britt fell down last night."

I noticed a few splotches of dark blood on the ground and wanted to ask the girl what they were doing out here at night, but instead said, "Ouch, I bet that hurt."

Scarf looked up at me. "I don't want Britt to go to jail."

"I know you don't." I patted the top of her shoulder, like I do with my niece and nephew, and then switched topics. "Have you ever walked a dog before?"

She shook her head.

"Would you like to walk Vira back to the cabin?"

She nodded.

I took one of those minimalistic leashes they utilize at veterinary clinics, which I'd lifted from Doc Rawson's place, out of a back pocket and attached it to Vira's newfangled collar, which Doc Rawson had tossed my way a few visits earlier. "Now, Vira knows you're not a giant, so she shouldn't yank you along too hard."

We made it all of ten yards before a bloodcurdling scream pierced the afternoon. "Run, Scarf! Run! They're—"

After a booming thud, the voice fell silent.

"The backpack of jewelry is in the car," Egan spoke directly to Kuznetsov. "Just take it and leave."

At Leather Jacket's bidding, Kippy continued hanging on to both pieces of luggage. At Leather Jacket's further bidding, Kuznetsov swooped around and relieved Kippy of her sidearm.

Kuznetsov sounded almost sympathetic when he replied to Egan, "But you know who we are." He then added, "Where's the girl and the dog man?"

"The police are on their way," Kippy cut in. "They went up to the road to flag them down."

Leather Jacket squinted at Kippy through his pistol sight. "Why police come to cabin?"

"To collect evidence."

"Evidence that girls eat and shit in cabin." He continued smiling at Kippy. She realized he was having the time of his life. "Call partner over; tell him 'chop-chop.'"

Kippy shook her head instead and said, "No."

While Kippy made her stand, Egan began to panic. She knew she had to make a move. These men—who she'd been dumb enough to summon to Galena—were not only going to kill her and Kippy and the guy with the dog . . . but Scarf as well.

Egan couldn't let that happen.

She twisted about, dropped all she'd been carrying, started to run, and screamed at the top of her lungs, "Run, Scarf! Run! They're—"

But the man in the leather jacket caught her in five paces, grabbed her by the back of her neck, swung her around full circle, and smashed her face into the wood of the cabin's exterior.

Egan dropped like a boat anchor.

Kippy released the luggage, began to turn, but suddenly her own Beretta was in her face.

"No," Kuznetsov ordered, his finger on the trigger. Then to Leather Jacket, "Go get them."

My heart caught in my throat. The hair on Vira's back stood up. Scarf's shoulders began to shake and quiver.

Out from the side of the cabin came the Russian gangster—the killer we'd met in town—a gun hanging from his right hand. He spotted us through the trees and took off in our direction.

A heartbeat later I had the three of us turned about. "Run, Vira!" I screamed. "Let's go, Scarf!" I egged the young girl on.

The three of us bolted as fast as Scarf's little legs could carry her. And though we had a lengthy start, there was no way we could outpace the Russian thug.

Not all of us.

I patted Vira's hip and yelled, "Go, Vira! Keep her safe, girl!

Keep her safe!" I peeled off from the herd as I screamed them along, "Go Scarf! Go with Vira!"

And then I swung around, turning back, jogging slowly toward the man in the leather jacket, my arms in the air.

CHAPTER 41

"Where's the girl?" Kuznetsov asked as his lethal associate marched me around the side of the cabin where I could tell no small amount of drama had taken place.

Kippy glanced my way. She appeared to be in mourning. Otherwise, she stood motionless as Kuznetsov, leaning back against the side of the cabin, pointed a handgun at Kip's center mass.

Britt Egan was in worse shape. She sat on the ground, lightly swaying, her legs splayed out in front of her—her face a crimson mess. She stared at our arrival with blank eyes.

"Girl in woods with dog?" the Russian killer said, watching Egan as she reached still-cuffed and quivering hands over her head, grabbed at fistfuls of hair, and pulled it downward. I was stunned as a blond wig slid slowly off. I'd figured she'd gotten a dye job somewhere along the line. Egan wiped the hairpiece across her face as though it were a washcloth. It did nothing but smear blood across her features, and Egan finally let it drop to the dirt.

I doubted the poor kid was even aware of what she'd done or if she'd done anything at all.

The young thug looked from Egan to his partner and snapped, "Why you not help whore."

Kuznetsov ignored his colleague's inquiry, saying instead, "If the girl gets to a neighbor, Dima—they'll call the cops. Let's get the fuck going."

We now knew the name of the Russian gangster . . . Dima. And Dima continued to fume as he stared down at Egan.

"Wash whore's face." He pointed at the cabin. "Get her pretty again." Then he motioned Kippy over with the barrel of his pistol. "Pub crawl's over."

"This new gun?" Dima had relieved me of my APX Compact semi-automatic pistol as soon as I'd surrendered.

"Yes."

Per Dima's instructions, Kippy and I filed slowly into the woods, a full yard apart, taking the same path I'd taken earlier with Scarf. Before commencing our forced march, the two men spoke briefly in their native tongue. Neither Kippy nor I required a translator or subtitles to comprehend what the two were discussing—something along the lines of how three of us would be entering the woods but only one would be returning.

Unfortunately, I didn't hear the only word I knew in Russian—*nyet* for *no*—and assumed we would receive no stay of execution.

Kippy glanced sideways and mouthed "I'm sorry." I shook my head in response and scanned the trees ahead of us. I'd been spoiled in the past. This was usually the part where, like at the end of a Tarzan flick, Vira appears as though she were Cheeta riding in on a herd of elephants to save the day.

But where the hell was she?

I prayed for a glimpse of gold—for Vira to tear-ass out from the brush and latch on to this murderous prick at thirty miles an hour.

But so far I saw nothing.

"Is gun good?"

"Yes," I repeated.

"I thank you for gun," he replied. "I take good care of it." Dima and his thick, Slavic accent were starting to grate on my nerves. His next words, though, stuck an ice pick into my heart. "This good place. Turn around."

We did as ordered, and I watched as Dima shoved his pistol

into the back of his belt. Enamored with my APX Compact, he bounced it in his hand a couple times and then aimed it at my face. I could have gone cliché and tried to talk him out of this—*you don't have to do this; really, you don't*—but *this* is exactly what Dima appeared to do for a living, and I wasn't about to waste my breath.

So instead I said, "You're really going to shoot a guy with his own gun?"

"I read a lot, and this is what they call *irony*."

I continued staring straight ahead as I said, "I love you, Kippy."

Dima lowered the firearm a few inches. "You love partner?"

"Yes."

He looked at Kippy. "You love partner, too?"

"Yes," Kippy said in a quiet voice. She'd figured out what I was going to do.

"Day not get better than this," the Russian said, more to Kippy than to me. "Day not get better." His face broke into a Father Christmas smile. "By powers vested in me," he raised the APX Compact, "I pronounce you dead man and wife."

The woman's forehead had taken the brunt of the blow against the cabin's log siding. Head cuts tend to bleed and Kuznetsov used a wad of paper towels he'd found on the kitchen countertop to apply direct pressure in order to slow the bleeding and allow her various wounds to clot. Her nose had survived the carnage, but her eyes swelled and Kuznetsov suspected she'd have quite the pair of shiners. Next, he worked a new clump of paper towels—this time wet—along with some antibacterial soap that'd been abandoned by the kitchen sink, gently across her face. Kuznetsov was pleased when she obeyed him by taking baby sips of water out of a coffee mug he'd unearthed in a cupboard.

Kuznetsov hoped Dima would be quick. Time was of the essence, especially if the Druckman child had, in fact, connected with a neighbor. With the little girl in play, it made no sense for Dima to waste time marching them too far into the woods.

At least the Druckman child hadn't seen their faces. Kuznetsov hoped the kid had, in fact, made it to the safety of a nearby cabin.

Druckman's mistress moaned in pain, another good sign, and caught Kuznetsov's eyes as he worked at her cheek, and hissed "motherfucker" at him, which, quite frankly, was also a good sign. Kuznetsov figured the young woman had a concussion. She had to have—he'd heard the sickening thump of her skull crashing against the cabin's exterior.

Not a pleasant sound.

After Kuznetsov cleaned the blood off her face, he turned his attention to removing the wig cap when the shots rang out. First one . . . and then another. The girl tensed at both gunshots— another good sign as it meant her brain still functioned and she likely knew what those shots indicated.

They indicated that it was over, that Dima had executed the two Chicago police officers.

It meant that Dima would be back soon.

And then they could finally get the hell out of here.

He pulled the trigger as I charged.

This is what Kippy had read into my declaration of affection— that I would be taking one for the team, that I'd rush him, and, as he shot me, she'd get her chance to attack . . . or make a run for it.

It'd give her a chance at survival.

Only I didn't plan on taking one for the team. I knew something Kippy didn't know. I knew my APX Compact semiautomatic pistol held no ammunition. The magazine was empty. It was as unloaded as it had been on the day I'd received my concealed carry permit, when Kippy gave me shit about not loading it. I saw his eyes widen as he pulled the trigger again and again, right on up until I tackled the son of a bitch, wrapping both arms around him as we sailed to the hard ground.

I twisted my APX Compact from his hand and swung it across his face, but he kept moving. He got fingers around my throat, so I hit him again. And again. His hand disappeared as he bucked underneath me, trying to toss me off, and I realized too late he was reaching for his own pistol from the back of his belt, sacrificing his face for a shot at his weapon.

But Kippy was on him, twisting the semiautomatic from his left hand until it was hers, and jamming the barrel into his mouth, hard.

"I expect this one's loaded," she said.

We tied his hands behind his back with his own shoelaces. Then Kippy yanked his leather jacket off his shoulders and pulled it down to his forearms for additional reinforcement. Unless Dima was Harry Houdini, there was no way he'd be getting his hands free. Nevertheless, I stripped him of his footwear and tossed his shoes as far as I could, each one in a different direction.

Dima's face was bruised and bloodied, and I imagined he'd need surgery for what I'd done to both his cheekbones, but when Kippy took the gun from his mouth, he spit blood and said, "Why no bullets, cop?"

The Russian hadn't checked the magazine or chamber of my APX. It was incomprehensible to the young thug that I'd waltz around with an unloaded gun—he made the faulty assumption I wasn't an idiot.

I shoved one of his own socks into his mouth and said, "It's a long story."

Kuznetsov worked fast, as Dima would be coming through the cabin door at any second. He teased the woman's natural brown hair with the tips of his fingers, letting it flow down to her shoulders, letting it block some of her facial bruising.

She whispered to him, "Why are you doing this if you're only going to kill me?"

Grateful she was putting sentences together, Kuznetsov looked into her eyes. He held up his hand and said, "How many fingers am I holding up?"

"Fuck you."

"Close enough."

Kuznetsov could feel it eating away inside him; his hypertension was off the charts—a shortness of breath, a pulsing headache, crippling anxiety. The way things were going, if Dima didn't get him first, he'd drop dead from a massive stroke.

He'd considered lying in wait for the Russian torpedo. He had the cop's Beretta and he might get lucky. Kuznetsov could pop Dima as soon as the man stepped foot inside the rental cabin. But he'd seen how quickly Dima had moved, a snake's strike, to stop Druckman's mistress from escaping or further warning the others. And if he did that to someone he'd expressed a prurient interest in, Kuznetsov could only imagine what the man might do to him. He also figured Dima would be full of adrenaline at this point, and perhaps a wee bit paranoid himself, getting his own ideas about what Kuznetsov might be up to.

Kuznetsov might not fare so well if he went mano a mano against the torpedo from Little Odessa.

So he decided a minor variation of his original plan was in order.

When Dima arrived, the three of them would grab the backpack of gems, cut through the woods, and continue up the gravel road to where the Econoline waited at the lip of a nearby driveway. As he stepped into the van, he'd palm the .38 Special from under the driver's seat and drop it into his coat pocket. Then Kuznetsov would make a huge deal out of placing the cop's Beretta in the glove compartment so Dima would assume all of the firearms were accounted for. Then, with a little luck, Dima would reach for a chocolate milk from the cooler between them as he did like clockwork . . . and that's when Kuznetsov would strike.

After, he'd shove the Russian's body out the passenger door. A second later, the Econoline would be on the road, heading toward the highway.

"I did my best," Kuznetsov told Druckman's mistress as he stood up. "Finish cleaning yourself."

He watched as she rose on shaky legs and made her way into the cabin's bathroom. Then Kuznetsov tucked the Beretta into the front of his waistband so Dima wouldn't get any notions that might run counter to Kuznetsov's health and well-being, opened the screen door, and stepped to the ground.

What the hell was taking Dima? The man should have been here by now.

Was he wasting time trying to track down the Druckman child?

Someone cleared their throat. Kuznetsov turned left and froze in disbelief. The dog cop stood at the cabin's corner, in a classic shooting stance, arms outstretched, firearm pointed at Kuznetsov's chest.

"Sorry if we kept you waiting," Kippy said, approaching from behind and retrieving her Beretta from the Russian's belt.

CHAPTER 42

Scarf clung tight to Vira's leash as the golden retriever slalomed between trees and cut through brush, leading the small girl to the refuge of a neighboring cabin. It had been a roller-coaster ride without the safety belt. Scarf's heart pounded; her lungs burned. The first time she tumbled to the ground, she looked back from where they'd run. She could no longer see Mace or the scary man who had been chasing them. The second time Scarf tumbled, she wasn't sure if she could get back up again, but then spotted the cabin sitting beyond the tree line.

Both that and Vira nudging her with a wet nose gave the girl a second wind.

She sucked in air, grabbed the leash, and pulled herself to her feet.

As the two busted through the thickets, she spotted an older man staring her way on the grass beside the cabin's driveway. His jaw dropped and eyes widened, and he knelt down to their level as Scarf and Vira approached.

"We need help," Scarf said, and then began to sob. She wiped an arm across her eyes and repeated, "We need help."

"I know," the older man said. "The police are on the way." He pointed toward a long black car, like the ones she and her parents were taxied about in. The driver's door was open; a younger man dressed in what appeared to be a chauffeur's uniform smiled her way and held up a hand in greeting. "We heard the commotion and my friend jogged over to see what was happening." He shook his head. "Some bad men were shoving your friends around, Eleanor."

Elle took a step closer to Vira. "You know who I am?"

The older man nodded. "Why of course—you're Eleanor Druckman. Anyone following the news knows that," he said. "My name is Audrick Verlinden, and I did a bit of business with your father." The man was about as old as her grandparents, she figured, and his suit seemed too nice for him to be vacationing in one of these pioneer cabins. He had gray streaks in his hair and stared at her through rectangular glasses. "In fact, it was through your father that I found out you were staying in a cabin out here." He looked at Elle a long moment. "My God, you look so much like your mother."

"Do you know my mom, too?"

"Not as much as I do your father, but I got to see her once, back in her modeling days, on a catwalk in Paris."

"You did?"

"I really did," Verlinden said. "I was there during their autumn fashion week some years back." It hadn't been his cup of tea—Verlinden wouldn't know a Louis Vuitton from a Givenchy—but a dear friend's wife lived in that world and dragged the two of them to the Carrousel du Louvre. "When your mother strode down the runway, there wasn't a sound in the room; it was one of those moments where you could hear a pin drop." Verlinden hadn't a clue who designed Calley Kurtz's clothing that day—couldn't have cared less—but he sat forward in his chair and gawked at Calley as though he were viewing his first sunrise.

It took his breath away . . . to be in the presence of such rare beauty. He remembered thinking of Helen of Troy, realizing how a face could indeed launch a thousand ships. Quite frankly, the only reason he'd invested with Druckman's financial group was because of Calley Kurtz and his memory of that day in Paris at the Carrousel du Louvre.

Verlinden turned his attention to Vira, holding out a palm for her to sniff. "Whom may I ask is this?"

"That's Vira," Scarf said. "Like 'Ira,' only with a 'V' in front."

"'Ira' with a 'V,'" the man named Verlinden said as Vira licked at his fingertips. "She seems like an awfully nice dog,"

"Vira's the best—she got me away from the scary man."

"The 'scary man'?" Verlinden looked off into the woods and then back toward his chauffeur, who stepped from behind the car door and headed in their direction.

"He was chasing Mace and me and Vira after Britt screamed."

"Who's Mace?"

Scarf patted Vira's head. "Mace is Vira's master."

Vira finished licking at the Belgian's fingers, turned around, walked back toward the tree line until the leash stopped her, and gave a low and lengthy whine.

"What is Vira saying?"

"I think she wants to go back and help Mace?"

Verlinden placed a hand on the leash so the golden retriever wouldn't pull away from the little girl as his driver stood at their side. "Vira," he called gently, and the golden retriever returned to him. He thumbed through the tags around her neck. "Well, look at that, you're from Chicago, and here's a phone number to call—I bet it's Mace's number." Verlinden looked from the dog to Eleanor. "The most important thing—what your father would want—is for you to be safe," he said. "What do you think will happen if Vira goes back?"

"She might help Mace and Britt and that police woman."

"She might do that, but golden retrievers are normally such kindhearted dogs," the Belgian said. "I'd sure hate for Vira to get hurt."

Eleanor gripped the leash with both hands, an anchor in a tug-of-war contest. "I don't want her to get hurt."

"I don't want anyone to get hurt, Eleanor. And I think it'd be safer if we all got in the car, just in case—"

A gunshot rang through the forest, followed moments later by a second shot.

Vira turned and bolted. Scarf clung to the leash for dear life as she flew forward. Verlinden and his driver grabbed at the leash for added support.

"We need to leave, Eleanor," Verlinden said. "It's not safe here."

"Vira," Scarf yelled as Vira tugged against the leash, wanting to be set free, wanting to sprint toward the gunfire. "Come on, girl," Scarf called as the three of them worked quickly to reel the golden retriever away from the tree line and then into the backseat of the Mercedes-Benz Maybach with Eleanor.

PART FOUR

GENEVA LAKE

The poor dog, in life the firmest friend.
The first to welcome, foremost to defend.
—Lord Byron

CHAPTER 43

Kippy switched handcuffs from Egan to Kuznetsov.

She cuffed Kuznetsov's hands behind his back and around the legs of a globe-shaped charcoal grill that had somehow survived the seventies and now sat unused and rusting on the patch of dirt and dead grass that was the cabin's front yard. We also tied Kuznetsov's ankles together with a couple of pillowcases. Even if the Russian hopped to his full height, it'd be worth the price of admission to watch him leap about the grass anchored to a barbecue grill as though he were some kind of demented Easter bunny.

I wish I could take credit, but it was Kippy's idea to fire Dima's pistol a couple of times in the air in order to give Kuznetsov a false sense of security, to let him think we'd been dispatched of posthaste.

As we ventured back into the woods, bearing additional pillowcases and dish towels to further hogtie Dima, I put a forefinger and thumb in my mouth and let loose a high-pitched whistle. Kippy stepped away, cupping a hand over her ear.

"Sorry," I said. "Just calling Vira."

"I thought a tornado was coming," she said. "How 'bout a heads-up next time?"

Dima, as it turned out, had somehow managed to rise to his feet—his bare feet—and make it all of ten yards from the spot where we'd left him. He must have stepped on something sharp, maybe a pointed stick or jagged stone, because he was standing on one leg while wiggling the other, a pained looked on his already bruised face. I don't know if it was the ludicrous image of the hobbled Russian mobster or a release of pent-up tension, but Kippy and I started giggling. After our chuckles died down, Kippy went over and gave Dima's chest a brisk shove, tripping him over backward onto the ground. We knotted pillowcases and kitchen towels around his ankles, and toyed briefly with dragging his sorry ass all the way back to the cabin, but figured we'd already done our cardio for the day.

On the hustle back to the cabin, I whistled again, this time stepping away from Kippy. My golden retriever did not appear. We'd not seen hide nor hair of Vira or Scarf during our trip to batten down the Russian thug. I figured Vira had done her job, as Vira always did, and both she and Scarf were safe and sound inside a neighboring cabin.

With a little luck, the police might already be on their way.

Back at the cabin, Kippy and Egan jumped in the Malibu and headed out in search of a phone signal, likely driving all the way back to Casey's. Kippy wanted Galena Police—including their chief of police—at the cabin ASAP. She wanted Special Agent Squires brought into the loop; after all, this was his investigation. Kippy also wanted an ambulance for Egan. The poor girl's face looked like something you'd see after a train wreck.

I, on the other hand, got to stay back at the cabin and man the fort.

Periodically, I'd let loose with another whistle and stand still for a minute, hoping to see my golden retriever galloping toward me across a horizon of trees, but, instead, I received silence in return. I started to worry because if Vira and Scarf were safe inside a nearby cabin, the folks there would have had plenty of time to contact the police, yet there'd been no sirens or squad cars pouring into the dirt of the cabin's driveway. I seriously considered checking out adjacent cabins—going door to door, I guess—but decided that'd best be done by the pros as part of an official police response.

Maybe they'd let me tag along.

But what if the two hadn't run to a neighboring cabin? What if Vira led Scarf to a patch of bushes or a woodpile or a downed tree? Then my golden retriever should hear my whistle, come running, and then lead me back to Scarf.

I walked a few yards into the brush and began shouting "Vira" and "Scarf," repeatedly, as though calling truant children home for dinner.

All my efforts were met with an unnerving silence.

Then it dawned on me that, like the cabin Egan and Scarf had been staying in, the other rentals may not have landlines. So, like Kippy, they'd have to drive up the road toward Galena to dial 911. They'd obviously bring Scarf along with them, for safekeeping, and maybe Vira as well—or perhaps they'd leave Vira inside their cabin until they returned.

That seemed the most likely scenario. Kippy and Egan were probably at Casey's General Store right now calling the police and, a few cars over, someone else was doing the same.

Stressing over Scarf's and Vira's absence, I'd tuned out Kuznetsov, but I stopped near the charcoal grill long enough to hear what the man was prattling on about.

The Russian saw he had my undivided attention and started in again. "Name your price," he said. "All you have to do is uncuff me and I'll transfer that amount into your bank."

I stared down at the man. His face was red, a sheen of sweat plastered across his features. "You can do that from your phone?"

"Your phone, my phone—all we need are account numbers."

"But they'll arrest me for letting you go." I pointed out.

"We kick apart this grill; make it look like I busted it up getting free while you were out searching for the Druckman girl."

"But how did you untie your legs?"

"I slipped the cuffs under my feet to get my hands in front, and then untied them and ran like hell." He said again, "Name your price."

I stepped toward the bound man. "Can you get a half mil into my checking account?"

Kuznetsov scoffed. "That's child's play."

"How about six hundred thousand?"

"Consider it done."

"Okay," I said, and scooched down by the grill in front of him.

Kuznetsov smiled, but I didn't get the sense his heart was in it.

I stuffed the last of the dish towels into his mouth. "Maybe next time."

Five minutes later, Kippy and what seemed to be the entire Galena Police Department—sirens wailing—arrived.

CHAPTER 44

The Belgian handed the Happy Meal and Sprite—the fast-food joint didn't serve 7Up—over the back of his seat to Eleanor. He also handed her a small cheeseburger and small water for her to divvy out to Vira as the two made themselves comfortable in the back of the S600 Maybach. Verlinden and his caretaker opted to wait until they'd arrived back at Geneva Lake to rustle up something more suitable for themselves to consume.

Verlinden was appalled by what happened to Calley Kurtz. Sickened. God forgive him, he'd read Druckman wrong. Since the investment banker had built his fortune bilking clients, it seemed apropos that he himself get taken to the cleaners. But Verlinden never thought the financier would spin out of control. Why on earth didn't the man stick with what he knew? Instead, the demented fool went with a home invasion . . . a kidnapping . . . and a murder.

Verlinden never saw that coming.

As part of his deep dive into all things Kenneth J. Druckman, Verlinden knew about the man's parents. Good people they were, but ordinary, and dull as yesterday's dishwater. Druckman's father's ambition had ended at selling discounted furniture at a strip mall a stone's throw off an interstate highway. Druckman's mother dithered about her Floridian retirement, filling her days with quilting and baking rolls and scrapbooking.

And as for Calley Kurtz's mother, the poor woman suffered from Parkinson's disease.

That was the pathway that awaited Eleanor Scarf Druckman, that was her future—badmintoned between a pair of dullards and a woman suffering a brain disorder.

And of course, the Belgian thought, there'd be no money. Not after the FBI and SEC found out what monetary follies the Druckman Financial Group had been up to lo these many years. Eleanor's paternal grandparents would be lucky if the authorities didn't come after their house in northwest Florida.

Verlinden sat sideways in his passenger seat and watched Eleanor giggle as she fed Vira pieces from the dog's cheeseburger. What a charming little girl, a delight, a Shirley Temple for these trying times.

Verlinden had no children of his own. He'd never been one for personal relationships, and, to be honest, he found sex off-putting, more than a touch repellent, even as a young man coming into his own, when he'd experimented with both women and men . . . and found them equally wanting.

No, Verlinden had his projects, his various hobbies, and, of course . . . he had his exquisites.

Verlinden had kept his friends in Taiwan on the payroll. After all, they'd proved quite the full-service operation—hacker savants who'd exploited vulnerabilities in Druckman's network system in order to provide Verlinden with enough evidence of financial fraud to sink a battleship. Taiwan continued monitoring Druckman's system per some kind of remote administration tool, and though Verlinden had only vague generalities of what RAT software entailed, he remained terrified of it ever being utilized against himself. And Taiwan's cyber intrusion continued bearing fruit as Verlinden was updated in real time regarding Druckman's frenzied activities these past weeks.

One item of interest had initially perplexed Verlinden: a rental cabin Druckman had reserved for two weeks in, of all places, Galena, Illinois. This transaction had been completed through one of Druckman's shell companies. After the financier had gone off the rails, Verlinden realized the Galena cabin was where Druckman had secreted his daughter. Verlinden assumed the poor girl was stuffed away with Druckman's mistress—always an endearing quality whilst employing a kidnapper—or some other accomplice.

Verlinden figured Druckman's mistress or accomplice would do the right thing once they'd heard of Druckman's passing.

And so Verlinden held back, leaving them a little time in which to *do the right thing.*

But an entire day had passed since the news broke of Druckman's death, and the faux kidnapper had yet to do the right thing.

Verlinden owed it to Calley Kurtz to make sure her daughter was safe.

He didn't like ripping the caretaker away from his duties at the Geneva Lake estate. Lord knows he'd done that several times these past weeks. The caretaker's primary responsibility at Geneva Lake was providing daily care and whatever medical attention he could offer for the patient housed at Verlinden's estate. It wasn't good for a person in such fragile condition, a person who could barely sit up on their own, to be left alone for a day here or a day and a half there. Parenteral nutrition—IV feeding—and Depends only went so far. Yet here Verlinden was again, pulling the man away from his primary responsibilities for yet another adventure, this time to Galena, Illinois, in order to make damn sure whoever was watching over Calley Kurtz's daughter did the right thing.

They had arrived in Galena that morning, around ten, and set up shop in the driveway of a vacant cabin next to the one Druckman had rented. The caretaker had cut through the woods and slid up against a side wall, and though it was hard for him to decipher what was being said, he'd reported back that it had been a pleasant conversation and that Eleanor clearly knew the woman she'd been with this past week.

The caretaker had scooched to the corner of the cabin and listened as the woman told Eleanor she'd be back as soon as possible but instructed Elle to jog over to one of the neighboring cabins if she wasn't back by two o'clock.

Evidently, the woman was, in fact, doing the right thing, but first had to run some errands in town.

The woman appeared to care about Eleanor, but her priorities were certainly skewed.

The Belgian smiled at Elle as she and Vira wolfed down the final remnants of their burgers. The little girl was going to be as jaw-droppingly striking as her mother. It was obvious the woman watching Elle had yet to inform her of her parents' fate. It pained Verlinden to think about how the poor child was going to be stigmatized—her life forever scarred. Every time she walked into a room, people would whisper *she's the one* and *her father stole from his clients,* and, of course, *her dad killed her mom and then offed himself.*

Sure, she'd have three grandparents to love her; however, they'd raise her to be commonplace and conventional when the child was born to be anything but. Whatever you might say about her father, the man had a great deal of gray matter upstairs. The smart money was on Elle's DNA . . . she'd be intelligent like him . . . and stunningly beautiful like her mother.

Quite frankly . . . Eleanor would be an exquisite.

A wave of melancholy washed over the Belgian. He had no end of riches, nothing in the world he couldn't have, all except for one trivial matter—there was no one to share them with . . . no one to hand them down to when he passed away.

And no one to mourn his death.

He watched as Eleanor popped the cover off the small cup of water and held it down for the golden retriever to dip its tongue into, and his mind turned to his private islet in the British Virgin Islands—Pequeño Espejismo, translated as Little Mirage—where he escaped the harsh Wisconsin winters, and which served as a rental gold mine the remainder of the year. He thought of how picturesque a place it would be for a little tot to grow into a delightful young woman, tucked far away from the ugliness of conventional life, from the ugliness that had claimed both her parents.

The Belgian thought how Eleanor's fate needn't turn out to be so hideously ordinary.

Elle's faux kidnapper had failed to do the *right thing* by not bringing Eleanor to the police station as soon as she'd heard of Kenneth Druckman's demise.

But in the case of Eleanor Scarf Druckman, was there an even *righter thing* the Belgian could do?

"Where to, sir?" the caretaker asked, bringing Verlinden back to the here and now.

"Geneva Lake." The Belgian had made up his mind. "Let's go home."

Human beings had never entered into Audrick Verlinden's pantheon of exquisites. The patient at Geneva Lake was anything but . . . quite the opposite, actually.

Besides, Verlinden's thoughts began to drift as he fixed his gaze on the road that lay ahead of them, Eleanor would never be part of his collection . . . far from it.

Eleanor would be his heir.

CHAPTER 45

I was now officially terrified.

I'd spent the last two hours tagging along with Galena police officers Brad Tyler and Marnie Hayes as we went door-to-door—more accurately, cabin-to-cabin—right up to the crossroad that led to Casey's General Store and farther on into town. Of the four rental cabins, the two farthest ones were currently occupied by tourists. Both included a husband and wife; one had a little boy, the other two young girls. Both families invited us inside, neither had seen a little girl or a golden retriever, and both households appeared sincerely concerned about the situation. While Officer Hayes quizzed the lodgers, Officer Tyler loitered about their driveways, calling in their license plates in case they tripped any triggers.

They didn't.

The two nearby cabins were not currently occupied. This was confirmed by phone calls to rental companies as well as Hayes and Tyler and me banging on doors, peeking in windows, and looking around back for any hidden vehicles.

As we trekked from cabin to cabin, I'd weave off into the woods, shouting and whistling for Vira. If she heard me, Vira would move heaven and earth to hustle her way back to me. At a minimum, she'd bark to let me know where she was hiding.

I left officers Tyler and Hayes to comb the houses on the opposite side of the road. Vira knew about streets, and she wouldn't drag Scarf across one unless there were no other options. And the Russian mobster had ceased pursuing them as soon as I'd surrendered to him. There was also no way Vira and Scarf could have doubled back without us spotting them. They'd have had to pass us in the woods or ignore us as they zipped past Egan and Scarf's cabin, which wouldn't have made a lick of sense.

It seemed like an eternity but had only taken fifteen minutes, twenty tops, from when I had sent the two of them sprinting away from that Russian killer to when Kippy and I had subdued Kuznetsov.

And at that point I'd immediately begun calling out for them.

How could the two of them have disappeared into the Bermuda Triangle within twenty minutes?

I'd been banking on Vira and Scarf having connected with some tourist family that, in turn, had driven up the road to get a phone signal. So it killed me when Kippy returned with the Galena cops in tow and informed me there'd been no other 911 calls regarding *our situation*.

It had become official—I was terrified.

Kippy and SAC Squires—who'd helicoptered in from Chicago with a handful of suits as soon as he'd gotten word—were deep in discussion by the barbecue grill when I trudged up. Galena Police Chief Lori Rieger, a tall woman of maybe fifty, stood nearby. Kippy glanced my way and I shook my head.

"I have no idea where they went. And there's no way Vira's going to jog Scarf ten miles that way," I said, pointing a hand at the woods behind me.

"We'll find them, Mace," Squires said. "Chief Rieger's bringing in their dogs, and her officers are going to fan out and shake this area up." Squires spotted doubt on my face. "We're going to find them, Mace."

I nodded and tried to perk up. "Anything new here?" I said, noticing Kuznetsov was no longer appended to the grill.

Kippy looked at Chief Rieger. "Lori's got the Russians at the station, sitting in separate rooms and thinking about their place in the cosmos," she said. "They've photographed and bagged the jewelry. And Len's going to the hospital to see if he can get anything more out of Britt."

"Did you tell him about Druckman getting extorted?"

"Yeah."

"Did you tell him your theory?"

"What's that?" Squires asked.

"Egan says Druckman seemed sincere when he told her he was being extorted. Egan also said Druckman and Calley were estranged, likely due to Druckman's affair with her." Kippy thought for a second and continued, "The two were only in the marriage for Scarf's sake; a divorce was on the way, so if someone was blackmailing Druckman over something sexual, perhaps another affair, that wouldn't have made him come unglued or play with fire."

Squires glanced at the cabin. "And have him do all this," he said. "You're thinking the extortion was more professional than personal?"

"That might make sense. What would a big-time investment advisor, who might not be on the up-and-up—in fact, could be shady—fear most?"

"Exposure—shown to be a fraud," Squires filled in the blanks. "His reputation shot, a lengthy stay in prison."

Kippy shrugged. "It's a thought."

"That it is."

"What happens with the Russians?" I asked.

Chief Rieger spoke for the first time. "That Kuznetsov's a real winner—he's already begging for a deal. Says he's a gold mine of information about his colleagues in New York."

"He's frightened," Squires said. Then added, "Not without reason."

"What about the other one?"

"Hasn't spoken a word."

"I still don't get how they found us," Kippy said. "I thought Kuznetsov dropped a GPS in Egan's backpack, but there was nothing there when we checked the jewelry."

"I'll have a mechanic inspect Egan's Honda," Rieger replied. "Maybe they stuck something on her car."

These were busy people, so I stepped away, let them get back to doing their jobs. But something gnawed at the back of my mind as I headed into the woods and began my whistling routine again. Sadly, I lacked Squires's optimism about the Galena police or his platoon of agents finding Vira and Scarf out here in the thickets.

Something was at play here . . . something else had occurred.

"Aw, Vira," I said quietly to myself. I heard footsteps behind me and felt Kippy's hand on my shoulder. We stood there saying nothing, lost in trepidation, and I thought back on how I'd attached the leash to Vira's collar so Scarf could walk a dog for the first time in her life before we headed back to town and moved on to the police station, where I knew the poor kid's existence would never be the same.

And that's when it occurred to me.

I twisted sideways toward Kippy.

"What have you got, Mace?"

"You know how Chief Rieger thinks they stuck a tracking device on Egan's car?"

Kippy nodded.

"You know how Doc Rawson tosses free stuff from vendors my way?"

Kippy nodded again; however, question marks lingered in her eyes.

"Vira's collar," I said. "It's a pet tracker—it's got GPS."

CHAPTER 46

Vira whimpered softly as she stared out the back window of the S600 Maybach.

Scarf held her palm against the golden retriever's shoulder. "Everything's going to be okay, Vira," she said, not for the first time. "It really is."

They'd been riding mostly in silence for much of the past hour. Mr. Verlinden and his driver stared at the road ahead of them, each lost in their own thoughts.

Scarf was terrified, not for herself as she felt safe, but for Britt and Mace and that female detective whose name she'd forgotten. Scarf hoped the police had arrived and saved everyone and gotten the scary guys put in jail and that no one got hurt or . . . well, Scarf didn't want to think about anything else that might have happened.

She hadn't wanted Britt to get into any trouble, even if she had done a thing or two wrong, and now Scarf didn't know what she'd do if something really bad had happened to her. Mr. Verlinden kept checking his smartphone, but he'd informed the car he'd seen nothing on the news. He said he would let her know as soon as he heard anything.

And now Scarf felt sad and sorry and horrible for Mace's dog. The poor thing was so brokenhearted at leaving Mace behind that Scarf felt herself begin to tear up. There was a little water left in Vira's cup from the drive-through place, so Scarf held it up to her. "Vira, do you want another sip of water?"

Vira looked at Scarf and let loose another soft whine.

"Aw, Vira, it's going to be okay." Scarf petted the golden retriever on the top of her head. "We're going to get you back to Mace," she said. "I promise, Vira. I promise we will."

CHAPTER 47

"This piece of shit can't be right," I said. "It has Vira in Wisconsin."

We'd fumbled around bringing the GPS app up on my iPhone and, with Kippy's technical know-how, finally got the damned thing working. The tracking device built into Vira's collar allowed us to locate her using the global positioning system to get a bead on her geographical location. But this reading was off the charts insane. Wisconsin? No matter how hard I'd egged them on in their flight from the Russian thug, there's no way in hell Vira and Scarf fled a hundred miles away.

"How could that be?" Agent Squires queried over the speaker of Kippy's smartphone.

"It's the Russians," I said. "There must be more than just the two of them bastards."

"But Kuznetsov is spilling his guts on everything he's ever known, because the *pakhan*, the big boss, in Little Odessa wants him dead." Squires had headed to the police department after checking in with Egan at Galena's Midwest Medical Center. He brought us up to date over Kippy's cell phone. He added, "Kuznetsov hasn't said anything about there being other Russians involved."

"Can you press him on it?" I said. "Wouldn't it make sense to have more bodies here to grab two girls and the diamonds?"

"Except we only dealt with Dima and Kuznetsov in town,"

Kippy said. "If there were more, why didn't they make them-selves known when we were tying up their buddies?"

"I can ask him, Mace, but Kippy's right—why grab Vira and the girl but leave the bag of jewels, which is what would have brought them to Galena in the first place?"

It didn't make any sense, so, of course, I grasped at more straws. "Druckman had someone else involved in the kidnapping, another accomplice other than Egan," I said. "At least someone else knew about it."

"If he did," Kippy said, "Britt wasn't aware of them, and she's been pretty straight with us."

My mind spun. I couldn't shake the thought that some ne-farious *other* was hidden in the weeds. If Druckman was be-ing extorted, would his blackmailer be at play here in Galena? I then flashed on Kippy's mystery man—we'll call him Mr. X—who may or may not have been with Druckman at the very end. The mystery man who may or may not have ushered the investment banker into the hereafter . . . the mystery man who, in all prob-ability, doesn't exist.

"I don't know," I said, my mind still spinning, "either this GPS app's a piece of crap or there's someone else we're unaware of."

"I agree with Mace," Kippy said. "The only other scenario is that a random guy out of nowhere happens to be in the woods, spots Scarf and Vira, and decides, *Hey, here's a kid and a dog, and I've always wanted to have a kid and a dog.*"

"Yeah," I replied. "I call bullshit on the random guy."

Squires asked, "Where in Wisconsin does the app say they're at?"

I poked at my smartphone. "Around Big Foot Beach State Park, right near Geneva Lake."

"How big is that park?"

"No effen idea, but I'm heading there now."

Kippy added, "I'm going with him, sir. In fact, I'm driving."

"Okay, I'll ask Kuznetsov if there could be other Russians at play, but, realistically, we need to think about who this third party could be . . . if there is a third party." The special agent then said, "How far away is Lake Geneva?"

"Two and a half hours," Kippy said. "We'll make it in two."

"We'll take the copter and make it in one."

"You're coming?"

"Nothing more I can do here," he replied. "Chief Rieger has everything under control, and if Vira and the Druckman girl found a cave to crawl into, her team will find them, but I no longer think they're here to be found. Your GPS lead sounds good to me, so damn right I'm coming."

CHAPTER 48

When they'd first arrived at his Geneva Lake manor, Verlinden walked Eleanor and Vira about the grounds.

"We'll take a helicopter ride to Madison in a couple of hours," he informed the little girl. "And then catch a plane to Chicago."

Eleanor nodded, but her attention had turned to peering over the edge of the hilltop's cliff into the blue-green waters of Geneva Lake. Vira stood at her side, peering as well.

"Can you dive in from way up here?" she asked.

Verlinden shuffled over from the helicopter pad. "I tried it once when I was about twice your age, but never again. Jumping was more fun. It's not that steep, but you better know how to swim," he said. "Do you know how to swim?"

Eleanor nodded again. "I can also hold my breath for almost a minute."

"You've got me beat—these days I doubt I'd last ten seconds."

Then they hiked inland on a thin trail cutting through the copse of trees and undergrowth, eventually stepping out onto a field on the opposite side. A smile the size of a billboard filled Eleanor's face as she spotted the hot air balloons.

"Can we go up in one?"

"Someday soon we'll do that. They need a bit of work, though, to be flight ready," he said. "When I stayed here as a boy, my mother's parents—my grandparents, God bless their souls—would take me up all the time." He added, "Some of my favorite memories."

The caretaker topped the flight of steps, carrying with him a bowl of water in one hand and a food bowl in the other. "I hope Vira likes green beans, Miss Eleanor."

"I bet she'll love them."

The caretaker led the trio away from the deflated balloons and set the bowls down on a patch of short grass. Vira strolled over, and the three watched as the golden retriever sniffed at the beans, nibbled briefly on one, then moved a few feet away, sat down, and curled up.

"She misses Mace."

"I'll bet she does."

The caretaker pressed a tent stake into the sod with the sole of his shoe. "Might I have the leash, Miss Eleanor?"

Elle looked at Mr. Verlinden.

"Vira's an outdoor dog—it might be best for her to get all the potty out of her before the helicopter ride."

The caretaker took the leash handle, worked it under the arch of the tent stake, and pressed the stake the rest of the way into the turf.

Later, as they ate popcorn and streamed *The Lion King* on Disney while they waited for the helicopter's arrival, the Belgian considered his plan. They'd fly to Madison, which made no sense if their endpoint was Chicago. Only their endpoint was not Chicago. Their endpoint was Verlinden's private island—Little Mirage. At Madison, they'd hop aboard a plane and it'd be a miracle if Eleanor, after the day she'd had, would be awake for that ride. If she was, she'd certainly fall asleep on the plane when the trip turned out to be a bit longer than anticipated.

Eleanor would wake up on Little Mirage.

He'd already had his property management people make the current lodgers—the kinfolk of some South Korean telecom mogul—an offer they couldn't pass up. If they'd cut short their stay, they'd be reimbursed in full plus receive a monthlong holiday at Verlinden's newly acquired ski lodge in the Swiss Alps over the Christmas–New Year's holidays at no cost. The Koreans were likely packing their bags this very moment.

Yes, tomorrow would be full of pain for Eleanor—as birthing often is—as he'd let her watch the news and read some of the articles on the Internet to her. Poor Elle would be crushed . . . she'd be destroyed.

How could she not?

But, like the mythical Phoenix, Eleanor would soon rise from the ashes of her past life.

It might take a month, it might take six—but Verlinden had all the time in the world.

And he had his housekeeper—an elderly Portuguese woman he could trust with his life—to help with Eleanor's *transformation*. After all, it was Madam Telma who'd put him in touch with those Portuguese physicians—a team of black-market specialists— he'd flown in on several occasions over the years to tend to the *particular* needs of his Geneva Lake patient, needs that through traditional medical channels might arouse curiosity . . . and in-quiry. These practitioners were a tight-lipped bunch and could help with any therapeutic aspect in the child's *recovery*.

Also, the golden retriever would not be returning to Chicago, whether her master remained alive or not. Instead, "Ira" with a "V" would be coming along with them to Little Mirage. The dog had bonded with Eleanor and would have a soothing effect on her, especially in the little girl's initial weeks on the island.

Eleanor turned from the movie and asked him, "Do you live here all alone?"

"Sadly, Elle, at my age, I've outlived my family—my American family, that is," he said. "The caretaker lives here year round, though, as he takes care of an ailing patient we have with us."

"You're taking care of a sick person?"

Verlinden nodded.

"What are they sick with?"

"This particular person is sick with life, Elle," the Belgian said. "I know that sounds quite odd, but our patient is sick with life."

CHAPTER 49

"Kuznetsov says there's no way Dima is running a separate squad of Russians in Galena without his knowledge." Agent Squires added, "Kuznetsov says Dima's been back-channeling with the powers that be in Little Odessa, but he's adamant that there are no other *Russian* players on the field."

I sat in the back of the Lake Geneva squad car with Kippy as Agent Squires relayed to us his just-completed conversation with Chief Rieger. I'd have enjoyed the helicopter ride from Galena to Lake Geneva had I not fretted the entire time about where in hell Vira and Scarf had disappeared to. When Dima marched Kippy and me out into the woods to introduce us to our maker, I prayed Vira would pop out of nowhere and save the day, like she'd done a few times in the past.

Sans that, I had no clue where she wound up, and I put the odds at this crazy dog collar GPS working correctly at about fifty-fifty.

"Anything on their search?"

"Nothing so far, but the chief has all her officers and a bunch of volunteers out scouring that patch of woods and neighboring cornfields."

We had touched down at the Grand Geneva Resort Airport, a couple miles northeast of Lake Geneva. The resort's airport is privately owned, but the nearest official airport was in Milwaukee, and Squires would have had us bungee into the lake before going that far out of the way. We were picked up by Lake Geneva Police Chief Michael Zogby—it pays to hang with SAC Squires— where I'd surrendered my iPhone so the chief could navigate us to where the GPS coordinates appeared to have dead-ended, as there'd been no movement since we'd coptered out of Illinois.

"This goes beyond Big Foot Beach State Park," Chief Zogby informed the car. The chief, a balding man with eyeglasses covered with clip-on sunglasses, assured us he knew the area like the back of his hand. "More like halfway around the lake, closer to a village called Fontana-On-Geneva Lake."

A minute later the chief pulled to the side of the road, checking my iPhone against a map on his phone. "Well, shit."

"What?" Squires asked.

"This road curves off toward some pretty major estates." The chief pulled back onto the street, took an immediate right turn, zigzagged a few times, and then took a left onto a paved road that ran alongside Geneva Lake. "There's real money here, Agent Squires. Lots of money, and I think those coordinates of yours are on one of these hilltops overlooking the lake."

The police chief kept driving, cruising twenty miles an hour as we passed several driveways, few and far between, leading up to what he'd informed us were recessed and shrouded mansions. Zogby stopped his squad car about fifty yards before the paved road wound to a dead-end at an intimidating set of wrought-iron gates. The chief turned sideways and said, "Any of you ever heard of a man by the name of Audrick Verlinden?"

The three of us shook our heads.

"This is Verlinden manor. It's been in his family, his mother's side, for about a million years. The man is richer than God."

I asked Zogby, "Why are you parking here?"

"We'd have to use their intercom system to get the gate open, and I'll bet you a thousand bucks there's a camera set up so they can see who's parked outside." The chief focused his attention on Squires. "I've met Verlinden a time or two—and to be honest, he seemed like a nice enough fellow; eccentric, a bit of an odd duck, but pleasant—so do you want Verlinden to know you're coming?

Or would you like the element of surprise?" Zogby flicked up his clip-ons. "It's all up to you."

Squires held the chief's gaze. "I'd like the element of surprise."

"We'll need a search warrant."

Squires nodded.

Zogby shrugged. "I don't think you'll get a Lake Geneva judge to warrant Audrick Verlinden—those guys have to run for office. Wouldn't want Verlinden on their ass on account of, you know, him being richer than God." He held up my iPhone. "Not based on Petco software, anyway."

"Do you have a go-to judge?"

"For suspected drug dealers and shit like that," Zogby replied and pointed at the wrought-iron gates. "Not for stuff like this."

"It's not just a little lost dog, and I'm sure your guy's been following the news," Squires pointed out. "Probable cause is that the Druckman child was last seen with the golden retriever literally hours ago."

"Well, we'll punch that home in the affidavit as well as how you—the head of the FBI field office in Chicago—are here personally to lead the investigation." Zogby then nodded his head. "I may have a judge."

"Hopefully, he'll grant it, otherwise I'll burn eight hours with the on-duty federal judge."

The chief put the squad car in reverse as I tapped his headrest and said, "Wait." I popped the back door open. "I'm staying here."

"As you wish," Zogby said, his foot on the brake. "Stay away from those gates, though." He handed my iPhone back. "I hope to God that app is working and not catching a read off some goddamned mutt from around here." He reached for his radio. "I'll have a squad back in under ten, just to get eyes on anyone trying to leave."

Kippy opened her door. "I'm staying, too."

CHAPTER 50

Another Lake Geneva police car appeared in under ten minutes. This one driven by a black officer named Wallace Cook.

"I'm going to park it back around the first bend," Cook said after Kippy and I jumped in, "so they don't notice a roadblock right outside their gate."

Cook shifted into reverse and backed the squad car up thirty yards, curved around the bend, and then jockeyed his vehicle so it blocked the entirety of the road. He popped the trunk, jumped from the driver's seat, fiddled about in the trunk as Kippy and I stepped from the car and joined him. Cook resurfaced from the cargo compartment with a sizeable tire iron—cops don't mess around with flat tires—and, though the tire on the squad car wasn't flat, he leaned the tire iron against the side of the vehicle.

Then Cook looked from Kippy to me and said, "So what the hell is this all about?"

"Did the chief tell you anything?" Kippy trumped Cook's question with one of her own.

"The chief said it had to do with that kidnapped girl from Chicago and that I shouldn't say a goddamned thing to anyone, but since you two aren't just *anyone*—I repeat, what the hell is this all about?"

"The girl was last seen with one of our police dogs," Kippy explained. "The dog has a GPS unit built into her collar and the coordinates led us here."

"They've got gadgets like that?"

"Yeah," I said. "They can get a bit pricey, but I got this one for free."

"And it points to Verlinden's house?"

I shrugged. "Or somewhere on his property."

Officer Cook waved an arm at the woods. "You know he owns a shit-ton of land here, both lakefront and back into the hills?"

"That's what we're trying to sort out," Kippy said, "whether the dog and the girl are with Verlinden or with some other perps hiding on his property."

"Where was the dog and the—"

"Mace," Kippy interrupted Cook, pointing to the sky above Geneva Lake.

I'd heard the sound, too, whirring rotors growing louder, but it registered—had to have after the events of the past couple hours—as I looked where Kippy pointed. Across the lake and heading our way came a black helicopter. The three of us followed its trajectory as it slowed to a hover over the peak of Verlinden's property, and then descended, disappearing beneath the tree line.

"I don't think your roadblock's going to work," I said to Cook, panicking now as I took off running toward Verlinden's private gate.

"Let Zogby and Squires know the man's got his own helicopter," Kippy told the Lake Geneva police officer and came sprinting after me. "What are you thinking, Mace?"

"I have no idea," I said, picking up speed, wondering if I'd have to climb the wrought-iron gates or see if the damned fence disappeared when it hit the woods. Something about the helicopter's arrival triggered me; I was convinced we'd found Kippy's Mr. X—that Audrick Verlinden was the missing piece of the puzzle. And I wish I could say I was thinking first of Eleanor Druckman; however, my foremost concern was for my golden retriever. "There's no way in hell Vira's getting aboard that copter."

CHAPTER 51

"Mister Verlinden?"

Addressing him with the title "mister" before his surname told the Belgian the Druckman child had indeed been raised correctly, most likely from her mother's side, which held true for Verlinden himself. "Call me Audie," he replied. "My close friends call me Audie."

Which wasn't true . . . it wasn't true at all.

"Did my father call you Audie?"

"Your father called me Audrick. I'm sorry I never shared my nickname with him."

"Do you like *The Lion King*, Audie?"

"I am enjoying it immensely, Eleanor."

"You can call me Scarf."

"I am enjoying it immensely, Scarf."

"Can I ask you something, Audie?"

"Anything at all."

"Are my parents okay?"

Verlinden was slow to respond. "You're hogging all the popcorn."

She handed him the bowl, her eyes never leaving his face.

"Thank you," he said, and shook the container as if he were mining for gold. "Do you like plane rides?"

"Yes."

"They are fun, aren't they?"

"Yes," the little girl repeated, her eyes lingering on his face. She was in search of the truth.

"Can we talk about it on the plane?"

"Why can't you tell me now?"

"We'll be leaving soon, Scarf," the Belgian said. "And there's another thing I need to talk to you about first."

"What?"

"You know those scary guys that were after you at the cabin? The gunshots?"

Scarf's eyes turned moist. "I hope Britt's okay."

"I hope she is, too," Verlinden said. As they'd been watching *The Lion King*, he'd been checking his smartphone every five minutes for any news out of Galena. He hadn't seen a thing, which might not bode well for Scarf's old nanny—Britt Egan, who'd been watching her at the cabin—or the two police officers out of Chicago who had found Eleanor, but it was the last thing he wanted to tell the little girl. Well, the second-to-last thing. "Until we know for sure Britt's okay, can you pretend to not be you?"

"Not be me?"

"Just until we know the police have all the scary guys in jail?" The caretaker had set a thicker-than-needed jacket for mid-September as well as a Green Bay Packers cap on the edge of the couch. "So if you could wear that coat and cap, and go by—who shall we introduce you as?—Matilda, that would keep the baddies from finding us."

"Matilda's a silly name."

"I suspect it is," he agreed. "What name would you like to go by?"

"Sierra."

"Sierra's a beautiful disguise name," he said, holding out his hand. "I'm pleased to meet you, Sierra."

They shook on it.

The Belgian's smartphone rang. He recognized the caller, stood, crossed the room, went into the hallway, and strode into the front kitchen before answering. "Verlinden," he said to the helicopter pilot. "Yes," he said moments later. "We'll meet you at the helipad in ten minutes. I'm bringing my niece."

Verlinden ended the call, turned to head back to Scarf, but caught the beep and LED flash coming from the cubbyhole on the far side of the kitchen, the small space that functioned as the estate's security center. Although this was the caretaker's domain—the man was currently hauling luggage up to the helicopter pad—Verlinden knew how to work the motion detectors and cameras. He first peeked at the monitor displaying the entry gates. The gates remained closed and no vehicles loitered on the road out front.

Verlinden then turned his attention toward the motion detector that had been triggered. The unit was set in Alert mode as Alarm mode omits an ear-piercing siren to frighten off potential intruders, but considering the amount of land he owned, Verlinden didn't want that hellishness unleashed whenever a deer tripped one of the sensors. He noted the detector that had gone off—the one closest to the front gate, opposite the lake—and then noticed a second motion detector had been triggered—this one near the fire pit and grill station.

Verlinden's notion of a stray deer wandering about his property began to fade.

Someone was out there.

He toggled through video from the outdoor cameras until he came to the security camera nearest the grill station.

And that's when he spotted them.

A man and a woman were heading toward the steps leading up to the flatland, where the hot air balloons lay.

Verlinden tapped at his smartphone and contacted the caretaker.

CHAPTER 52

Turned out we didn't need to climb ten feet of wrought iron after all. The perimeter fence petered out about eighty yards inland, where the hill steepened with patches of rock outcroppings. Once inside, Kippy and I doubled back, down and inward as fast as the terrain allowed. Soon after we stumbled upon a brick walkway leading toward the highest incline on Verlinden's property—the peak of which continued to display Vira's GPS coordinates on my iPhone app.

In theory, my golden retriever hadn't moved.

"It can't be this easy."

"Actually, it's a good layout to stymie burglars," Kippy said. "Hard to haul a ninety-inch flat screen back from where we came or swimming it beyond the entry gate."

"A thief would have to come by boat."

Kippy shrugged. "I'm sure the house itself is wired six ways from Sunday."

We paused at a fire pit surrounded by an array of well-designed lawn chairs. Then we migrated past some kind of outdoor kitchen large enough to feed Rhode Island, and from there the walkway led to a slanting sequence of stone steps that worked their way up the hillside.

At the foot of the stairway, I said, "Should I whistle and see if she comes?"

"I think we need to get up there," Kippy replied, her eyes prodding me onward.

With an hour before dusk, I figured the only thing breaking our way was that we wouldn't have to suffer through this in darkness. I took the first step and began to climb.

We were a third of the way up the incline before I spoke again, "Long ass day, huh?"

"Tell me about it."

We were halfway up the incline when I spotted a man with pitch black hair at the top of the steps, arms folded across his chest, stern look on his face, and staring down our way.

A second later, a voice from below said, "Might I ask what you two are doing on my property?"

CHAPTER 53

The Lion King ended and Scarf looked over the back of the sofa to see if her father's friend had returned to the family room.

He hadn't.

"Mr. Verlinden?" Scarf called, and then a little louder, "Audie?"

He must be getting ready for the flight back to Chicago, so Scarf took a moment to put on the jacket, which must have been made for an adult as it hung down nearly to her knees. She giggled as she put on the Packers cap. She couldn't wait to have her father see her wearing it. Scarf didn't know much about football, thought it was boring, but she knew her dad, and he'd probably take the hat and toss it into the fireplace.

Her father was a lifelong Bears fan.

Scarf sat patiently as the credits came to a finish and the big screen TV faded to black. Then she ventured out of the family room, worked her way into the kitchen, and spotted the popcorn bowl on a countertop. He'd been here.

"Mr. Verlinden?" Scarf called again to no reply.

Mr. Verlinden lived in a big house and Scarf thought she'd go exploring. She trekked back down the hallway until she came to a staircase. If Audie was getting ready for tonight's trip, maybe he was upstairs.

Scarf started up the flight of steps.

CHAPTER 54

Vira lay in the evening sun, head resting upon her front paws. She'd not touched the water dish or the beans after her initial sniff. She wasn't hungry. After Scarf crossed the field with the older of the two men they'd encountered today—disappearing into a grove of trees—Vira had curled up on the grass with a whimper.

And except for some minor shifting about here and a soft whine there, Vira had remained in the same spot ever since.

But now she watched quietly as the younger of the two men came sprinting out from the tree line and across the field. She stood up as he flew past and continued watching as he ran by the hot air balloons before finally coming to a halt at the hill's edge. Vira's ears perked up as she followed in his wake. Almost immediately her leash grew taut . . . and she strained against it with all her might.

Why wouldn't she?

Her best friend had just arrived.

Mace was here . . . and Vira began to bark.

CHAPTER 55

"I'm looking for my dog," I said, holding up my cell phone as though that clarified everything.

The man at the bottom of the steps wore a dress suit and black shoes, and stared up at us through designer glasses. He, too, held a smartphone in one hand, likely ready to tap in 911. I took him to be Audrick Verlinden.

He stared at me a long moment. "Are you Mason Reid?"

"Yes," I said, stunned. "How did you know that?"

"I called the number on Vira's dog tag and it kicked over to your answering machine."

That made perfect sense. The answering machine on my landline in Lansing is all decked out for business. It makes me sound as though I was running some kind of canine empire out of my trailer home.

I'd long since given up correcting people over the proper pronunciation of "Vira." No one gets it right. Ever. And I can't blame them because they're not aware her name stems from the Oak Ridge Boys' song "Elvira," so they pronounce it "Vera." Not that I'd have corrected Mr. Verlinden, but I didn't have to. The man pronounced my golden retriever's name correctly right off the bat.

Like "Ira," only with a "V" in front.

Verlinden pocketed his smartphone. "How did you know your dog was here?"

"She's got a GPS thing in her collar."

He nodded and started climbing the zigzag of steps when Vira began barking. A ton of weight dropped from my shoulders. It was all I could do to keep from blowing off our current predicament and sprinting up the side of the hill. "Hey, Vira," I called back, letting her know we'd heard her, "it's all good. We're here, girl. We're here."

Vira's chorus of barks and woofs trailed off, allowing the man I took as Verlinden to ask, "Why didn't you ring me at the gate?"

"The app has generalized coordinates, and we cut in through the woods before hitting your property," Kippy spoke for the first time.

Verlinden looked confused. "How far back did you cut in?"

"About halfway between the road up to your neighbors and your driveway." Kippy held out her badge. "I'm a detective with the Chicago Police Department."

"Then you of all people should respect our trespassing laws," he said, not caring a whit about Kippy's badge. His eyes didn't bulge, he didn't reach for a hidden firearm, and he didn't turn and flee the scene. "You know, quaint little customs like not entering the premises without consent of the property owner." His gaze worked its way back toward me. "Your answering machine said you trained dogs. I assume K-nines for the police?"

"Now and again. Mostly, I run an obedience school," I said, hoping we'd not have to revisit the portion concerning our sneaking about on his property. "I also train HRD dogs."

The man I assumed to be Verlinden had arrived at the step directly below us. He held a hand my way and said, "What in the devil are HRD dogs?"

I shook his hand. "Human remains detection dogs."

He stared at me a moment. "Cadaver dogs?"

I nodded.

"I've read about them in the paper." His attention turned to Kippy as he confirmed my assumption. "My name is Audrick Verlinden, by the way," he said, swinging an arm in a quarter circle, "and this is my humble abode." He shook Kippy's hand.

"I didn't mean to get off on the wrong foot, but we've dealt with more than our share of vandalism these past years."

"The Thompson boy, sir?" the man at the top of the hill spoke for the first time. I took him for Verlinden's butler or manservant or whatever they call them in homes that have a hundred rooms. Fortunately, the manservant's arms now hung at his sides, a less menacing look and feel.

"Yes," Verlinden said with a nod of his head, "the infamous Thompson boy. He egged our entry gate when he was a wee lad, didn't realize we had security cameras. I shared the video with his parents and he's been our nemesis ever since. Our cars have been key scratched in town, and, last fall, someone in a Halloween mask tossed our lawn chairs in the fire pit and torched them."

"Did you go to the police?"

Verlinden shrugged. "Dan and Lydia live down the lake. I've known them for decades and Dan's parents since I was a wee lad. We keep expecting their son will *mature* or head off to college, whichever comes first." A smile crossed Verlinden's face. "Although, since we're speaking openly, I don't view the Thompson boy as a *head-off-to-college* type."

I took another step up the hill. "I'd hate to take up any more of your time, Mr. Verlinden," I said. "Let me grab Vira and we'll be out of your hair."

"Of course," he said, stepping around Kippy and myself to lead the way. "Let's go get Vira."

"How'd she even show up here?" I asked as we neared the pinnacle.

Verlinden pointed at his manservant.

"Yes, sir," his underling said, and turned to me, all very proper. "While wiping down the grill station, Mr. Reid, I heard a car door slam, and then I heard it *peel out* as the vernacular goes. I didn't give it another thought, but a minute later Vira burst through the tree line, her leash trailing behind her." The man turned back to his employer. "I assumed it was the Thompson boy driving the vehicle."

Verlinden's brow wrinkled. "I can't imagine he's upped his game to include dog snatching." Verlinden said to me. "I presumed you were visiting the state park and Vira made good an escape attempt. I planned to call again and leave a message, but her tag displayed a Chicago address and, like I said—I assumed you were at the park."

As we topped the hill, another surprise was in store for us. A string of deflated hot air balloons lay out on the grass, colorful—yellow and green and red and more. Breathtaking. A wicker gondola sat next to each hot air balloon; the nearest gondola lay on its side, evidently under repair.

Kippy and I looked to Verlinden.

"Not so much a hobby," he said, "as it's been in my mother's family for generations. I keep the balloons out of respect for the past. We should all respect the past, wouldn't you say?" The question was rhetorical and Verlinden continued, "We do take them up once or twice a summer, especially when Lake Geneva hosts the Fourth of July festival."

I got over the hot air balloons as soon as I spotted my golden retriever. There she was, tethered far enough away from the balloons so she couldn't mess with them. I jogged toward her and watched as Vira leapt the height of the leash. "Yes, girl, I'm coming. Did you think I wouldn't find you?" I said. "As if that could ever happen."

"Let me get a screwdriver, Mr. Reid," Verlinden's servant said. "To pry up the tent stake."

He shuffled about his toolkit, but I was busy showing Vira some love, hugging her, scratching at the back of her ears, and shaking front paws. "No worries," I said as I unclipped the leash from Vira's collar.

Vira shot toward Kippy as though out of a cannon. They rubbed noses and wiggled as if it'd been a thousand years since they'd seen each other.

"We can get you to your car quicker if we head this way." Verlinden pointed toward a clump of trees on the far side of the balloon field.

Vira continued twisting and spinning about, still ecstatic. She ran to me, and then zagged back to Kippy as I meandered toward the two of them. Verlinden's story made a certain degree of sense, and neither he nor his manservant were acting fishy or threatening, and Vira appeared anything but ill-treated—even a bowl of food and water had been left near her tether stake.

I wondered who the hell dumped her off on the lake road. Had Vira put up a fight? Had Scarf's abductors figured out what the added width of her collar meant?

"A heartwarming reunion," Verlinden observed. "I do hate to give you the bum's rush, but I'm a little short on time. If you could follow me, I'd appreciate it."

Kippy and I took steps in Verlinden's direction. Part of me wanted to jog down the hill and get the hell off the man's property as fast as humanly possible, or at least be gone before Special Agent Squires and Chief Zogby showed up with a search warrant and squad cars full of police officers and FBI agents. I knew we were knee-deep in the middle of what was about to occur and hoped there'd be no legal entanglements in my foreseeable future.

At least that's one good thing about living paycheck to paycheck—there wasn't much Verlinden could sue me for.

Verlinden's man was still fussing about with his toolkit, in search of that elusive screwdriver his OCD demanded he find to pry up the tent stake and get that cheap leash the heck off his grounds. He stood in victory, evidently holding the longest tool his Phillips set had to offer.

Vira was still full of the dickens. She circled me twice, like a shark prepping an attack, barked once, and then slipped past Kippy and on toward Verlinden's manservant. Her bark tore me from my thoughts. Something was up in the world according to Vira, and I turned sideways to watch.

My golden retriever came to a rest a few yards in front of Verlinden's man. She sat down and began patting at an exposed patch of dirt with one paw. Kippy was closer than I and began heading to Vira. I looked at the dead grass and dirt she sat near, squinted my eyes, and swore I spotted cinder and soot and ash in the mix.

It dawned on me at the same time it hit Kippy. She turned my way, her eyes wide open. Verlinden's manservant had been tracking the goings-on. He dropped his screwdriver and scooped up some kind of metal contraption.

"A cadaver dog, eh?" I heard Verlinden say from behind me.

CHAPTER 56

There were a lot of rooms upstairs to explore.

Fortunately for Scarf, most of the doorways were open and the little girl strode the hallway, alternately calling out "Mr. Verlinden!" and "Audie!" A handful of times she snuck into the open rooms, always on the lakeside, to gaze through bay windows over Geneva Lake before returning on her quest.

Where could Mr. Verlinden have disappeared to?

Was he outside with the helicopter man? If so, what was taking him so long?

Scarf took a second trip around the four-sided hallway of the second floor, this time jogging and yelling for "Audie!" between giggles until she found herself back by her starting point at the top of the staircase. She sat down on the top step and tried to catch her breath.

She wasn't certain if Mr. Verlinden's home was bigger than her mother and father's house, but it sure had a lot more bedrooms. Mr. Verlinden's home would be the perfect place for a championship game of hide-and-seek. Playing that in this house, Scarf figured, would take hours.

Was Mr. Verlinden playing hide-and-seek?

No, that would be silly, and Mr. Verlinden wasn't a silly man.

Scarf wandered about the main floor, a whopper of a dining room, an assortment of family and living rooms, several offices, each one with a view of the lake, and two complete kitchens, including tables for even more people to eat.

And a little off to the side in the back kitchen, beyond the walk-in pantry, there was another door.

Scarf was good with doors.

She opened this one slowly and peered down a set of wooden steps that seemed out of place—dingier—than the rest of the household. Much older, too, if that were possible. Where Scarf lived, her mom and dad had a separate cottage where their staff could sleep overnight if they wanted to. Carlos, or "Carl," the gardener often stayed there, as did Henri, or "Henry," the chef—don't you dare call him a cook—and, even sometimes, Mrs. Dorsey, Scarf's current nanny.

Did this basement stairwell lead down to rooms where Mr. Verlinden's staff lived? Maybe the nice man who drove Audie's car had a room down there?

"Mr. Verlinden?" Scarf whispered into the darkness. She'd said it like a little mouse, so she repeated it louder, "Mr. Verlinden?"

Scarf stepped back. She'd heard something . . . or at least Scarf thought she'd heard something.

She flicked on the light switch, which illuminated the wooden steps, but the light also illuminated how steep the wooden steps were. Suddenly, Scarf was uneasy. She didn't want to search for Mr. Verlinden down there, but she still called out, "Audie?"

There it came again. A human sound, a low moan, like someone was sick. Or maybe someone had fallen down these steep, steep stairs and hit their head.

Scarf shivered.

She didn't want to go down to the basement; in fact, Scarf felt chilled just having the door open, but someone down there moaning meant somebody needed help.

Then she remembered what Mr. Verlinden had told her—that a *patient* also lived in this big, old house.

A patient who was *sick with life*.

But even if a patient was sick with life—whatever that

meant—you couldn't keep them down in a cold and dark and scary basement, could you? It'd be awfully hard getting them up these steep, steep stairs whenever the patient needed to go see a doctor or get to a hospital.

But what if it was Mr. Verlinden down there?

He'd been gone an awfully long time. What if he'd fallen down these wooden steps and hit his head and crawled off into the darkness?

Then he'd need help.

Scarf clung tight to the railing . . . and began her descent.

CHAPTER 57

"Run!" I screamed, scrambling forward.

Kippy went for her Beretta—no time for that—and I plowed into her, sending us both tumbling across the grass like bowling pins. A geyser of fire occupied the area we'd just vacated.

Scorching, blistering heat, searing air, impossible to breathe, I screamed, "Roll!"

Maybe I meant it as a way to smother flames, maybe I meant for us to make it to the hillside for cover—maybe I meant both—but it didn't matter as Verlinden's manservant adjusted his aim, a new wave of fire heading our way.

Every inch sunburned, eyebrows singed, my face a washcloth of sweat. Kippy spun toward me but . . .

. . . the conflagration ceased.

I blinked my eyes against the haze.

Verlinden's manservant and my golden fought in a blur of motion—Cheeta with the herd of elephants saving the day.

Vira dropped from a thrashing forearm, darted back, and sprang for his wrist, but he turned a shoulder. The man shook, shimmied, then snapped an elbow into the side of Vira's temple. She dropped again, and he slammed his contraption—some make-shift flamethrower—into her side as though swinging a baseball bat. Vira yelped and rolled, but his eyes were back on us.

He rotated our way . . . his metal device once more spitting flame.

Three shots rang out—boom, boom, boom—pounding the manservant's rib cage, center mass, blood flowed. The flamethrower dropped to the ground, no longer spraying death, and he stumbled backward into the upended gondola. His head turned toward his employer—their eyes locked a long moment—and I swear he mouthed "I'm sorry, sir" before slipping to the ground.

Kippy was on her knees, but she also stared toward Mr. Verlinden, her Beretta now pointed his way.

"Ahhhhh," came from Verlinden in a gruesome exhale—a hot air balloon deflating—his mouth a perfect circle. I waited for a scream, but, instead, he sank to the lawn and looked our way. "Who's going to watch the patient?"

We spotted the helicopter as we exited the trail cutting from Verlinden's hot air balloon field through the crop of trees. Vira was out in front, leading our motley crew. Then came Kippy, her left hand on the shoulder of a handcuffed Verlinden, her Beretta in her right hand, barrel pointed at the ground. I brought up the rear, my APX Compact out, still bereft of ammunition, also pointed down. My firearm was more a bluff, a show of force, in case Verlinden had additional *lethal personnel* in his employ.

Evidently, the pilot spotted us as seconds later the helicopter lifted off from Verlinden's private helipad and cut left across the lake.

"You may have spooked him," Verlinden said.

Kippy asked, "Is Eleanor aboard?"

"No."

"Is she okay?" Verlinden had not said a word since he'd been placed in cuffs and Mirandized, not so much as a sneeze on our short jaunt from his balloon field, and I figured Kippy wanted to keep the rich man talking.

"Eleanor is just fine. Last I saw, she was watching *The Lion King*," he replied. "I hate to disappoint you both, but I won't be waiving my right to remain silent until I have legal counsel."

"Don't worry—I'm not as *disappointed* as I'd have been had I'd gotten flame broiled." Verlinden kept his word about remaining silent; still Kippy asked, "You going to show us how to open the front gate?"

Verlinden nodded his agreement.

Kippy'd had a short phone call with Squires as we worked our way out of the hot air balloon field. It took one minute to tell him our tale, another two minutes to answer his questions, and a final ten seconds to get his assurance that, yes, he and Chief Zogby were on their way, search warrant in hand.

I was lost in my own thoughts, wondering how long those ashes had been gracing Mr. Verlinden's balloon field. They obviously belonged to someone who'd not been as fortunate as Kippy and I had been. Verlinden and his servant had been kind to Vira, even providing her food and water. More significantly, it appeared Verlinden and his manservant had also been kind to Eleanor Druckman.

If Elle had been mistreated, Vira's demeanor would have been completely different.

And when it came to human remains detection, no matter how Verlinden or his manservant had removed the *larger chunks* or raked over their cremation project, the scent remained, so Vira was letting all of us know about the trace signature she'd caught in the grass and soil, ash and cinder.

Unfortunately, there's no scent DNA in a cremation—no dots for Vira to connect.

But she got immediate feedback from me—my warning mode— and witnessed the manservant's attempt to harm us . . . and took immediate action.

We were halfway down the paved stairway leading to Verlinden's lake cottage when Vira shot down the remaining steps, cut across the terrace, and launched herself at the back door.

A split second later, we heard Scarf scream.

Verlinden looked at Kippy and broke his vow of silence. "I think she met my father."

CHAPTER 58

Scarf stepped down into the secluded staircase at the back of the cottage. "Mr. Verlinden?"

In return, a low and lengthy moan. Scarf took two more steps down the stairwell. Thank God no one lay broken at the bottom, she thought. That was good, wasn't it? If Mr. Verlinden or his driver or whoever was down there had fallen and hit their head, maybe they were in good enough shape to crawl up against a wall and rub their owie, like Scarf's mom had taught her to do with her bumps and bruises.

She took two more steps. "Mr. Verlinden—can you hear me?"

In response, another muffled moan.

It seemed whenever Scarf called out to him, she'd get a hushed wail in return. She sure wished Mr. Verlinden or his driver or whoever was downstairs would say something in English to let her know they were alright, even if they had an owie or two from falling. If only they would talk to her, then she'd feel safe enough to scamper down the rest of the stairs two at a time in order to help.

Scarf took a few more steps—nearing the bottom—and wished Mr. Verlinden had let Vira come into his house instead of leashing her on the hilltop. Sure, Mr. Verlinden had a nice house and nice things, and Vira might bump into something or maybe even drool on his carpet, but Scarf wished Vira was at her side right now.

She really did.

Scarf felt safe when she was with Vira.

The light dimmed at the bottom of the steps, and Scarf hoped to find another switch on the basement wall. A few seconds later, she was there, stepping down onto the concrete floor. "Where are you, Mr. Verlinden?"

"Aaaaah," came a groan from farther down the hallway—a corridor that shadowed into darkness. Scarf wanted to flee, to sprint back upstairs, run to the TV room, and wait for someone big to come and help. But the wailing cried out to her again, "Uuuurgh."

Scarf ran a hand along the wall, finding a light switch, flicking it. Halfway down the hall a single overhead bulb winked on. It sure didn't kick off much more illumination than what filtered down from the staircase.

She no longer thought of Mr. Verlinden's house as being a great place to play hide-and-seek. Scarf no longer thought that at all.

"Mr. Verlinden," she called again, blinking back tears. "Can you please say something? Please. I'm getting scared."

"Aaaargh."

It was a slightly different moan this time. Maybe Mr. Verlinden or his driver or whoever was calling out to her had hit their head so hard in the fall that they'd crawled into the room for a pillow or towel or something to hold against their owie, or maybe they were trying to find a phone so they could call for help.

Scarf took a few steps into the hallway and the wailing came again. "Aaaargh."

It was close by now. Scarf could tell.

Real close.

She forced herself to take a few more steps down the poorly lit corridor until she came to a rest in front of the hallway's first door, or only door as far as she could tell. And if Scarf wasn't scared enough already, what she spotted above the handle almost sent her flying back up the staircase.

Of the room from which she knew the wailing originated . . . there was a lock on the door.

This was crazy. Why would you lock someone in?

Scarf stood in front of the door an eternity, glued to the floor, too terrified to speak, but she knew she had to. And though she no longer thought it was Mr. Verlinden or his driver in the basement room, she said, "Mr. Verlinden—are you in there?"

"Aaaaah . . . uurgh."

Two long groans this time. Was whoever behind the door trying to put words together? Was his head starting to hurt less so he could speak?

Scarf tried the knob and, yes, the door was locked. It was hefty, too, much like the front door of a house, both thick and heavy, to keep the bad guys out. But Scarf knew how to twist open locks, and she inched her hand upward and turned the deadbolt.

Though it barely made a peep, unlocking the door elicited another, "Aaargh."

Scarf's heart lodged in her throat as she ginned up the courage to swing open the door. She didn't want to be down here. And she didn't want to do this. She was so scared and just wanted to go home. She wanted her mom . . . and her dad . . . and she knew people were keeping secrets from her—Mr. Verlinden, and even Britt—because they saw her as just a dumb kid.

She knew there was something awful they weren't telling her.

And maybe that scared her most of all.

Scarf twisted the doorknob and pushed the door open a few inches.

"Aaaargh." The wailing noise grew louder, excited, and frantic.

Scarf shoved the door all the way open. Unlike the murkiness of the staircase and hallway, a bright light shone inside this most unusual of rooms.

Scarf spotted what had been making the wailing sound.

And Scarf began to scream.

CHAPTER 59

Verlinden mumbled something about his right front pocket as Kippy pressed him against the brick of the cottage's exterior. A second later she had his keys and tossed them my way. Vira was on two feet, pawing at the wooden entry door as Scarf continued screaming. I caught the keys, worked the lock, and Vira squeezed inside as soon as the door was open.

It seemed an eternity since we'd headed out from my trailer home first thing this morning, but, somewhere along the line, Scarf had become part of Vira's pack and—as I can bear witness—you don't mess with Vira's pack.

I scuttled behind my golden retriever, spotting her tail as she cut right into a kitchen, then a quick profile as she threw herself into a stairwell. I followed, palming the bannister as I took the steps four at a time, then leapt to the cement at the bottom.

Ahead was Scarf, hands to her face as she backed out of a room. Vira, growling now, cut in front of her, between her new friend and whatever terror lay inside the basement chamber. Vira darted into the room and I followed suit.

Vira, silent now, froze in front of me. I stopped next to her. A second later Kippy was by my side, her pistol at the ready.

The three of us had been expecting another fight—it had been a long afternoon of hostilities—but we weren't prepared for what lay in front of us.

Vira recovered first, realized there wasn't a threat after all, turned around, and trotted over to comfort Scarf.

"Jesus Christ," I said.

I may have spotted a hospital bed situated along the right-side wall. I may have spotted a toilet with safety rails and an oversized stainless steel scrub sink and what may have been a walk-in bathtub situated along the left-side wall. I may have noted how the tiled floor pitched slightly and contained a center drain for easy cleaning. I may also have noted how everything seemed to sparkle and shine as though scrubbed daily.

And I may have even noticed how every wall in the basement room, the ceiling as well, were papered over with pictures from the past—pictures of some beautiful young woman on what had to have been her wedding day. Oddly, the images were only of the young bride as there were no corresponding photographs of a groom on this landscape of nuptials. The walls and ceiling contained only images of the young woman in white—numerous poses, but only of her.

All those things may have registered on some subconscious level, but what stole the show was what perched before us in the center of the underground chamber.

The man swam in a hospital gown, his lap and legs shrouded in a dark wool blanket, and shriveled deeply into what appeared to be a top-of-the-line wheelchair, that is, were the year still 1960. The man was of advanced years—quite frankly, he looked to be in his upper hundreds. He was gaunt, wrinkled beyond repair, completely bald—as in no hair, no eyebrows, and no eyelashes— and his face a sagging patchwork of liver spots. This impossibly ancient man wore Coke-bottle glasses, and, though no eye contact was made, he stared in our general direction, his mouth wide open in a continual moan. I wasn't sure if he could tell we were even there—I suspected he might be reacting to our sound and move- ment . . . his arms stretched toward us.

"Aaaargh."

At the sound of his wail, it dawned on me. We had just found the groom—the man missing from all of the marital images.

"Jesus Christ," I repeated.

Kippy holstered her Beretta. "I'll have Squires get an ambulance."

We backed slowly out of the basement room.

Scarf was busy hugging Vira. She looked up at us, perhaps still in shock from her discovery, and said, "Is that a monster in there?"

"No," Kippy said, taking a knee next to the little girl. "He's just a sick old man who needs a doctor."

"I beg to disagree," Verlinden piped in from the foot of the staircase. "Our sweet, little Eleanor is right—there is a monster in there."

CHAPTER 60

Kippy and Scarf sat on a couch in the room where Scarf said she'd finished watching a Disney movie. Vira sat at their feet while I stared out a window. The paramedics had hauled the ghost that was Verlinden's father away in their ambulance, off to the local hospital in Lake Geneva. Turned out both the male and female EMTs were as weirded out by whom they'd been summoned to help as I'd been upon finding him in his basement chamber. I could see it in their eyes as they carried him away, secured to a stretcher, out to the ambulance.

"You're a charming little girl, Eleanor—a true exquisite," Verlinden said before Chief Zogby perp-walked him out to the police cruiser, both heading to the police station in town. "And I wish you all the luck in the world."

"Thanks, Audie," Scarf said softly.

Chief Zogby had taken our initial statements, which lasted all of ten minutes as Zogby had basically been involved since the get-go. However, Kippy and I were expected to hightail it over to the Lake Geneva Police Department as soon as things wrapped up here for a more in-depth *grilling* by a guy named "Zeke" something or other, who happened to be the district attorney for Walworth County. Since it involved a shooting and the death of Verlinden's employee, I imagined we'd be in Lake Geneva well into the evening.

I'd have to call Dick Weech and let him know I'd be tied up

longer than expected, and that he could eat anything and everything he finds in my fridge, pantry, or freezer.

Hopefully, Bill wasn't driving Dick apeshit.

Speaking of things wrapping up here, we were waiting on a social worker to arrive. Squires had flittered about Verlinden's mansion, coordinating next steps with both Lake Geneva PD and his team of agents. He planned to land his helicopter on Verlinden's helipad and fly Scarf back to Chicago where three concerned grandparents awaited her arrival. The social worker would come along and, hopefully, make any twists and turns and bumps in the ride home a little less turbulent for the poor kid.

Scarf had settled into a somber silence, head down, glancing from her lap to her shoes to Vira and then back again. I suspected I knew what was clanking about in the young girl's mind—why no one seemed inclined to call her mother or father—and, as I bumbled about the room, I tried to distract her with silly questions about Disney movies until Kippy gave me a quick shake of her head.

Squires came in to inform the room that someone named "Suzette" was about a minute out and that they'd be boarding soon after.

I returned to my spot at the window, briefly, as I heard a sob and turned around. Kippy had an arm over Scarf's trembling shoulders; Vira's head rested on Scarf's lap.

Tears washed down Scarf's face as she looked up at Kippy and asked in a nearly imperceptible voice, "Are my parents dead?"

CHAPTER 61

TWO WEEKS LATER

I shook my head. "No, Bill."

My bloodhound peeked back at me, sheepishly, as he edged nearer the sand of the swimming beach. Sue barked once and Bill spun on a dime, scampering back to the picnic bench where my German shepherd and I sat, near where Maggie and Delta wandered about the trees and tables, charcoal grills and playground. It was a little after nine o'clock in the morning, a school day, and Lakefront Park was nearly vacant. With only the periodic jogger or bicyclist flying past—and no strangers to call me out—I let the dogs roam free.

Scarf's grandparents on her father's side and her grandmother on Calley's side sat several picnic tables away, talking quietly among themselves. That was fine by me as I wouldn't dare intrude on what the trio was going through—attempting to pick up the pieces if only for the sake of their mutual granddaughter.

Plus, the three grandparents had a hundred logistical items to work out, and, quite frankly, they didn't know me from Adam.

I stared off into the distance and watched as Kippy, Scarf, and Vira paced along Lake Michigan, closing in on a beach house. Except for the periodic round of questioning, Kippy had been on leave from CPD following the shooting and had brought Vira to Glencoe darned near every day to visit Scarf in a heartfelt effort to cheer up the little kid. Scarf's world had been shattered—how could it not have been?—and, between tears, if Kippy and Vira were able to wring a smile out of the little girl, it was well worth the travel time.

Scarf was flying to Florida later this morning, where she'd be staying with her father's parents, so I tagged along to introduce her to the other dogs in my pack as well as to say goodbye and wish her well.

"I love Vira," Scarf told me.

"She sure is special, isn't she?" I replied.

Scarf nodded.

"Do you think your grandparents will let you have a dog?"

"I don't know."

"Well, if it's okay with them, I can start scouting out a puppy for you."

"You would?"

"It'd be my pleasure."

"Would you and Kippy and Vira bring the puppy down for me?"

"Of course—who wouldn't want to go to Florida when it starts getting cold up here."

She shot me a grin and then ran off to barter with the powers that be. A minute later her grandfather tossed a none-too-pleased glance my way, and I hoped word of the fissure I'd inadvertently created would not work its way back to Kippy.

I scratched at Sue's back as Maggie and Delta sauntered over and sat in front of us. My farm collies stared up at me, looked over at Scarf's grandparents in disapproving unison, glanced at each other, and then looked back up at me.

"Really?" I said. "I've never met Scarf's family before in my life and may never see them again, but you guys are saying they're plotting against me." I picked up Maggie and shook her remaining front paw. "I've got to say it's a pretty feeble scam this time. I usually get better from you two con artists."

It was good that Druckman's parents were spiriting Scarf back to the Florida Panhandle with them as yet another boot was about to drop. The FBI had seized the computers at Druckman Financial Group as well as any and all paper documentation.

SAC Squires had his financial crimes unit dig in, and, per my favorite G-man, a preliminary look indicated that falsification of financial information as well as securities fraud and wire fraud were merely the tip of the Kenneth J. Druckman iceberg.

I sat on the ground with Maggie in my lap and watched Kippy give Scarf a long hug as Vira darted about the water's edge.

Kippy shared with me that after all was said and done, Scarf still had love in her heart for her old nanny, Britt Egan. She didn't blame Britt for her mother's death. Scarf even told Squires that Egan had not hurt or threatened her in their entire time together at the cabin outside Galena. Our statements regarding Britt Egan had also been positive—truthful, but positive. Kippy even stressed how Egan had taken a beatdown from Dima the Russian Gangster after she'd screamed to warn me and Scarf away.

However, Britt Egan would not be walking away scot-free from what had occurred during the past month.

Egan was nearly twenty-four years old. Kippy and I hoped she'd be out of prison before she hit thirty.

Dima—psychopath that he is—would not be so lucky. Attempted first-degree murder, committed with aggravating factors, tends to up the correctional ante. No jaunts to Mother Russia for him in the foreseeable future. Squires informed us that Dima'd kept his mouth shut, that is, except for asking every police officer he stumbled across if they loaded cartridges into their magazines or left them empty.

I had to smile at that.

I suspect Dima may have a few more years tacked on as Armen Kuznetsov is spending his days in FBI custody singing like a canary. Evidently, Kuznetsov borrowed a chunk of dough from his old pals in the Russian Mob in New York City to provide Druckman a down payment on Calley Kurtz's soon-to-be stolen jewelry. After the heist went south, Dima had been sent not only to help Kuznetsov recover the missing Russian funds and/or get the gems, but to put two in the back of Kuznetsov's head once all was said and done. Kuznetsov knew this for a fact as it was basically all Dima jabbered on about throughout their road trip to Galena.

As a result, Kuznetsov was sharing with SAC Squires everything he knew about his Little Odessa chums. I imagine Kuznetsov hoped the Federal Witness Protection Program could score him a sweet little antique store in East Corncob, Nebraska.

The three girls headed back our way as the Druckmans would need to leave soon in order to make the airport in time. I glanced over at Sue, still sitting by the bench, and then at Bill, now heading toward Kippy and the gang, and my thoughts turned toward the exceedingly mysterious Audrick Verlinden.

Verlinden had his very own dream team of criminal defense attorneys working around the clock to justify his having Eleanor Scarf Druckman at his Geneva Lake mansion. First off, the billionaire vehemently denied extorting money from Kenneth Druckman. As a recent investor in Druckman Financial Group, per his lawyers, Verlinden had confronted Druckman over inaccurate figures in his most recent financial return and demanded his full investment back. Verlinden did, in fact, get his funds back, but that act of reimbursement crippled Druckman's elaborate Ponzi scheme—leading him down the point of no return— because Druckman contacted Verlinden a few times afterward, late at night, intoxicated and virtually incomprehensible, to inform Verlinden how he'd ruined Druckman's life.

Per Verlinden's dream team, the last call Druckman had with their client was on the final night of Druckman's life. Druckman was again intoxicated, nearly unfathomable, but he apologized during this call, and informed Verlinden it was all coming to an end. When questioned about current issues headlining the news, Druckman told Verlinden his daughter was fine—she was with a friend—and that she'd be home the next day. Druckman even slurred out an address in Galena, Illinois, which Verlinden hustled to jot down.

When news of Druckman's death broke, and Druckman's daughter remained missing, Verlinden and his late manservant set out for Galena and drove to a nearby cabin in order to peek about and see if Eleanor Druckman was there or if it had all been more of Druckman's drunken musings, but then the little girl herself came tearing out from the woods as though the devil himself were on her tail. Eleanor's arrival was quickly followed by gunshots, so Verlinden, his manservant, Elle, and my golden retriever jumped in the sedan and got the hell out of Illinois. Verlinden brought her back to his lake house where he knew they'd all be safe. In fact, Verlinden was making plans to fly Eleanor to Chicago, and from there to the Chicago Police Department, when the authorities arrived.

That was Verlinden's story and he was sticking to it.

Yup, I thought, a jury might buy that, especially a jury of Audrick Verlinden's Lake Geneva peers who may know of the good his family had done for their community over many decades.

In regard to Verlinden's manservant trying to flame broil us, Verlinden's team of attorneys stated that their client has no idea what happened. In fact, their client lives at his Geneva Lake estate only half the year—he winters on an island somewhere, endless business travel—whereas his caretaker lives there fulltime. Who knows what *unspeakable* things the man had wormed his way into whenever Verlinden was away. His lawyers stated that Verlinden claims he realized at the exact same moment we did that Vira had found human remains in the soot and ashes next to the hot air balloons. Verlinden's dream team speculates that his caretaker panicked when he realized he'd been found out, and tried to kill us. Verlinden, they say, believes if his caretaker had succeeded in killing Kippy and me, that he himself would have been next on the madman's kill list.

In other words, Verlinden tossed his loyal and longtime manservant under the bus.

Though a bit harder to swallow, this might squeak by a jury of Lake Geneva residents.

However, the hardest thing for such a jury to swallow—no matter which dream team member spoon-feeds it to them—was how Verlinden's father had been held in captivity in a basement chamber for nearly half a century.

SAC Squires provided the backstory. Audrick Verlinden's mother had hung herself from a basement rafter in their Antwerp home, only to be found by Verlinden himself when he was a mere lad of sixteen. Geneva Lake neighbors who had known the O'Fallons—his mother's family—for decades had shared the rumors and gossip with inquisitive FBI agents. The story went that Verlinden's father had driven his mother to suicide via abuse and neglect as well as a recurrent, and not-so-hidden, series of affairs with much younger women.

Six months after his wife's death, Father Verlinden had taken his sailing boat out on the open water off the seacoast as he was wont to do. A day later his dinghy was found floating about, abandoned. Father Verlinden had gone missing and was, eventually, declared dead.

Verlinden's dream team laid everything at the feet of Verlinden's deceased O'Fallon relatives as Audrick Verlinden had not yet been of legal age at the time of Father Verlinden's abduction. An uncle and grandfather and cousin on the O'Fallon side had grabbed Father Verlinden off his schooner, got him to shore, and then flew a secured Verlinden back to their Geneva Lake estate, where plans had been made for him to spend eternity locked inside a basement room papered with images of his young bride.

Father Verlinden had initially proved a difficult captive. However, with the aid of minor sedatives, as well as being tethered to the wall via welded chain, he'd been manageable enough until around the beginning of President Clinton's second term, when it became increasingly clear that Father Verlinden had lost his mind. They'd gone to great lengths to keep the man alive as physicians and surgeons had been flown in from Portugal whenever the captive patient was in need of medical attention.

Audrick Verlinden had been surprised that his father outlived the O'Fallons directly responsible for his confinement, thus the upkeep for Father Verlinden had, regretfully, fallen upon him. Not wanting to risk a scandal—which would taint the O'Fallons' good name—Verlinden provided the best care his father, under these peculiar circumstances, could possibly have asked for in his final years. As it turned out, Verlinden's manservant was a licensed vocational nurse and, like his father before him, tended to the day-to-day needs of Audrick Verlinden's father.

There must have been a kernel of truth in all that as Father Verlinden didn't make it two days at the Lake Geneva hospital before he passed away.

Like I said, the case of the old man in the basement chamber will be a bit more difficult for a Lake Geneva jury to swallow.

Druckman's parents were a bit standoffish as we made our good-byes, but Calley's mother called to us as we turned to depart. Lucinda Kurtz was in her early sixties, stricken with Parkinson's disease, and walking with the assistance of a cane; nevertheless you could still see where Calley got her good looks.

"I wanted to thank you for finding Scarf," she said.

"It was our honor," Kippy replied and I nodded.

"I don't know what I'd have done if I'd lost her as well."

While Kippy gave her a hug, Vira trekked over and stuck her nose at the base of Lucinda's cane. Last thing I needed was for my golden retriever to knock over a handicapped woman, so I knelt down, put a hand on Vira's shoulder, and whispered, "Come here, girl."

Lucinda had one of those specialized canes similar to the kind my grandfather used after knee surgery. I recognized its anti-slip rubber base which pivots to stay flat on any terrain. It certainly got Grandpa through his convalescence and likely helps Lucinda maintain her balance despite the effects of Parkinson's. These canes were of great aid to anyone with mobility issues, and all such canes did was leave an imprint of four circles in any patch of dirt or soil.

More specifically, a small square with a circle in each corner.

That's when it came to me.

Kippy's mystery man—Mr. X—who may or may not have been with Druckman at the very end.

The circular holes in the ground I'd spotted at the scene of

Druckman's suicide, the ones Vira had been sniffing at—they may not have come from the leg of some piece of forensic equipment after all.

I slowly stood, not really listening as Lucinda and Kippy made their final farewells. Instead, my thoughts turned to Scarf . . . and how she'd lost both of her parents in a matter of days . . . how the poor girl's life had been turned upside down . . . and how that was more than any kid should ever have to go through.

Then I thought of a single mother raising her only daughter, of the love between the two . . . of a bond that transcends death.

And I thought of that first morning, when Vira and I discovered Lucinda's daughter—the once-lovely Calley Kurtz—lying alone in the ravine, cold and lifeless beside an oversized stone.

Five minutes later, Kippy, the kids, and I were in the F-150 heading home.

CHAPTER 62

"Did you get extra napkins?" Like most guys, I never purchase napkins; instead, I lift them from a variety of fast-food restaurants and suggested that Kippy do the same. "You pocket an inch of them when no one's looking."

We'd driven the kids back from Glencoe to my trailer in Lansing, a solid hour, where Kippy volunteered to take her car and fetch us a bag of tacos for lunch while I dinked around the yard with the pooches. A half hour later she'd returned, two bags in hand.

"Yes," Kippy replied. "I got plenty of napkins."

I grabbed two cans of Coke from the refrigerator and turned to bring them to the table, but there stood Kippy—in front of me, blocking my path—with Vira at her heels.

"I've been meaning to ask you something, Mace. Something I think we've both been avoiding."

"Shoot."

"Remember when Dima marched us out into the woods?"

"Not something I'll ever forget."

"When Vira didn't show, I figured we were as good as dead."

I nodded my head.

"You said something to me right before he tried to shoot us. At the time, I took it to mean you were going to rush him and, you know, give me a chance to live."

"Actually, I was going to shove you into him and give me a chance to live."

"Yeah, right, but let's get back to what you said." Kippy stared into my eyes and asked, "Do you remember what you told me?"

I nodded again.

"Did you mean it?"

I stared back at Kippy a long moment. "Are you sure you got extra napkins?"

ACKNOWLEDGMENTS

First, I am forever grateful to the gang at St. Martin's Press—from Senior Editor Daniela Rapp to Copy Editor Lani Meyer to Assistant Editor Cassidy Graham to Marketing Manager Sara Beth Haring to Associate Director of Publicity Hector Dejean. You are all incredibly talented and a joy to work with. Second, I must recognize my agent—the unsinkable Jill Marr at the Sandra Dijkstra Literary Agency. Finally—a ton of thanks to my photographer, Beta Reader Extraordinaire, and wife, Cindy Archer-Burton, as well as my sounding board, editor, and father, Bruce W. Burton. You are lifesavers one and all.